THE CREEPYPASTA COLLECTION

THE CREEPYPASTA COLLECTION

MODERN URBAN LEGENDS YOU CAN'T UNREAD

Edited by MrCreepyPasta

ADAMS MEDIA
NEW YORK LONDON TORONTO SYDNEY NEW DELHI

Adams Media
An Imprint of Simon & Schuster, Inc.
100 Technology Center Drive
Stoughton, MA 02072

For information about special discounts for bulk purchases, please contact Simon & Schuster Special Sales at 1-866-506-1949 or business@simonandschuster.com.

The Simon & Schuster Speakers Bureau can bring authors to your live event. For more information or to book an event contact the Simon & Schuster Speakers Bureau at 1-866-248-3049 or visit our website at www.simonspeakers.com.

Manufactured in the United States of America

11 2023

Library of Congress Cataloging-in-Publication Data has been applied for.

ISBN 978-1-4405-9790-9
ISBN 978-1-4405-9791-6 (ebook)

DEDICATION

For everyone who strives to grow.

CONTENTS

INTRODUCTION

Hey there kids.

It's me, MrCreepyPasta!

And I've finally managed to break myself free from the comfort of YouTube and onto the shelves of bookstores! What you're holding is a collection of some of the darkest, goriest, and most terrifying Creepypastas that the Internet has to offer. As you continue through these pages, you unleash more and more of these creatures from the Internet's unknown into your imagination. The culmination of all types of horror from ages long past up to modern day lies in this book. I've compiled some of the most talented creators of nightmares and the most dangerous creatures for you to enjoy. Isn't that fun?

Oh! I think I see a few of you are confused. *Creepypasta* is somewhat of an odd name isn't it? And myself, MrCreepyPasta. I bet you think I'm some kind of kook or something. No, no, I'm nothing like that. See, I'm a storyteller. Let me explain:

The art of telling ghost stories around the campfire is slowly losing steam. Sure, back in the day that's all we had; telling ghost stories and sharing urban tales were always done in this way. Kids like you would huddle against each other as monsters and shadows were created using words. As those kids grew older, those same creatures would grow with them, and their shadows would spread as their stories were told over and over again by the firelight. Those horrors, birthed from imagination, would become larger and stronger than humanity because of the power words gave them.

These days, we have a new kind of campfire. Today you're more likely to find people sharing stories and creating monsters in front of their computers than by a fire. From that new glow of storytelling, a new breed of creation has been born. Nothing can snuff out imagination, and as long as human beings have a way to scare each other with words, our imagination will find a way. These new stories and these new creatures have found new ways to travel across the globe and infiltrate their way into our lives. Today, rather than being spoken to only a few individuals at a time, these stories are shared across websites and across oceans through technology. These tales are copied and pasted (or copy pasta-ed), and e-mailed, posted, and narrated. The art of storytelling—in an age where the art is thought to be lost—lives on stronger than ever.

An Internet community of writers, artists, and actors surfaced to bring these new horrors to life. This book contains the work of many of the most talented artists and authors of today. These creators have summoned ideas and monsters that the Internet has embraced, loved, and feared. These creatures are the new shadows that overpower humanity, and I've collected the best of them here for you. The all-powerful written word broke these monsters free and unleashed them onto the world. The term *Creepypasta* has become a way to not just describe a story, but also a way to describe a nightmare that was born on the Internet and seeded itself in a person's dreams. Nightmare after nightmare flowed from computer screens and tablets directly into the hearts and minds of kids and adults, not unlike yourself.

And now you hold in your hands the gateway to that world that words created. If you place this book back on the shelf now, you'll save yourself. The horrors stay within this book. The terrors that are told from person to person, and travel from country to country, will never see the light of your imagination. Likewise, you will never know of what true horror has to offer. You will be safe.

However, if your curiosity is high, and you really want to see how far and how dark the rabbit hole goes . . .

Prepare yourself.

Turn the page.

And Sweet Dreams.

PICTURE THIS

Vincent V. Cava

Picture this.

90,000 people are reported missing every year in the United States alone. You heard that number correctly. Don't believe me? Look it up: 90,000 people. A staggering 2,300 return home safely or are family abductions. The latter of which occurs when either the mother or father runs off with the little ones because of a domestic dispute or divorce.

As far as adults go, a làrge portion of missing cases typically involve people who are suffering from drug or alcohol abuse. These addicts have a tendency to go on benders, disappearing from their friends and families for days on end while they pump their bodies full of booze and illegal narcotics. A shockingly high number of reports concern senior citizens suffering from dementia or Alzheimer's. You'd be surprised how often they wander away from their caretakers and get lost. Usually it doesn't take very long for the police to locate the disoriented old-timer and bring him or her back to the nursing home.

Given these facts, we see that the number of people (both children and adults) who are abducted by strangers is actually relatively small. Only about 150 of these kinds of abductions are estimated to occur in the United States annually.

Now picture this.

You were an artist—a painter who specialized in Impressionism. You loved art all your life. You saw a coffee-table book when you were twelve years old that had a picture of *Blue Dancers* by Edgar Degas and you couldn't look away from it. You were mesmerized by the colors, the brush strokes, the way the girls in the painting contorted their bodies. To you, they didn't even look like dancers—they were a meadow of morning glories swaying in a gentle breeze. You knew right then and there that you wanted to create something as gorgeous and spellbinding as that picture.

You studied the greats: Renoir, Degas, Cézanne, and of course Monet. When you turned fifteen, you started taking art classes after school at the local community college, but you never shared your passion with anyone—not even your closest friends and family. You were afraid of what they might say. What if they laughed at you? What if they told you that your paintings were sloppy or ugly? What if they told you that you didn't have talent or that you'd never create your own *Blue Dancers* one day?

So you hid your passion from everyone you knew. Whenever you finished a piece you tossed it in the garbage because seeing your art in a dumpster was better than the possibility of hearing your friends make fun of it.

You wanted to study art in college, but society told you that only morons do that. Instead you opted for an engineering degree. Your parents were happy. You graduated from school and got a job where you sat in a cubicle and made $55,000 per year. You spent all day every day musing about what it would be like to wake up each morning and do nothing but paint. You tried to keep up with your art, but you never had the time. Your boss asked you to work weekends every chance he got and when you did have a second to yourself you were too tired to do anything but watch TV or surf the web. You started to hate yourself for being so spineless—for not pursuing the only thing in life that ever made you feel good. You fell into a depression.

Picture this.

An estimated 1 in 10 adults suffers from depression. That means there are at least 24 million people in the U.S. who feel lost, who feel hopeless, who feel like the world would be a better place without them, and you were one of those people.

You wore a mask in front of your friends and family. That part was easy. You had been hiding your passion from them all your life; you could hide your depression too. Nobody at work could see how much you were hurting, but when you got home you lay in bed and you cried. You thought about downing an entire bottle of aspirin, but you were afraid of what people would say if you survived. You stood on the edge of your bathtub with one end of a belt looped around your neck and the other fastened to the metal rod of your shower curtain while you weighed the pros and cons of suicide. You spent hours surfing the Internet, visiting forums, looking for a way to save yourself. You even went so far as to post questions anonymously, pleading for help.

Then you got the piece of advice that you believed you were searching for—from Reddit of all places, a website famous for stupid cat pictures and bastardizing the word *meme*. It came in the form of a comment in a thread you made about feeling suicidal. You didn't see the commenter's username; in fact, you were so excited after reading their advice that you closed your browser's window before checking where it came from. It didn't matter who they were in real life anyway; as far as you were concerned those words were sent straight to you from your guardian angel, watching over you from heaven.

"Try finding a creative outlet," your web-surfing savior said. "I picked up painting as a means to channel my depression.

Whenever I'm feeling down, I grab a brush and get to work. It helps to serve as a fantastic distraction."

So picture this.

You took that guardian angel's advice and ran with it. You swore off suicide, called your mom and dad and told them you loved them. The very next morning you woke up and headed to the library where you spent the entire day reading about your favorite artists—the painters you had idolized your entire life. For hours you looked at photos of their works and it made you feel young again. Then you stumbled upon a book with a picture of *Blue Dancers* and you found yourself awestruck, just like that time when you were twelve. It was that moment you decided to quit your job and follow your dreams.

Your mom and dad weren't happy, but they understood when you told them about your depression. They always thought art was just a mild hobby and had never actually seen one of your finished paintings before. It took all of the courage you could muster to show them a piece you prepared for them. After all, it was more than just a picture to you. It was your heart, your dreams—it was a piece of your soul. It went better than you expected. The painting made your dad smile and your mother tear up. Since you had no job, they let you move back in and turn your room into a studio until you could figure things out.

And picture this.

You turned back to the Internet for advice, only this time you weren't looking for someone to talk you off a ledge. You wanted tips on color blending and assistance on applying primer. You started posting pictures of your work to various forums looking for guidance, but you got more than you bargained for. You began receiving compliments—total strangers telling you how much they loved your art.

A few people even commissioned pieces from you. You sold your first painting for $300 to a newly wed couple in Minnesota who said your art would be perfect for their new home. It was surreal. All you ever wanted to do was paint and now people were paying you for it. You opened an online store, started a blog, and even built a website with links to all of your social media accounts. You began to rack up followers on Facebook and Twitter. A couple of your paintings were blogged around the Internet thousands of times. An art enthusiast magazine even did a feature on one of your pieces. It wasn't on the cover or anything, but it was an honor just to get a tiny blurb.

Eventually, you made enough money to move out of your parents' house and get a small apartment of your own. You certainly weren't rich, but you got to wake up and do nothing but paint every day, just like you always dreamed.

One morning you opened your eyes to see a half finished commissioned piece staring back at you from across the room. Rays of early morning sunshine shimmered in through the window, falling on the partially completed painting. It glimmered in the daylight. You thought about how lost you would have been if not for that guardian angel on the Internet who convinced you to paint your sadness away. You smiled to yourself—the first time in a long time that it wasn't forced because you knew that you were finally happy.

But picture this.

When one begins to receive admirers one also starts to attract critics—people who question how or why you got to where you were in your career. Some of them were jealous. They wanted what you had. Many of them were artists in their own right who didn't receive nearly the amount of attention you got. You found their hate silly. After all, it's not like your paintings were touring museums around the country. You were barely scraping by, but they couldn't support themselves with their art so they hated you.

Some of your other detractors weren't artists at all. They were trolls who couldn't stand to see another person happy so they did their best to knock you down a peg. They used the cloak of anonymity to message you through Twitter just to call you names. They told you that your work was "crap," but when they said that they weren't just insulting your paintings, they were insulting you. Remember, your art was a reflection of your heart, your dreams—it was a piece of your soul and these sorry excuses for human beings, hiding behind idiotic user handles, were shitting all over it.

And then something strange happened. You no longer heard the praise and the compliments. They were still there, but almost muffled in a way—suffocated and drowned out by a vocal minority who only wanted to see you fail.

You fought to prove yourself—to paint something that would make even your most overly zealous hecklers change their minds about you, but the more of your heart you poured into your work, the harsher their words became. The closer you got to creating your very own *Blue Dancers*, the more hate and vitriol they spewed at you.

It began to consume you. It was all you could think about.

Picture this.

Hacking isn't nearly as difficult as Hollywood would have you believe it is. You don't need to be a zit-faced computer whiz that spends eighteen hours a day in a dark basement eating Cheetos and drinking Mountain Dew to learn how to do it. You don't even need to know how to get around firewalls or disassemble code. All you need is patience. Patience and the understanding that people, even anonymous Internet trolls, get a little too comfortable and give away personal information without even thinking about it.

Now picture this.

The haters kept coming for you. Every time you posted a picture of your work or announced another sale on Facebook, there they were, popping up like a rash of pus-filled herpes sores. One commenter in particular really got under your skin. His username was Dark_Painter97 and every remark he made on your art blog was rude and spiteful. "Overrated," he called you—"unoriginal" and "uninspired" as well. You could see the resentment seething out of every comment he left underneath your posts.

You had grown sick of his cyber-bullying. Part of you wanted to see what this keyboard warrior looked like in real life, so without thinking you clicked on his username. The link directed you to the profile page of his blog, but he didn't have any pictures uploaded to it. However, a caption in the "about" section caught your eye.

It said: Follow me on twitter @Dark_Painter97.

You checked out his Twitter account to see if this anonymous jackass had posted any photos of himself. He hadn't, and his profile picture was just some stupid cartoon character, but you did notice he was very active on his account. He went back and forth, tweeting jokes with one particular user quite frequently—a teenager whose user handle included his real name with a very clear face pic. They appeared to be good friends. You realized then that the

"97" in Dark_Painter97 was most likely a reference to the year your tormenter was born. It made sense. It takes a certain amount of immaturity and free time to cyber-bully someone, and teenage boys have both of those in spades. You performed a Facebook search of his friend's name and found him pretty easily. His profile page had the privacy functions disabled so it wasn't hard to poke around.

This teenager only had about 125 friends on Facebook so you began filtering through his list, looking for boys who were born in the year 1997. It only took about an hour of sifting through profile pages until you found something that struck a chord with you. It was a boy who fit the bill. He was a smarmy little weasel who looked like he hadn't been outside a day in his life. Everything about his face irked you: from his bird's beak of a nose to the pair of bulky, camouflage-print Oakley sunglasses he was wearing in his profile pic. You wanted so badly to smash his smug smile into paste.

Then you looked at the info section of his page and you felt the light bulb in your head slowly begin to brighten.

Likes: Gaming, Manga, and Painting

Okay, that's a check, but liking to paint doesn't automatically make him the culprit.

Birthday: June 26, 1997

Double check.

And of course . . .

Follow my art blog @Dark_Painter97

Checkmate, bitch.

You had him. You knew what that insufferable little troll looked like, where he lived— you even knew what high school he went to. In just over an hour and a half you had learned everything you could ever want to know about him. But what were you going to do with your newfound information? According to his Facebook page, he lived a state away. That's a long way to go just to tell someone off. You told yourself that driving over state lines for the sole purpose of yelling at some idiot kid was crazy, but you couldn't stop yourself. It was like someone else had taken control of your body. Before you knew it, you were on the Interstate, half-way between the teenager's hometown and your apartment.

You stopped off for a burger when you hit his county and looked his parents' information up on your cell phone. Finding their home address was easy. The time was around 4:00 P.M. when you pulled up to his house. According to their Facebook pages, his mom and dad both worked nine-to-fives so you figured they wouldn't be home yet. You could see the little brat through the window fiddling around on his computer, probably leaving another disparaging comment on the latest picture you uploaded to your blog—either that or looking at porn. Things had worked out too perfectly for you. You had come too far not to give him a piece of your mind so you pulled your car into the driveway and knocked on the front door.

You could tell he was confused when he answered it. He had no idea who you were, which was something you found funny. If you had spent as much time as he did harassing someone on the Internet, you figured you'd at least recognize them if they were standing at your front door.

You opened your mouth to speak. You even pointed an accusatory finger at him, but his entitled little face made you so damn angry. You blacked out.

When you came to your senses you were standing over him in the foyer. Now that arrogant look on his face was gone. Instead, it appeared as if a cherry bomb had exploded in it. His nose had been mushed into pulp and his left eye was completely swollen shut. You were taken aback with yourself. How had it happened? You weren't even a violent person. In fact, you had never planned on causing the kid any sort of physical harm.

You looked at the grandfather clock against the wall; it was 4:30. Where had the time gone? Who knew how long you had before his parents got home? Charges started to rattle off in your mind: aggravated assault of a minor, burglary. Who knows, maybe even attempted murder? If they caught you then you'd do the next fifteen years in prison for sure. Goodbye art career. Then you had another thought. If you just ran off, the snotty little shit might be able to identify you once he came to. So you panicked.

You slung his unconscious body over your shoulder and carried him outside to your car. Lady luck must have been on your side because there was no one else in sight. You dumped him in your trunk and backed out of the driveway as fast as you could before speeding off to make your getaway.

Only about 150 people get abducted by strangers in the United States annually. Now this kid was one of them and he was locked in the back of your trunk.

Picture this.

One in every 15,000 people is murdered in the U.S. each year. Doesn't that number sound high? It's true, though. Don't believe me? Look it up: one in every 15,000 people. Calculate those stats over a 75-year lifespan, and that means there is a 1 in 200 chance that someone will try to kill you.

It's a terrifying thought, really. In comparison, your chances of getting hit by a car are only 1 in 600, which means you're three times more likely to get gutted by a knife-wielding maniac or shot by a jaded ex-lover then you are to get run over by a minivan whose driver was texting while speeding through an intersection.

Now picture this.

You made it back inside your apartment with the kid. It was late so you were able to smuggle him up to your unit under the cover of darkness. To your knowledge, no one had seen you. You were safe for the moment, but you were sick to your stomach about what had transpired. You remembered the warm fuzzy feeling you got after reading the advice of your guardian angel and you were pretty sure the mixture of emotions that was now brewing inside you was the exact opposite. You wondered what kind of guidance that anonymous angel of the Internet would give you this time. But what were you going to do? Start a thread on Reddit about it?

Today I Fucked Up By Assaulting And Kidnapping A Minor

The kid was bleeding profusely from the mutilated chunk of flesh hanging off his face that used to be a nose. You placed him in your bathtub to prevent him from gushing all over the floor of your apartment while you thought about how to rectify the situation.

Tears began to well up in your eyes once you realized how screwed you were. You were no criminal; you were an artist. But artists don't beat their critics to within an inch of their lives.

"I'm sorry!" you cried out to the kid, whose body, a broken pile of pulverized meat, lay motionless in your tub. "I never meant for this to happen."

You feared he would die in your bathroom before you could muster up the courage to call him an ambulance. You knew you had made a terrible mistake and needed to own up to it, but you were so afraid of going to prison.

Between your sobs you heard a whimper. You peered up to see the kid begin to stir. The eye that wasn't swollen shut made contact with yours. His sclera was as red as a dog's dick and you could tell he was straining to focus, but he was staring right at you. The teenager's whimpers transformed into something that resembled a low gurgle—almost as if he was drowning on the blood that had pooled in the back of his throat. But you realized he wasn't drowning, he was laughing, causing your concerns to give way to confusion. He forced out a few grunts in an effort to say something, his voice whistling through the broken teeth, jagged shards of bone, that you had shattered with your fists.

"Y-you're that fucking shitty artist, aren't you?" he groaned.

His gurgling laugh began again and you understood it was directed at you. He had won. With nothing but an Internet modem and a laptop he had successfully derailed your career and he knew it too. You were going to spend the rest of your life in prison. With that thought, a fiery rage swelled inside your chest. You didn't deserve what the little shit had done to you. All you wanted to do was make art, to paint your own *Blue Dancers*, and this entitled piece of trash had taken it away from you.

There was no blacking out the second time. You were fully aware of what you were doing when you mounted his body and began to pummel his face. With each blow, you could feel his cheekbones collapse more and more underneath your knuckles. You clawed at his eyes like a rabies-stricken animal, then forced your hands inside his mouth and pulled at his jaw, popping it from its hinges. And when your arms got sore, you stood up and let your boots take a turn at the kid's cranium.

Picture this.

It takes 200 pounds of pressure to crush a human skull.

By the time you had finished whaling away on the teenager his head looked like a plate of pink and purple mashed potatoes. One in every 15,000 people in the United States is murdered every year and now the kid whose brains were currently spilling down your bathtub's drain was the newest casualty of that statistic.

You washed his blood off your hands in the sink and tried to calm down a bit. After looking back at the headless corpse in your tub you realized you were a little frightened with yourself, but it wasn't because you had just murdered a teenager in cold blood. It was the sensation of ecstasy washing over your body that worried you. It felt amazing, like you had just lived out a fantasy. Not a sexual one—stomping the kid's skull in didn't get you off, but it was more than a little empowering. The snotty turd deserved everything he got, but now you had a new problem on your hands.

It didn't take a criminal mastermind to know that keeping the kid's body in your tub was a bad idea, but getting rid of it wasn't as simple as chucking it down the trash chute. You were an artist, though, and artists have creative minds. So you did what creative minds do. You got creative.

Picture this.

On average, 75 people are arrested in the United States for having sex with the deceased every year. Don't believe me? Look it up: 75 people. This is especially concerning considering there are four states, Louisiana, Kentucky, Oklahoma, and North Carolina, where necrophilia isn't even against the law.

Of the 75 people arrested for making love to the dead annually, nearly half of them work in mortuaries. Given these facts, one can assume that funeral homes are a magnet for necrophiliacs. It makes sense when you think about it. After all, it seems like the dream job for someone who indulges in that kind of fetish.

Many psychologists believe that only a small fraction of these people actually have sexual attractions to dead bodies. Most engage in necrophilia due to social anxieties. It's the fear of rejection or the body's inability to perform under pressure that causes people to stray down this path. Corpses can't laugh at the size of your penis or roll their eyes if you can't get it up, so people find comfort and safety in the dead. It is for that reason that a staggering 94 percent of necrophiliacs are men.

Just like any sexual fetish, necrophilia has its own dark little community on the Internet. If one looks hard enough, they'll be able to find forums where users anonymously trade pics and tell stories of their latest sexual conquests. Well, I say anonymously, but as I explained before, when it comes to the Internet, people have a tendency to get a little too comfortable and give away their personal information without even thinking about it.

So picture this.

You opened up your laptop and did a little digging. Google is magic; within minutes you were perusing a forum full of cadaver-loving freaks. An hour or two of browsing and you stumbled upon a thread that sparked your interest. In an off-topic, throw-away comment, one of the perverts claimed to regularly visit a pizza joint not more than five miles from your apartment before engaging in his morbid sex-capades.

After scanning his comment history you saw that he often bragged about how his job supplied him with an endless stream of what he called his "real love dolls." It turned out he was a mortician who really enjoyed the alone time he spent with the corpses he was supposed to be beautifying.

You created an account and messaged him, claiming to be a nineteen-year-old girl who was really into watching guys screw stiffs. When he asked for verification you scrounged up some pictures of your friend's little sister and sent them to him. People are gullible when they want to believe something and this guy really wanted to believe that a cute coed was interested in perverts who fuck dead bodies.

He sent you a face pic. When you performed a reverse image search it directed you right to his Facebook page. The idiot had even messaged you his profile picture. His Facebook page did indeed confirm that he was a mortician and even listed the name of the funeral home he worked in. You smiled to yourself when, after looking the place up, you read that it had a crematorium. However, there was something else you found out about him after digging through his information—something you found very useful. The pervert had a family too—a wife and an eleven-year-old son.

You sweet-talked the mortician through the night, encouraging him to tell you about the disgusting things he does to newly arrived cadavers. He said that he wanted to fuck you on top of them. It turns out he was one of the few necrophiliacs that didn't have a fear of performing. This sicko was just genuinely attracted to dead bodies. You told him all the nasty things you knew he wanted to hear. When you asked for a dick pic, he was more than happy to oblige. The picture he sent you was a full-body nude with his erect cock and face clearly visible in the frame.

The two of you made plans to meet up at the mortuary after hours for a little ménage à trois with a twenty-four-year-old model who had recently died from a coke overdose. For some reason, he always seemed really excited to tell you how his "real love dolls" had passed. You assumed it was part of the fetish.

You showed up at the funeral home the following evening with a manila folder full of hard evidence. He broke down and started crying when you explained to him that he'd been duped. You presented him with the photos he sent you and explained to him that you had screenshots of the previous night's conversation saved and backed up. The mortician begged you not to show his wife. Apparently she had caught him once on top of a seventeen-year-old girl who had perished in a car wreck. His wife was pregnant at the time and only stayed with the mortician for the baby's sake, but she had informed him that if she ever found out he was doing it again, she'd call the cops and take his son away from him forever. He tried to make you go away by writing you a check, but you refused the bribe. You hadn't come for money.

You explained that you needed him to help you make a body disappear. The plan was simple. The funeral home had a crematorium and all you needed was access to it. The mortician reluctantly agreed to help you in exchange for keeping his revolting secret under wraps, so the two of you headed out to your car and hoisted an oversized duffle bag containing Dark_Painter97's body out of your trunk. You carried it inside, but when you asked the mortician to direct you to the furnace he waved his hand.

"I've got it from here," he told you.

You shot him a suspicious look and informed him that if he was planning on going to the police, your evidence would be in his wife's inbox the next day.

"Don't worry," he said. "You're safe. The kid will be ashes by the end of the night."

He asked you how the teenager died so you told him your story.

"Wow, I get murders from time to time, but that sounds especially brutal," he responded after hearing your grisly tale.

When you were finished, you thanked him for his help and started out the door.

"No—thank you," he said.

His remark left you puzzled. It wasn't until after you started your car and pulled out of the parking lot that you realized what the mortician was showing his appreciation for. You had delivered him a new play toy—a "real love doll"—and he was going to have some fun with it before he sent it off to the incinerator.

Picture this.

Roughly 85 percent of the country's population has access to the Internet. That means approximately 270 million people in the United States alone are connected to the world wide web. Of that 270 million, a little over half have profiles on active social networking sites, which makes the number of people using Twitter, Facebook, Snapchat, Tinder, and all the other flavors of the week tally somewhere around 135 million.

You were one of the 135 million. So what did you do after having just gotten away with murder? You hopped on social media to help yourself forget about the past couple of days. The problem was, images of Dark_Painter97's caved-in skull kept flashing through your mind. Even worse, you couldn't help but picture what that perverted mortician was most likely doing to the partially headless cadaver you had brought him.

Your thoughts turned back to your guardian angel. You hadn't revisited your old suicide thread since that anonymous hero of the Internet had rescued you from your depression. It wasn't necessary. Up until a few hours ago, you had believed yourself to be relatively happy. But the day had been a traumatic one so you decided to check in on the cyberspace superman to see if he was still crusading around, searching for lost souls to save.

It took a minute for you to remember your password, but once you logged in you began to navigate the site, looking for the familiar forum. It stung more than you thought it would to reread the post. It reminded you how black the world seemed back then. You scrolled down the thread, searching for your guardian angel—the one person on the planet who seemed to understand you.

The comment was still there so you began to read it, hoping that you would again be able to pull something useful from the sage advice that had once saved your life, but you stopped halfway through. You had seen something that made your heart rise in your throat because for the very first time, you had read your guardian angel's username.

Dark_Painter97

You rubbed your eyes and looked again just to make sure you weren't hallucinating, but the text on your monitor hadn't changed. You came to a realization that made you feel physically ill.

Approximately 135 million Americans are active on social media sites and you murdered the only one that had given you a reason to wake up in the morning.

It was utterly ridiculous. How could a human being be so sympathetic and understanding one day and such an obnoxious little twat the next? It was like a bad dream. You felt as if a war for your sanity was being waged inside your head. Part of you wanted to laugh at the irony of the situation. Another part of you wanted to cry. You ended up spending the entire evening staring at an unfinished piece leaning up against the wall of your apartment, not even able to remember whom you were even painting it for. Did it matter? It was like the whole damn world had lied to you.

It wasn't until morning that reality started to sink in. Perhaps the sun helped to burn off the fog that had been shrouding your brain since your revelation, but for whatever reason you no longer felt helpless. You realized that all this time, you had been using your guardian angel as a crutch—leaning on his words of wisdom whenever you felt like you couldn't stand on your own. Unfortunately, it turned out you had been worshiping a false idol. In reality your champion had been a chump all along—just another jealous wannabe who only cared about seeing you fall. The sick part was, you knew Dark_Painter97 was just the tip of the iceberg. You had other critics. Worse ones—and they deserved everything he got. Maybe even more. That strange feeling of ecstasy had once again returned, only this time it didn't make you feel frightened. It made you feel unstoppable.

Picture this.

Every avalanche starts with a single snowflake. Contemplate that for a second. It's a crazy thought, but it's absolutely true. The fact that a force so deadly and dangerous can come from something so innocent and harmless is remarkable.

When you first started snooping around that annoying Internet troll's Twitter account you couldn't have had any idea what it would lead to. There was no way to predict that mere hours later you would be passing off his headless corpse to a mortician with a fetish for the dead. There was also no way to anticipate the other murders it would lead to, but after discovering that you had killed your guardian angel, you felt like there was no point in simply ignoring the rest of your critics.

So you sought them out and made them pay for every hurtful comment they ever messaged you. You started with those who only lived a day's drive away. Like a predator hunting its prey you'd stalk them, lying in wait for the perfect time to strike. Their deaths were usually agonizing ones. You made sure that each and every one of your victims suffered painfully. The mortician was in your back pocket. You still had the ability to blackmail him. He feigned frustration with his predicament, but both of you knew he was happy with the arrangement. After about the third or fourth "love doll" you brought to him, he began making requests.

"I'd really appreciate it if the next one you brought in didn't have teeth," he would say to you. "Can you get me someone who maybe has a genetic birth defect?"

You entertained his bizarre fetish. After all, it didn't matter to you what happened to the bodies you were bringing in, as long as they were a pile of ashes in the morning. The mortician had a network of people like him—hardcore cadaver-humpers across the country. Many of them also worked in funeral homes and had access to their own crematoriums. Things probably started to snowball out of control when you found yourself going on vacation just to off another critic.

Painting had become secondary to you. It no longer thrilled you the way murder did. You only kept painting and posting photos to the Internet as a means to find more people to kill. You no longer strove for perfection in your art. *Blue Dancers* had drifted further away than ever. You started to purposefully make mistakes in order to attract more negative opinions. After a while, you didn't even care if the people you were hunting were offering genuine constructive criticism or not. No one was safe.

But even an avalanche finally reaches the bottom of the mountain.

One day a detective showed up at your apartment and started asking questions. He was trying to connect the disappearance of two of the people you had killed. You could tell by the look in his eye that he didn't consider you a suspect yet, but you knew that he was smart. It would only be a matter of time before he put the pieces of the puzzle together and realized what you had done.

So picture this.

You packed up your belongings, emptied your bank account, and left town that night. You didn't want to rot in prison so you moved to the other side of the country and changed your name. With a haircut and a pair of colored contact lenses (you always wanted hazel eyes) you started a new life for yourself.

In a few days you would read about yourself in the news—an up-and-coming painter who suddenly disappeared without a trace. 90,000 people are reported missing every year and now you were one of them. A few days after that you were the main suspect in the deaths of the two people that detective had questioned you about. The cops were never going to find you though. You were too smart for them.

But there was a problem. People still needed to die. Lying low for the rest of your life just wasn't an option, but you knew the police would be looking for a painter so you picked up a new type of art, one that was sure to attract its fair share of critics—writing.

Given your actual motives, you figured horror was an appropriate genre to publish in. You created new social media accounts under your fake name, and even used photos of a guy you went to high school with who had died in a motorcycle accident for your profile pics. People seemed to enjoy the stories you posted on the Internet and after a little while you began to get popular. Your tales were read on forums, translated into other languages, and some of them were even published in short story collections.

Now that your work had become well known, you began to do little things that you knew would encourage criticism. You used run-on sentences and purposefully made small grammatical mistakes in hopes that someone would try to correct you. From time to time, you even wrote stories in a second-person narrative, knowing full well just how polarizing it can be for readers.

You stayed connected to the mortician and his network of perverted funeral workers. Your trap had been set and now all you had to do was wait for critics to come along who couldn't resist tearing your work to pieces—and along they came. Like a moth to a flame, people were drawn to the flaws you had engineered into your writing. They pointed them out, under the cover of anonymity, but the masks they wore were as flimsy as papier-mâché.

There is no privacy anymore—no way to truly remain faceless. If someone wants to dig hard enough, they can learn as much about you as your closest and dearest friends.

So let me ask you a question. One that I'm sure a lot of you will laugh off once you realize whom this story is about, but one that you'd be wise to take very, very seriously the next time you post to the Internet.

Are you picturing it yet?

CREEPING CRIMSON

Michael Marks

The Hedges Motel and Motor Lodge was the kind of tucked-away place you don't find on purpose. It's not mentioned in any roadside guides or travel pamphlets, it doesn't advertise, and it doesn't have a webpage for booking—in fact, if you blink as you make the turn around the bend where it's nestled you'll miss it altogether.

That being said, it's not at all an unpleasant-looking place—a single-story motel and restaurant built with the aesthetic of a log cabin. It sits nestled in a surrounding forest of sweet-smelling redwood and pine, and when mixed with the scent of rain—like when I went—it seems downright heavenly. The burnt orange of the tree bark surrounding the stained wood buildings stands out—even when darkened by the rain and dim light of dusk. Yet a sinister tone can be felt and glimpsed if you're looking hard enough. The red sign reading VACANCY casts its light on the surrounding area, giving the sap leaking from the redwoods the tone of blood seeping from open wounds.

When my wife and I made the turn that brought that place into our view I was already road weary. We had plans to meet some friends of ours at a cabin; it was getting late and we'd already been on the road a long time with plenty of miles left to go. I should have kept driving; no matter the miles between me and sleep, I should have just kept on down the winding road and on to my destination. My empty stomach and heavy eyes had other plans, though, and I pulled into its parking lot.

I wish I would have blinked.

• • •

"Are you sure you want to get a room? I mean, I could just take over driving while you get some sleep," my wife Helen said. I answered her before I spoke by putting the car in park and shutting off the engine.

"I'm exhausted, and hungry, and honestly I just want a real bed for the night." I smiled and leaned back in my seat, rubbing my hands over my face, before continuing. "Besides, it's getting dark and pouring rain. On these roads, I'd rather not chance it."

Helen sighed, "I suppose you're right." She looked out of her window and up toward the sky as if diagnosing the weather. "I hope it clears up a bit by morning."

A quick flash of lightning filled the air and thunder rolled above our heads.

"I think that's the weather gods saying no." I smiled and grabbed my jacket from the backseat. "I'll get us a room."

• • •

I shook the rain from my jacket and stepped into the lobby. A portly older man behind the counter looked up from his portable television to greet me with a cheery smile. He groaned as he got to his feet and composed himself by straightening his flannel shirt and running his fingers through his thin silver hair before speaking.

"Good evening, young fella." He dropped his hands to the counter and leaned forward toward me as I approached. "What can I do ya for?"

"Hey there, I'm gonna need a room for two for the night." I smiled back and took in the decor. A fireplace burned in the other corner of the room and everything still had that log cabin charm inside. I could smell brewing coffee and that added to the warmth of the place.

"Sign in here." The old man plopped a huge register down on the counter and held a pen out toward me. The ledger was full of names but only two above mine had the same date.

"Busy night?" I asked, half joking and hoping the jovial tone came across in my tired voice.

"Couple others, a family with a couple of kids and them other fellas." He looked past my shoulder like he was looking for someone as I leaned down to sign. "'Tween you and me I think them other two might be a little light in the loafers, if ya catch my meaning." He whispered and met my eyes with a slow nod.

I chuckled, a bit caught off-guard by his antiquated turn of phrase. He stood up straight, looked over my shoulder again, and then limply flicked his wrist down as if to further explain. His eyes flicked around the lobby as if he were going to be caught making his gesture and a hint of worry crept up behind the otherwise cheery face.

"Yeah . . ." I handed him back the pen as I finished writing my name. "How's the coffee in your restaurant?"

"Better than what we got here in the lobby, I'll tell you that much." He grabbed the register and put it back under the front desk. He reached behind him and moved his hand along a row of keys before plucking one off and handing it to me. "Room 1-C, enjoy your stay Mr. . . ." He paused to lean down beneath the front desk and read my name off the register. "Mr. Gamble."

"Call me Tom," I said, taking the key from him and putting it in my coat pocket. "Mr. Gamble never really suited me." The old man laughed heartily at my statement as if he were in on some joke that went over my head.

"Well Tom, if you need anything just call the front desk and ask for Otis." He pointed a pudgy thumb at his chest with pride. I nodded and thanked him. As I headed back out into the rain, I looked back only once and saw him returned to his seat and watching his little TV with a satisfied smile.

• • •

After dropping our things off in the room, my wife and I went to the restaurant. It was little more than a dining counter being worked by one man who served as both waiter and cook, but it would do. As we took our seats we saw the family Otis had mentioned, a little further down the counter. The father—a man in his late 30s wearing a polo shirt and board shorts during a thunderstorm—nodded to me as we sat down. His daughter was running around with her arms outstretched making plane sounds as her parents focused on their cheeseburgers.

"She's adorable." Helen put her hand on my shoulder and looked over at the little girl with a smile. The girl noticed and became suddenly shy, hiding behind her mother's legs. Helen waved at her anyway and took a seat next to me as I looked over the laminated menu.

"Sorry, she's shy!" The girl's mother chimed in with a soft voice. She too was in her late 30s and far more appropriately dressed for the weather in a heavy jacket and jeans. "Say hi to the lady, Lydi beans."

"Lydi beans" poked her head out briefly from behind her mother's legs and waved before retreating. It was an act so adorable that even in my tired and half-starved state it made me smile.

"Hi, sweetheart," Helen said, looking across me at the little girl before switching her attention back to the mother. "How old is she?"

"Lydia is six." She looked down at her daughter as she spoke; the little girl stuck her head out again, realizing that she was now the focus of the adults' attention.

"And a half!" she chimed in.

". . . and a smart-aleck. Sit down and eat your grilled cheese, Lydi beans," Daddy board shorts chimed in.

"How you folks doing tonight?" A gruff voice suddenly came from in front of us and I looked up to see a gaunt bearded man in a greasy apron now standing there as if by magic. "What can I get you?"

"Coffee and a burger is fine. Hun?" I tapped Helen on the shoulder and she broke her gaze from the little girl long enough to react.

"Oh, I'll just have the same."

"You got it." The cook shuffled back into the kitchen just as the family was finishing up their food. My wife and I said goodnight to them as they passed and they wished the same to us. Lydia turned around as she stepped out the door and waved goodbye to us before throwing on the hood of her jacket and extending her arms out like plane wings once again as she ran into the rain with her parents.

• • •

After dinner we headed back to the room. I took a nice long shower and Helen laid back on the bed clicking through the channels. When my shower was over and I was getting dressed I noticed that I could hear the family from the restaurant talking in the next room—pretty clearly, too, considering they were talking at normal volume.

"Can you believe how thin these walls are?" I said to Helen as I stepped out of the bathroom in a cloud of steam.

"I know, right?" Her eyes looked behind me noticing how fogged up the bathroom was. "Jesus, did you take a shower or create a sauna?"

"There's no vent in there, no window either." I tossed my towel and rummaged through my bag for my cigarettes and lighter. "Guess we're going to have to skip the sex tonight."

"What does a bathroom window have to do with that?" she said with a confused laugh.

"No, you goofball, because of the walls." I found my cigarettes and Zippo finally and zipped my bag up. I turned toward my wife with a smile and held them up in offering.

"No, no, I don't feel like getting up." She splayed out taking up as much of the bed as possible and closed her eyes. "Hurry back, though. Sex is still on the table; we just have to be really, really, deathly, quiet."

"Maybe they sleep with earplugs?" I said. I heard my wife laugh as I stepped out beneath the overhang in front of the line of rooms and closed the door behind me.

• • •

I sat in a chair by the ice machine and had my cigarette. The storm continued to pound down on the little roadside motel and the red light from the vacancy sign made it look like blood was falling from the sky. My attention was drawn to the other end of the walkway as someone stepped out of 1-A and started heading my direction. He nodded and raised one hand in a wave as he approached; in the other he had an ice bucket.

"Hey there." He smiled as he stepped past and opened the ice machine.

"Hey, how ya doing tonight?" I took another drag off my cigarette and blew it out into the streaks of red rain.

"Pretty good." He set down his filled ice bucket and looked at my cigarette with longing. "Would you mind if I have one those?"

I reached my pack out to him and he took one. I lit it for him and he sucked in a deep drag with a look of long lost satisfaction.

"My boyfriend is always on my case to quit, but nothing beats that after a long day."

"Amen." I agreed. "So are you here with your boyfriend?"

"Yup." He took another drag and scratched his stubble. "We were just talking about how paper thin these walls are."

"No shit!" I agreed. "My wife and I were just saying the same thing. It's nuts."

"Why do you think they stuck us all together like this? I mean we have to be the only three rooms booked. Why would they put us all right next to each other?"

"I dunno." I twirled the cigarette in my hand while I thought. "Maybe it's easier for the cleaning service. No one around here looked too spry."

"Yeah, maybe . . ." He trailed off clearly thinking deeper about it. "My name is David, by the way."

"I'm Tom." I shook his hand and finished my cigarette.

"Hey, I found a good movie playing." I heard someone call from down the walkway. I looked to see a man peeking his head out of David's room. "Did you get the ice? Wait . . . are you smoking?"

"Busted." I said with a laugh.

"Yeah, I guess so." David flicked his cigarette out into the storm and grabbed his ice bucket. "Guess I better get back. Good to meet you, Tom."

"You too." I responded rising from my chair. David ran off to his room and I could hear his boyfriend on his case before he even reached the door. I went back to my room, more than ready to lie down and finally get some sleep.

• • •

I hadn't been asleep an hour when I woke to the sound of a PA system kicking on with a screech. My wife and I both sat up in bed confused as hell as to what was happening, but before we could even get our bearings the chanting started.

It droned out of some unseen speaker and filled the room. The words weren't English—in fact—they weren't any language I recognized. The voice speaking them was low and weighty drawing out each sound as it was made.

"What the fuck is that?!" I shouted, getting out of bed and hunting around the room. I could hear the family next door waking up too. The voice echoed from their room as well and I realized Daddy board shorts was doing exactly what I was doing, only with more expletives.

I looked over at Helen, who had already picked up the phone and had it to her ear.

"Shit! There's no dial tone." She slammed the receiver down and got out of bed, rushing over to her purse while I continued to hunt for where the sound was coming from. It was reverberating around the room making it hard to track down. I went to flick on a light to help in the search but nothing happened.

"Are you kidding me, the power is out too!" I slid my jeans on and got ready to storm to the front desk to ask cheery Mr. Otis exactly what the fuck was going on.

"No cell phone signal either." Helen held her phone up to me as if I wouldn't believe her. I could hear Daddy board shorts next door slamming against something—an expletive following each hit. Further down I could hear David or his partner yelling something I couldn't make out.

"Stay here, I'm going to find out what the fuck is going on." I reached for the knob but it wouldn't turn. I shouldered against the door but it felt sealed shut. It was like slamming against a brick wall.

"What are you doing?" Helen came to my side and watched me press pointlessly against the door.

"It's locked, it's fucking locked." I gave up and stepped away from the door frustrated.

"What do you mean it's locked? How is it locked?" Helen started to check for herself and I didn't bother to stop her.

"I mean locked, from the outside or something. It won't fucking open!"

"Well, grab the key!"

"There is no keyhole on the inside of the door, Helen! I turned the lock and the deadbolt already, the thing isn't budging!" I flipped over a chair, even more frustrated.

"You guys are locked in too?" I heard Daddy board shorts yell through the wall. "What the hell is going on?"

"No idea!" I yelled back. "Are the guys on the other side of you locked in too?"

"Yeah." He responded and I heard him move away from the wall.

The chanting felt like it was boring its way into my skull. In a fit of anger, I grabbed one of the chairs and threw it against the window as hard as I could. The chair simply bounced off and landed upside down next to the bed, so I picked it up and started slamming it against the window as hard as I could. I could hear my wife screaming at me but didn't care. I didn't like feeling trapped and it was driving me insane fast. I needed out of that room.

On the fourth hit the chair shattered into pieces, and not a mark was left on the window.

"It's bulletproof." Helen walked over and touched the glass. "It's bulletproof fucking glass, Tom. Why does a hotel room have bulletproof windows?"

I opened my mouth to say "I don't know" yet again but my response was cut short by the sound of someone screaming bloody murder. Not screaming in anger or frustration like myself and Daddy board shorts had been, but someone screaming in pure agony.

• • •

"What's going on?" I shouted through the wall. I could hear the little girl Lydia crying on the other side and beyond her the sounds of screams and cries for help.

"I don't know," said more sensible Mommy. "Jesus, it sounds like someone is killing them in there. Teddy is trying to see from the window."

I figured Ted must be Daddy board shorts's real name. I walked away from the wall and peeked out through the window, I did my best to crane my neck at an odd angle and see down the walkway but it just wasn't possible—all I saw was crimson rain. Suddenly the screams of pain stopped and only the sounds of the chant remained.

"Oh God, I can hear one of them crying, he's saying—David's dead. Oh God, did someone die?" Sensible Mommy was talking to me through the wall. I could hear Ted talking to someone one further down the line, presumably David's boyfriend. I sat on the bed and tried to listen as Helen pressed herself against the wall to hear better.

"He says—the red came and got him. He's babbling, making no sense," Helen said, "I can just barely hear them. Jesus, Tom, he's begging for someone to get him out."

"Shhhhh, honey. It'll be fine; just cover your ears. Okay?" Sensible Mommy was talking to little Lydia. I could see them cuddled together on the bed in my mind's eye, talking to a wall, confused and scared.

Then the screams started again. Even through the family's room, I could hear him loud and clear begging for help and scrambling around his room like a madman. I could hear things breaking as he desperately tried to get away from something in a locked room with no way out. The girl and her mom next door were crying, and so were Helen and I as we listened to the man's screams die out in pained gurgling as he begged for us to help him.

• • •

The next few minutes were a mix of confusion, fear, and desperate attempts to escape. The chanting continued over the hidden PA system as Helen slammed her fists against the window shouting for help. I could hear Ted from next door doing the same thing, just kicking fruitlessly at an unyielding door. I sat on the bed staring at the floor, my thoughts swirling around and trying desperately to find a place to land. I'd never heard anything like the sound of those two men dying and my brain didn't seem capable of processing it.

"I wonder what movie they watched," I said, just loud enough for Helen to hear. My thoughts had picked a strange place to land. Helen stopped her pounding on the window and came over to the bed.

"What?" She knelt down in front of me. "What the hell are you talking about?"

"I met one of them outside. His name was David, he and his boyfriend were gonna watch a movie." I looked up from the floor and met her eyes. "I wonder what the last movie they watched was?"

"Tom . . ." Helen collected herself realizing she needed to help me get myself together. "Tom, you need to snap out of it. I know what your brain is doing right now, running in circles. I need you right now, though; we have to find a way out of this fucking room."

Her words barely had time to sink in when we heard a new sound from next door. Ted and his wife suddenly started shouting through the wall to get our attention.

"Something is coming through the wall!" Ted shouted. I could hear the whole family talking and shouting.

"What the hell is it?" Helen got up from kneeling in front of me and ran over to our wall to hear well. "What do you mean it's coming through the wall?"

"Jesus Christ, I don't know." Sensible Mommy was crying as she yelled. I could hear her go back to comforting Lydia, telling her not to look at "it."

The sound of the family's panic suddenly went wild—sobs were replaced by screams and shouts for help. Ted was telling his wife and daughter to get as far back from it as they could. I heard them bump along our shared wall as they attempted to move away.

Helen lost it in that moment and looked down at me with wild tear-filled eyes before grabbing the brass lamp off the nightstand and ripping the cord from the wall. She started using it like a hammer in an attempt to break a hole in the wall.

"We have to help them!" Helen shouted at me. "Tom, get the fuck up and help me, we have to do something to help them!!"

I heard Ted scream in pain as whatever they were trying to avoid finally got to him. The sound of Lydia screaming for her father—as I could only assume she was watching him die—finally snapped me out of my trance and I grabbed one of the broken chair legs to help my wife smash a hole in the wall.

We tore through the wallpaper, stucco, and drywall with our makeshift tools in a rhythm that made quick work of our side of the wall. Helen slammed the lamp against one of the cross beams and it bounced off, nearly hitting me. Ted's screams were suddenly cut off and Sensible Mommy must have gone into pure protection mode. There was no more screaming or crying as she realized what we were trying to do, and we heard her start smashing something against the wall on her side. The hole on our side might be just enough to squeeze Lydia through, the crossbeams being the only thing that worried me. Suddenly a hole opened up on Sensible Mommy's side too and their room came into view.

Directly in front of us was the woman I'd seen in the restaurant, her face now pale and streaked with tears. She worked furiously to tear through the wall, like a trapped animal doing whatever it took to protect its young. Over her shoulder I saw something far more disturbing.

There was a mass of red that looked almost like moss except it pulsed and breathed as it moved closer and closer to them. It had covered most of their room, and I could tell they didn't have anywhere to go but through. Offshoots like vines shot out, groping blindly and sticking to whatever they touched as it crept closer. The worst part was what was sticking out of the center of the crimson mass.

It was Ted, his body half melted. His skin was mostly sloughed off and the crimson was crawling all over what meat there was left. His ruined body still reached for its family, a hand outstretched toward his wife as she desperately tried to escape. My eyes met hers—only for a second, but it was enough to crush me inside. I worked just as furiously as she and Helen to make enough room to get them through, then I wanted to find a way out of that fucking room.

I needed to find a way out of that fucking room.

• • •

"Mommy, it's really close." The terror apparent in Lydia's voice sent chills down my spine. There was no way we'd made enough of a hole to fit the mother through and it was dubious as to whether Lydia would fit. Still, we worked furiously, portions of the wall falling away and piling at our feet. Those damn support beams made the amount of space available for anyone to squeeze through minimal.

"Okay . . ." the mother said, stopping her work suddenly. "It's too close, please, please take my daughter. Get her out of here however you can."

"No!" Helen screamed, still smashing her lamp against the wall. "We are all getting out of here."

"It's too close, I need to help get Lydia through. If it gets me before I do we'll both die." Her eyes were filled with tears as she lifted her daughter and told her to climb through the hole. The look of abject terror on the child's innocent face was enough to send tears streaming from my eyes. Helen and I both reached through and took her hands. As Lydia tried her best to squeeze into the hole, I could hear her mother speaking behind her.

"Go honey, it's gonna be okay . . . it's gonna be . . ." Her words turned into screams and Lydia followed suit. The girl was kicking and screaming as I heard her mother flailing wildly behind her and shouting. Lydia screamed for her mother as Helen and I worked together to try and pull her into our room.

"It hurts, Mommy, it hurts!" She was stuck and yelling for her dying mom. It was too much to bear and I felt like my heart was going to beat out of my chest.

"Pull, Tom!" Helen was screaming at me.

"I'm fucking trying—she's stuck!"

The mother's screams turned into wet choking sounds and gurgles just like everyone who'd been caught before her, and the creeping crimson mass had nearly finished its meal. It would undoubtedly be looking for the next.

"You're hurting me!" Lydia screamed.

"It's okay, honey, just a little more." Helen tried to sound soothing but her voice was filled with panic. She wasn't moving, then suddenly something was pulling her in the other direction.

Lydia was no longer screaming words, just screaming. In my head I remembered the first time I saw her pretending to fly around the restaurant. Her shyness, her sweet demeanor. Now here she was stuck in a wall screaming as something I could barely wrap my brain around pulled her toward it to be dissolved into a pile of soft bones.

"Oh God, Tom, she's going the other way. It's got her! It's fucking got her!"

"I know, just keep pulling! Don't give up."

The growls of Helen's and my efforts mixed with Lydia's screams of pain. Suddenly the girl came free and we all fell backward onto the floor. I looked up first and was shocked into silence by what I saw—made all the worse in the dim red light that shone through the window.

"You're going to be okay, honey, you're going to be okay." Helen hadn't looked up yet, and she hadn't noticed the girl was no longer crying or screaming. I tried to tell her, as she lay there with her arms wrapped around the little girl's body, but the words were stuck in my throat.

When Helen finally sat up and opened her eyes, she looked down and saw what had caused me to freeze in my spot on the floor in horror.

Lydia's lower half was gone, and patches of crimson tendrils were stuck to what was left. Helen's screams and tears came far more freely than my own.

• • •

We both staggered against the far wall as the tendrils consumed what was left of Lydia's body; I turned away, unable to watch what was happening. My mind tried to focus on something else other than the sound of her body dissolving less than two feet away from me. I scanned the room for anything that could help us get out, anything at all. The chanting was making it hard to focus; with each loop it seemed to get just a tiny bit louder, and at this point it was like being at a shitty rock concert.

"It's coming through the wall!" Helen gripped my shoulder and twisted me to see the slime pouring through the hole we'd made and the vine-like tendrils reaching through and sticking to the wall with an audible "thwack." I returned to scanning the room, and as soon as my eyes landed on Helen's hairspray I felt a click in my brain. I hunted around in my pockets for my cigarette lighter, and once I felt it in my palm I grabbed Helen by the wrist and dragged her with me to grab the spray can.

"I hope this works like in the fucking movies." My palms were sweaty as I pulled the lighter from my pocket, and when I flicked it I thought it was going to fly out of my hand. It took two tries for the spark to become a flame but once it was there I aimed the hairspray can behind it and walked toward the spreading mass of red hell.

I pressed down and the stream of hairspray caught the flame, sending a jet of fire forward. But the range was short and it didn't touch any of the thing that was starting to cover the whole wall between us and our former neighbors. I started to walk closer and Helen—who'd been gripping my arm like a vise—suddenly let go and started rummaging through my bag.

I got within range of the thing and tried again to douse it in flame. This attempt was more successful. I watched as the fire licked against the wall, burning away the wallpaper and searing the spreading red mass to a charred black. In the dim orange glow of my makeshift flamethrower, a small smile must have crossed my face as my heart filled with a feeling of justice, no matter how small. It was quickly replaced with fear as the thing made a sound . . .

. . . It screamed. Not like a human being would scream, mind you. It was more ethereal; it echoed what sounded like a thousand voices through the walls and made it seem like it was all around us. It even drowned out the horrid chanting. I nearly dropped my makeshift weapon to cover my ears but managed to endure. Helen, on the other hand, stopped her search and clapped her hands over her ears to protect them from the hideous noise.

"Keep going!" she screamed. "Get closer to the door." I watched her take her hands off her ears and grit her teeth as she returned to tearing through my luggage hunting for something. I looked back to see the wall in flames, but the tendrils still spread out; they had started to cover the floor in that disgusting pulsing moss. I pressed down the aerosol can again and started to cover as much of it as I could in fire. The screaming sound continued and Helen and I did our best to press through it.

I had to step over what was left of Lydia to get to the other side and next to the door. I pointed the flame down and burned the now gorging mass of tendrils and moss that had covered her. I apologized under my breath as I backed up closer to the door. Helen suddenly raised her hand up and in it I saw a yellow canister of lighter fluid, the stuff I used to refill my Zippo. She ran over to me and started squirting the flames on the bed and wall. They burned brighter for a few seconds as the room started to fill with a horrid stench. I then realized we were stuck in a burning room as my eyes started to sting from the smoke that rose up all around us.

"The door!" Helen shouted as if trying to explain how we were going to get out. She sprayed the door down with lighter fluid, as much as was left in the canister. I caught on to her lead and turned toward the door with my makeshift flamethrower and set it ablaze. The lighter fluid helped the wood catch quickly as Helen ran to the bathroom and started soaking towels in water. I looked over at her while she worked, her mind going a mile a minute in survival mode. I mouthed the words "I love you" and saw her make a brief terrified smile before she mouthed them back.

A tendril flew from the flames and landed against my leg before Helen finished with what she was doing. My leg erupted in pain as soon as it touched me, and I screamed my lungs out before turning my flame thrower on the grasping thing. I burnt my own leg as I torched it free, but the feeling of the fire was nothing compared to the way the crimson set my nerves alight. I could smell my own flesh burning and it was preferable to being taken by that thing. A few more tendrils groped blindly for me, landing with audible smacks against the dresser and the window.

Helen dodged them as she ran back toward me with two wet towels in her arms. She threw one over me and then leaned down and kissed me.

"Bust through that fucking door, Tom."

• • •

The thing's screams felt like they were going to make my ears bleed as I stared at the burning hotel room door like a rival. I pulled the soaking-wet towel around me and crossed it over my face like I was doing an impression of classic Dracula. I could feel Helen behind me, wrapped in a towel of her own and ready to follow me through the hole I was hopefully going to make. I looked back toward the shared wall and it was covered in a mixture of the crimson mass and flames that now licked up toward the ceiling. The fire was spreading fast and we had no choice but to try and bust through the door. If the crimson didn't consume us the fire would, and either was only moments away.

I got into a runner's stance and took one last look back at Helen, whose face held a stern yet encouraging look—as if to say

"You can do this" and "You better fucking do this" at the same time. I lowered my head, trying to get it clear of the smoke, and took a deep breath; the air was hot and stunk like boiling blood. I let the burning breath out and charged forward, putting all my weight into my shoulder.

I lowered my head as I struck the flaming door and felt it splinter apart despite more resistance than I was hoping for. I went spilling through the hole in a dive and rolled off the walkway out into the rain. I threw the towel off and scrambled back toward the door as I tried to stand. My hands were outstretched for Helen as I saw her make a rush toward the hole I'd made.

She leapt through the fire with her head down, much like I had, but suddenly fell flat on the surface of the walkway. I heard her crash down hard; it looked as if she'd been dragged down mid-jump. I ran over to her, and as I reached down to help her up I saw the red tendrils embedded in her leg. More fired out from the hole in the door, and just beyond it I could see a great flaming mass rise up and take ownership of the scream that had been permeating throughout the hotel. Helen tried to get to her feet but the thing started dragging her backward. She wrapped her arms around me tight and I did the same to her, refusing to let go.

"The sacrifice must be completed!" I heard someone yell from the direction of the lobby. I quickly looked to see chubby hotel manager Otis waddling toward us with a knife in his hand. The sight would have been almost humorous under any other circumstance, but as he got closer I realized I couldn't hold Helen and fend off that fat little monster at the same time.

Everything that happened next happened too fast for me to even do anything in reaction.

"Look what you've done to my motel!!" Otis screamed as he lunged forward with the blade. Helen looked me in the eyes for one brief moment and I knew what she was going to do—God help me, I knew. She released her grip on me and I tried my best to hold on. I was dragged a few inches across the rain-slick wood walkway as the crimson pulled her back toward the room. I felt the knife come down and strike my arm, causing me to recoil in pain and lose my grip, as I fell backward off the walkway from momentum. Helen quickly grabbed the fat little monster by the collar and I tried to run back over to them. I was too late, though, as the crimson pulled Helen's legs with one quick motion and Helen held firm to Otis's collar. I reached out for her as I watched them both vanish into the flames of the room. I could hear Otis screaming in sheer and absolute pain as the thing devoured him or the fire burned him, I'm not sure which. My wife, on the other hand—my strong wife, my beautiful Helen—didn't scream.

The creature howled in either triumph or pain as the room started to collapse down around it. I sat under the red neon light of the NO VACANCY sign, the NO very clearly lit up to keep people away from here while Otis was performing his sacrifice. The chanting still playing through the unburnt speakers in the other rooms was slowly winding down as the rain pelted my skin. The fire spread quickly through the hotel as I watched.

I stood in the rain for hours and watched it burn to the ground.

TEENY TINY

Max Lobdell

My doctors asked me to tell my story so other girls could read it and learn from my mistakes because I'll be dead soon. That makes me pretty sad to think about. I don't want other girls to be sick like I am. I guess they won't be sick exactly like me, because that would be crazy, but maybe they can read this and avoid making bad decisions.

When I was little, Mom used to hold me and say stuff like, "Oh Katie, you fit so perfectly on my lap! You're so teeny-tiny!" I loved it. She'd keep me warm and hug me and I felt so great. I'd always go to Mom if I felt sad or scared and she'd just scoop me up saying, "What's wrong, my teeny-tiny girl?" and I'd tell her what was making me upset and she'd always, always, *always* make it all better.

The most vivid memory I have was the day I turned ten. It wasn't of my party, which I vaguely remember being great, it wasn't the presents, some of which I still have, but it was when Mom had me in her lap that night and had tears in her eyes and said to Dad, "Katie's getting to be a big girl, huh?" I don't remember what my dad said, but there was no denying it: I wasn't her teeny-tiny girl anymore.

At ten years old, I was about 4'10", maybe 100 pounds. I was growing fast. Both my parents are tall. I remember being scared. The scale kept going up, and by the time I was eleven I was 5'2", 120 pounds and I started getting boobs. At that point, when I was sad, Mom would hug me tight and say the right things, but it all felt different. She never cradled me. She never had me in her lap. I felt cold and lonely even though I was never really cold or lonely. I just wanted to be closer to her like I was when I was little. So I decided to get little again.

Mom started to notice when I pushed my food around on the plate, trying to pile it up on one side to make it look like I had eaten more than I really did. "You're a growing girl," she said, kindly but firmly. "You need to eat." I couldn't leave the table until I was done.

That night after dinner, I remember lying on my back on the bed, staring at the ceiling and feeling the food in my stomach. Mom's words "you're a growing girl" echoed in my mind and I felt so sick that I ran into the bathroom and threw up. I was really glad I had my own bathroom so they couldn't hear me puking. After I was done, I felt so much better. Lighter and smaller, even.

Mom was so happy to see me eating normally again. She worried aloud that I might be getting the flu, so seeing me chowing down like my old self pushed those worries right out of her head. What she didn't see was how I went to bed afterward and while the bathwater ran, I threw it all up. I did this every day for years.

One of the sad truths about throwing up your meals is you don't lose all that much weight. I actually gained more. Sure, I'd get rid of what I'd eaten, but probably twice a week I'd be lying in bed, wide awake, fingering my collar bones, hip bones, and ribs, and obsessing over food. Something inside me would snap, and I'd run to the fridge or the cabinets and eat until I felt like I was bursting. Then, exhausted, I'd go back upstairs and pass out on my bed. Calorie-for-calorie, after those twice-weekly binges, I was eating more than I would if I was healthy. Except I really, really wasn't healthy. And nobody knew.

All this built up to the last few months after I graduated high school. I was 5'11", 175 pounds, seventeen years old. There was absolutely nothing I hated more than my body. I was constantly lonely and wanted to take my mind off it all. I decided to get a job. When I told Mom I found a position at a place that recycles old medical gear, she was really proud of me for taking the initiative. It was bittersweet; I knew she was starting to see me as an adult. Not her teeny-tiny girl. I felt like a complete and utter failure.

The recycling place where I worked dismantled big machines that hospitals used and sold the parts. I was the receptionist. I took phone calls and helped set up deliveries. The people I worked with were really nice and after a few weeks they gave me a key so I could get there early and have coffee ready and work orders printed out. One night, after everyone left, I went back there and let myself in. I still feel bad about breaking their trust.

A couple of days earlier my coworkers had brought in an old machine. They all were wearing heavy gloves and had on breathing gear like scuba divers. When they were done, I asked what it was. Apparently it was something hospitals use to give radiation therapy to cancer patients. I didn't know too much about that, so when I got home I went on Wikipedia and did a lot of research and then I got an idea.

When I let myself in that night, the place was empty. I made a beeline for where they had the radiation therapy machine and I investigated it. Most of it was completely dismantled. What I was looking for was conveniently labeled and brightly marked in a massive lead container. It took me a while to get the cover off. Lead's so heavy! But after I did, I saw a round metal part that looked like a wheel. I picked it up, rotated the mechanism, and it opened a little window in the front. A faint blue light was inside. I held it up to my eye and looked in. Nothing but that light. I thought it was probably what I was looking for.

I brought the object home with me and locked the door of my bedroom. I worked to pry the thing open with a screwdriver but it seemed locked from the inside. Eventually I got frustrated and I turned the wheel again to open the window and pushed my screwdriver into the blue stuff and tried scooping it out. It turned out to be pretty soft. A lot of it broke as I poked it with the screwdriver, and when I turned the wheel upside down, the pieces tumbled out onto my desk. Now I could see how pretty it was. It was like chunks of glowing blue clay and sand. I gathered it up as best I could and put it away, save for the little bit I was going to use tonight.

One of the things I'd read about radiation therapy was that it made the poor people with cancer really skinny. They just totally lost their appetites. I couldn't believe it was true. I'd always had such a big appetite. I kept telling myself I need to be really careful when I take this stuff because if I get too much of the radiation I could get cancer myself. I took a pinch of the blue clay, put it in my mouth, and swallowed it with a gulp of water. It felt warm going down even though the water was cold. Since I'd gotten home from the recycling place I'd been pretty warm, in fact. Cozy. Like a little puppy under a blanket.

That night I woke up sweating worse than I'd ever sweated in my life. The bed was totally soaked. Gross. Water weight wasn't really what I wanted to lose, but it was better than nothing. I took a shower and changed the sheets and went back to bed. My stomach ached a little.

When I woke up the next morning, my stomach hurt and I threw up a couple times. But, I wasn't even remotely hungry. That fact alone made the pain in my tummy pretty much go away. I didn't need to eat! Mom asked if I was bringing leftovers to work from last night's dinner and I lied and said we were going to get a pizza. I hate lying to Mom, but I didn't want her to worry. There was no need to tell her I wasn't hungry. At work, they'd finished disassembling the machine and started sending it out to wherever they send those things. I'd been really careful to put the canister back exactly as I left it. No one checked to see if the little wheel was still there.

The next few days were uneventful, aside from my stomachache getting worse and having to puke once or twice. I'd barely eaten anything since I started taking the radiation medicine. Whenever I got woozy from lack of food I ate an apple or a fat-free yogurt and I was fine. I was still sweating a lot. When I got on the scale, it said 168.

After a week of eating nearly nothing and faithfully taking my radiation medicine nightly, my stomachache got really, really bad. I'd stopped throwing up, but this time it felt like I needed to go to the bathroom. I went, and it was awful. There was so much—I was shocked. I'd apparently eaten and kept down more than I thought. I got on the scale after, though, and that helped me feel a lot better. 161.

Over the next couple days, one or two people told me how pretty I looked. They asked me if I lost weight and I said yeah, maybe a few pounds. I beamed. Over my whole adolescence I'd done nothing but get bigger. Now, finally, I was shrinking and on the way to teeny-tiny. I didn't feel too great, though. My tummy was constantly having me run to the bathroom and it still hurt afterward. I figured I was getting rid of all the extra fat. 158.

I was in the shower about ten days after I started taking the medicine and I was horrified to see some of my hair coming out. That was bad. Really, really, really bad. I stopped washing it immediately and let just the water rinse away the remainder of the shampoo. I got out of the shower and took almost an hour blow-drying my hair because I was too scared to use a towel that might pull more out. When the mirror was unfogged and my hair was dry, I checked to see how noticeable it was. There was a good-sized patch of bare, red scalp about 2" wide above my left ear. I pushed the hair around it to cover the patch. Some more fell out. It had to be a nutritional deficiency from all the meals I'd been missing. I put on my Titans hat and got dressed. When I brushed my teeth I noticed a little blood in the sink. I made a note to get some multivitamins after work.

I didn't shower the next day because when I woke up that morning, there was more hair on my pillow. My scalp was getting pretty visible. It looked prickly and raw but it didn't hurt. Since I was off work I stayed at home and looked online for all the nutritional deficiencies that might cause my hair to fall out and my gums to bleed. Most of the ones were covered by my multivitamin, so I tripled the amount I took just to be on the safe side. I had to go to the bathroom five times during the fifteen hours that I was awake. By the last time I was incredibly light-headed and so thirsty. I weighed myself before I started downing water and my radiation medicine. 150. The medicine helped me lose 25 pounds in less than two weeks.

Mom hugged me the next morning before I went to work. She ran her hands up and down my back and she made a remark about how skinny I'd gotten. Then, she said it: "Remember when I used to call you my teeny-tiny girl? I miss those days but I love you just as much as a grownup." Then she let me go. Pain, nausea, and despair washed over me. Without warning, my lightheadedness came back with a vengeance and I stumbled and fell on the kitchen floor. My hat fell off. With my head spinning, I vaguely remember Mom gasping, "Katie what happened to your hair?" before I violently threw up on the floor and myself. It was all blood. I passed out to the sound of Mom screaming.

I don't know how much time went by at the hospital. I wasn't completely unconscious, but all I remember—up until recently when they used drugs to wake me up—were images of doctors in the same scuba gear as the guys at work saying meaningless words like "cesium" and "sloughed" and "gray" that didn't mean the color.

Today, I can't move or talk and I'm writing this using a cool keyboard that can pick out letters using the movements of my remaining eye. Like I said in the beginning, I'll be dead soon. I'm not too fun to look at anymore. My hair's gone. And my lower jaw. And my skin. The nice doctors are giving me medication that helps me manage the pain and keep me alert. They asked if they could do tests and experiments on me to help understand what ingestion of the radiation medicine does to the human body. Apparently there was a Japanese man a few years ago named Hiroshi Ouchi who got a similar level of exposure and the same stuff happened to him. They said it would help other people in the future if they could compare our two cases. Of course I let them.

I can't eat food anymore. My esophagus got cooked away. Same with my stomach. The doctors are keeping me hydrated with a tube in my butt. I don't really like to think about it. I guess all the excitement I get as I wait here is when they weigh me every six hours to see if I'm able to retain the fluids they give me or if it all seeps out into the sheets. They hoist me onto a pad and a little machine voice says a number. This morning it said 72. The next time it was 69.

Mom and Dad have to wear those scuba suits when they come visit. Mom's always crying because she's not allowed to touch me. Dad just stares. Right before I started writing this, Mom bent down and started whispering to me some of the stuff I remember her saying when I was small. I closed my eye and imagined being warm and safe on her lap. "I love you, my teeny-tiny girl," she sobbed. I would have smiled if I had a mouth.

THE HORROR FROM THE VAULT

Isaac Boissonneau

Part 1.

The following conversations, audio recordings, and testimonies all pertain to the incident that occurred from October 1st to November 2nd, in the Alden County National Reserve and its outlying towns, Alden and Greenvale.

This first part contains a series of e-mails between researchers Michael Hayes and Richard Harris.

From: @Hayesresearch.gmail.com
To: richardharris@AldenNationalResearch
Subject: IMPORTANT FIND!!!

Richie.

I know that we haven't spoken in a long time and that you need your space, but, earlier today, while me and my crew were digging for new mineral samples, we stumbled upon something huge.

Get back to me as soon as you can.

Michael.

From: richardharris@AldenNationalResearch
To: @Hayesresearch.gmail.com
Subject: What is it?

Despite the creeping feeling that you're trying to get me to respond, I'll bite. What did you find?

Oh, and what do you mean by "new mineral samples"? What happened to the old mineral samples?

From: @Hayesresearch.gmail.com
To: richardharris@AldenNationalResearch
Subject: The Vault.

Richie, what happened to the old samples isn't anything to worry about right now, we've got bigger things to discuss.

As I had said in my previous e-mail, me and my crew—that is to say, a crew of twenty bored college grads—were digging up at the base of the tallest mountain in the park—I can't remember its name—when we found the entrance to the vault.

Most of the kids were more interested in the view, which was, granted, a very nice one, but some of the kids were actually trying to earn their credit for a change and it was this little group who called me over, rather suddenly, just as I was about to call it a day.

Their voices were so loud, and their collective tone was both excited and frightened. I leaped from my chair and ran past a little cluster of trees to where they were.

I found them all crowded around something that I couldn't make out until I was close enough, but when I saw what it was I understood their reactions.

The ground had collapsed where they had been digging, the loose soil falling away into a hole that had appeared out of nowhere.

So I pushed past the whispering, frightened students and looked down, trying to see if someone had fallen in, hoping that no one had—we're on a shoestring budget as it is without having to deal with a lawsuit.

But I didn't see some deep, dark pit, I saw a set of stairs descending down into the darkness.

A faint rush of cold air hit me when I leaned in for a closer look and I backed away. I've heard stories about toxic spores found in the tombs beneath the pyramids, so I went to my tent and retrieved my bandanna, which I tied around my face, as well as my gloves, which I put on.

I mean, I just had to see what was down there, I had to.

I returned to find that some of the kids were already starting toward the stairs. I warned them off it in my best "stern teacher" voice and made sure that they had some form of protection as well as lights.

I swear I must be the only one who thinks these things through.

I had one of the kids, a girl by the name of Lori Summers, go tell the others what we had found and what we intended to do and when she came back we started our exploration.

The stairs led farther down than I had anticipated, the descent halted only by a few landings where we stopped and talked among each other. Or, rather, the kids talked. I was too busy examining the floor, walls, and ceiling, and what I found is pretty damn strange.

The material looked like obsidian. Now, I'm not an expert in archeology, but I've never heard of a temple made of obsidian. Maybe you could share some of that knowledge with me?

The stairs ended after a bit and we found ourselves in an antechamber. It was colder than a frost giant's scrote down there, but the air was so still, stagnant even.

Probably a good thing I wore my mask and gloves, eh? Anyway, from the antechamber we emerged into a short tunnel that led to a surprisingly spacious chamber.

Everything was so dark that our flashlights did less than we'd have hoped. Thankfully nobody got hurt.

As it turned out, there were five chambers in total, just five, which strikes me as more than a bit weird.

But, believe me, it got weirder from there.

You see, the first four rooms held nothing: no dust, no furniture, no bodies, and no signs of animal life; I didn't even see a single spider or cobweb while I was down there.

But the fifth room was different. The fifth room had something in it. I honestly have no idea what the hell it is. At first glance I thought it was a sarcophagus of some kind due to its shape, but, when I got closer, I saw that this wasn't the case at all.

It had a rudimentary face and body etched into it, but, unlike the mummy's tombs that I've seen, the overall picture didn't add up to something human.

I honestly can't really describe what was wrong with it, but everything about it looked off despite how it looked from a distance.

The coffin is also made of metal, though I'll need to run a few tests to determine just what type of metal it is.

We brought it back here and have been setting up the necessary equipment, but I think that this one will give us a bit more trouble than the usual fare, mostly because I can't see any way into the damn thing.

I feel like one of those handsome adventurer scientists you'd see in a B-movie, looking over something new and interesting, waiting with bated breath to see what will come of this new find.

It's so interesting, maybe we can talk more in person, say, over dinner?

Michael.

From: @Hayesresearch.gmail.com
To: richardharris@AldenNationalResearch
Subject: sorry

Sorry I missed dinner. Work at the lab has yielded some unforeseen results and I and most of my team have been feeling under the weather.

I'm glad the kids let my team do the rest of the work, don't think that I could stand to hear them whining about how much their heads hurt or how sick they've been feeling.

I feel like crap in the usual flu-type way, but I haven't stopped working on opening that damned coffin or whatever it really is. It seems as though we've stumbled across something new. How many of us get to say that?

So, yes, my health is worth it.

The samples—the metal from the coffin and the stone from the chamber—came back yesterday. I can safely say that I've never seen anything like it.

As it turns out, the stone is obsidian in appearance only. It was apparently filled with microscopic bands of frozen liquid, which has yet to yield a match to any known chemical compound and, I swear this is true, it's . . . warm, not room temperature, it's consistently stayed at 37 degrees Celsius.

And the metal? Every one of our tests has come up negative. Every. Single. One. It looks and feels like metal, but it isn't. I don't have any idea what it is.

This could be big, Richie, really big.

(This last e-mail wasn't ever sent, it was found as a saved draft on Mr. Hayes's computer.)

From: @Hayesresearch.gmail.com
To: richardharris@AldenNationalResearch
Subject:

Have you ever had a dream that was so bad you woke up in tears?

I did last night. It was so awful, so real.

At first I thought I was on a seashore, but the ground was warm and moist beneath my feet and, when I looked down, I saw that instead of sand, there were pores and tiny hairs and purple veins.

I looked at the sea and saw something that looked like water, but was stagnant and stank like an infected cut.

And above me I saw a dark, cloudless red sky without stars or moon.

It was so real. I didn't think that I was going to wake up.

Today, at the lab, everyone went about their business without talking. I knew that something was wrong, something was hanging over everyone's head like a guillotine waiting to fall.

Some of my colleagues are irritable today, many smell like they haven't washed, and all have bags under their eyes. They're not listless, though. If anything, they're more intent on their work than they usually are. Most of them aren't even talking to each other.

We've decided to open the coffin using strong acids to weaken the metal—or whatever it is—before taking a saw to it.

We'll have it open in a few hours and then we can all rest.

The following is a transcription of the testimony of police officer Edmund Moore, who was called in to investigate the research facility after two weeks of no outside contact.

Questioning Officer (QO): It is November 7th and I am here with the witness. State your name and badge number for the record, sir.

Edmund Moore (Moore): Officer Edmund Thomas Moore, my badge number is . . . hold on . . . 0902453.

QO: All right, you may proceed with your testimony.

Moore: Oh, can I? Can I really? It's only been three hours since we started. You FBI agents are exactly as uptight about rules as the movies say . . . either that or you're unbelievably shitty at figuring out how recorders work.

QO: The testimony, Officer Moore.

Moore: What, is this newfangled computer-thing too much for you to handle? You look like you're, what, twenty? Twenty-one? How the hell do you not know how to work a computer?

QO: . . . The testimony, Officer Moore. I have all day.

Moore: Obviously.

QO: Officer Moore!

Moore: All right, all right . . . just . . . just give me a minute.

QO: Officer Moore.

Moore: Do. Not. Rush. Me. You weren't there, kid. You didn't see it, so, with all due respect, shut the fuck up and give me a damn minute!

(The testimony begins after a minute has passed.)

All right, I was called in on October 10th. I'd been anticipating some time alone with my wife, so I was a bit ticked when I got the call.

I wanted to tell them to get another officer, but the recent flooding in Alden had left the station understaffed and stretched pretty thin. What my little town lacks in population it makes up for in overzealous whining. I cannot count the times I've been called out because some old lady thought she saw a wolf or a bear or Bigfoot.

Despite their pleading, I wanted to let them handle it, but Andrea, that's my wife, told me to go. So that was that.

Now, my little town lies farther from the national reserve—Alden is the town closest to it—but some of that wilderness reaches us and makes it pretty as a postcard, so we were constantly ranked pretty high up on the lists of prettiest towns, right next to some in Vermont and Maine.

I used to agree with popular opinion on that. The summers out there were warm and full of every shade of green you could think of, the falls were cozy and the local kids made a hell of a lot of profit from leaf raking. The winters sucked, though, but when do they ever not?

I'm stalling . . . sorry.

It was early in October, so the cold was creeping in and the leaves were clogging the gutters. It had rained all that week and all the weather reports were saying that it'd keep raining.

It did rain a bit on the way to the lab, but it cleared up pretty quick, New England weather and all that.

The lab was a big, four-story, concrete and metal monstrosity that looked out of place in all that wilderness. Like a scar, almost.

I got out of the car and noticed that the lights were still on. I went up to the door, hoping that all the people there were just too deep into their work to talk to the outside world, but I got no response no matter what I did.

So I called in our resident lock-pick, who overcharged me before he did his job, and went in.

I looked around, gave myself a tour of the facility. I knew that something wasn't quite right from the moment I stepped foot in there. It was far too quiet, there were no sounds except the pattering of rain on the roof.

More signs started appearing as I worked my way through the place. A kitchen full of spoiled food, a spilled cup of coffee near the stairway to the third floor that was feeding a mouse, an upended wastebasket near a bathroom, and a whole lot of open doors.

They were little things, but each one put an extra weight on my mind. But I wasn't scared, just . . . unnerved.

And then I got to the fourth, and final, floor. I was walking down the hall when I felt a draft through one of the open doors. I looked in and saw that the largest window in the room had been shattered.

I went in to investigate and immediately noticed that there were no trees near the window that were high enough to reach it, there was no debris on the floor and no glass on the inside, and the outer edges of the window frame were bent and cracked.

QO: And that was what scared you?

Moore: So it finally talks, and no it wasn't. It was what I found, lying in a heap off to the side, away from the window.

QO: What did you find?

Moore: Clothes. A big pile of wet clothing just lying there soaking up the rain. That was when I started to get scared. It was an image that just struck me as unnatural.

I rummaged through them and found the wallets and jewelry and money all intact, too, so whatever it was, it wasn't a robbery.

QO: Was there any blood?

Moore: None. The clothes were ripped, but that was it. At this point I was sufficiently ready to call in backup, so I went out of the room to see if I could get a better signal outside and I was about halfway to the stairs when I saw a shadow on the wall opposite me.

I turned around and there she was, standing in a doorway, dirty and mad, like a rabid dog.

The instant she saw me, she bolted. I decided to err on the side of caution and call in backup.

I didn't follow her. The look in her eyes was warning enough, but I did take a look at the room where she had come from.

The room had probably been one of the swankier labs, but everything, all of the equipment, the beakers and the chemicals in them, were smashed and shattered.

And at the center of the room was a tall metal thing, looked like a coffin, but there were way too many sides and the metal bulged out in weird ways.

I went up to get a closer look and I saw that the front . . . at least I think that it was the front, was decorated with some kind of ghoul or monster. One whose face was gone.

QO: Could you elaborate?

Moore: There was a hole where the face used to be. It was like something had punched through it, but the edges of the metal were bent outward.

QO: Just for the record, do you have any theories as to what might've been in that coffin?

Moore: Even after what's happened, I still don't know and I don't want to know. Leave it at that.

QO: And the woman?

Moore: We later found out her name was Lori Summers, but it took some doing, considering she was far too violent to let us fingerprint her. We eventually got lucky and another officer managed to get some hair from her as she was trying to tear hers out.

She didn't really tell us anything that we thought was important; when I asked her what had happened to her colleagues, she only said, "They were taken."

Part 2.

Moore's testimony continues.

Moore: After what happened at the lab, everyone at the station—myself included—was a bit on edge. We had a bunch of missing people, the family and friends of whom were breathing down our necks within a day of rumor spreading, and our only witness wasn't in the right mental state to tell us anything.

I was more unnerved than the others because I was there first. So, when the call came and I heard what was going on, I felt like I was gonna throw up.

Over the course of one night, we received about a dozen emergency calls from Alden, all of which sounded legitimate.

Alden is too small to have a real police force. The most they have is a sheriff, a car, and a few guns inside a puny former office building, so they call us for the big emergencies.

The calls started at 8:45, when a local hunter called from his lodge to report that his friends hadn't returned from what was supposed to be a short trip.

An hour later an old woman called to say that she saw something moving outside of her summer home, and fifty minutes after that, a little girl called us to say that she had seen a monster outside her window, her parents had gone out to calm her down, and they hadn't come back.

The calls kept coming in after those first three, but the others were pretty similar. Eventually the calls stopped. I was called in after the last one had been recorded.

It was a woman; she said her name was Sandra Williams. She said that she and the rest of the town had huddled up in the high school.

"There's something outside," she said, "We keep hearing it out in the streets. It sounds big."

We went to Alden at dawn and found a school full of very frightened, very tired people.

Once that was done we all formed search parties to go out looking for the missing townspeople. I was in charge of the second-largest group and we took to the alleyways and backyards, but all I saw was a trampoline with its mesh siding ripped apart, a few cars with their doors opened, and seven piles of clothes, all torn, all bloodless.

QO: I see. Now, before we take a break, I need to bring up something you said previously. You mentioned having a nightmare the same night, can you tell me about it?

Moore: Why? They're just dreams.

QO: Just, please tell us.

Moore: Why do I need to?

QO: (Sighs) All I can tell you is that the scientists who were working on the coffin may have experienced nightmares similar to yours. Now, will you please recount your first dream?

Moore: All right.

I was standing in some kind of field or plain surrounded by trees on all sides. It was dusk, so the light was getting dim, but I could still see the ground beneath me and the horizon.

I knew something wasn't right almost immediately. It was so quiet, the air didn't move, there were no signs of life all around me, and I got this feeling that the place, wherever the hell it was, was a dead place, a place where nothing could grow or thrive.

I started walking, but the ground never moved when I did. It was like I was walking in place.

And then a shadow fell over me and I got this feeling of being watched from someplace high up.

I looked up and there, above me, where the sun should have been, was this big, swollen tumor that moved like a heart, and as I looked, it got closer and closer, making the ground tremble as it did.

Then something moved just underneath the ground. Something I couldn't see, but I could still feel through the soles of my shoes. Something very large. Something that kept me from running.

And then I heard something pierce through the quiet, something tore it up and filled my ears and I wanted to cover my ears, but I couldn't!

QO: What did you hear?

Moore: Screaming. Men, children, women, all of 'em screaming like the skin was being pulled off their bodies. Screaming like they had been set on fire.

The tumor was right above me now, and when I looked up again I got a good look at its surface.

It wasn't a tumor. It was a mass, a mass of people, all naked, all fused to each other with their own blood and skin, all bloody and mutilated and screaming and struggling to tear themselves free as something beneath them—more people I think—pressed up against them.

And Andrea was among them. I picked her out almost immediately.

I told you about Andrea. We've been married for almost twelve years now, she's the light of my life, I'd do anything for her, and to see her . . . like that . . . begging and screaming like that, I . . . I'm glad the phone woke me up.

QO: I see.

Moore: Are you married? You got a girlfriend? Boyfriend?

QO: Not as of right now, Mr. . . .

Moore: Then you don't know shit.

(Moore gets up from his chair.)

QO: Mr. Moore, we're not done yet, please sit d—

Moore: I'm takin' a smoke break!

(A door slams)

This next testimony was given by Sandra Williams, who recounts her night in the school.

I'm not a heavy sleeper. I've been living alone for about five years and I guess I'm a bit paranoid. Even out in Alden, which is, by all accounts, totally nice and pleasant, I never felt exactly safe at nighttime.

I dunno, maybe it was just how close to the woods my house was. I've never been a big fan of the great outdoors; I just don't like the idea of being alone out there, in the dark. Even before that night I heard things near my backyard and the constant mention of wolves and bears and snakes didn't help either.

So I guess my paranoia paid off.

It was around midnight when I woke up. My house is a little, one-story place with a big backyard. I'd heard and seen animals in there before—raccoons and cats mostly—but what I heard, moving around in the dark, sounded a lot bigger.

I got up quickly, got my socks on and went to the window in my bedroom. I didn't see anything but a tree trunk, so I went to the back door and looked out.

It was so dark out there. The trees grow pretty tall out there, and the moon was hidden. My porch lights had been getting on in their years and weren't as bright as they used to be, so when I turned them on, they barely lit up the porch.

I couldn't see anything out there, so I thought that maybe whatever it was got scared off or moved on or something.

I had just started to go back to bed when I heard something bump into the side of the house, farther away from the backyard, near the bedroom.

A second later the window in my bedroom shattered and I ran out the front door as fast as I could.

I tried my neighbors' house, but they were gone for the week and I had left my car behind, so I ran all the way into town.

I got to the sheriff's office and told him what had happened. He promised that he'd send someone to check out my house and had me wait and fill out some paperwork and give a statement.

So he sent someone out and I sat back and waited.

But the officer didn't come back.

And then the calls started coming in, one after the other, each one making the sheriff more and more stressed. I tried to ask him what was going on, but he told me to wait at the station while he went out and looked things over himself.

I honestly didn't expect him to come back, but he did, he came back into the office clutching his side and huffing like an asthmatic.

I went over to see if he needed help, but he grabbed my shoulders and said, "Sandy, something's happening here, something bad, we need to go to the school and meet up with the others. Something's out there and it's taking people."

As you can expect, what he said made my heart leap into my throat and I beat him to the car.

We rode in silence, with me staring out the window, taking in the empty houses and cars. A few times I thought I saw something moving in the alleys and on rooftops, I tried to dismiss them as just shadows and my exhaustion kicking in, but after what happened I think that whatever it was that came into our town was following the car.

Our town has a school that had obviously been designed by someone who thought that Alden was going to become some massive city. It's a big, four-story brick building with a lot of very tall windows. We were able to fit most of what was left of the town in the gym.

Everyone looked scared and tired, and the mayor looked like he was about to have a heart attack. Everyone was just standing around looking worried or crying because someone they knew or loved had gone missing.

I wasn't feeling very talkative, so I left the main group and wandered over to a nearby window.

Everything was so still. There wasn't a breeze, there wasn't a sound from outside. It was like someone had pressed the mute button on the world. I had even tuned out the people in the gym, trying to just . . . just get a hold of myself.

I didn't bother trying to see who was or wasn't there, but I later learned that, out of a thousand, only five hundred and twenty three people were left.

A few hours passed and my eyes started to get heavy. Everyone else had quieted down and were just milling about, looking unsure of what to do. The families were all clustered together, trying to comfort each other.

The full weight of what had happened hit me right then, I think, and I just leaned against the window as my knees got weak.

Outside the moon was hidden by clouds and pretty low on the horizon. It was that time of night when dawn wasn't too far away, but it still wasn't light out.

The window overlooked both the playground and the street that passed the school. I decided to stare out into space and try to keep myself calm. I kept telling myself that help would come soon, but I honestly didn't know if that was true.

Maybe the calls hadn't gotten through to the real police, maybe they didn't believe us or maybe whatever was out there in the darkness had gone to Greenvale first.

That last thought made me want to throw up. I was about to go ask someone for their phone when I saw something outside move. I didn't see all of it, but I saw how big it was and how . . . I honestly can't really find a word to describe how its silhouette looked besides "wrong."

I couldn't spend too much time trying to piece together what I had seen. The thing, whatever it was, had found us and was right outside the school.

I alerted everyone and they all set about going into the depths of the school to lock the doors and barricade the windows with whatever they could find. I commandeered a phone from someone and called the police in Greenvale.

After about an hour the people who had fortified the school came back and we all sat, huddled together in the dark, listening.

I honestly didn't expect to hear anything. It was getting lighter outside and I guess—I guess I was remembering all those childhood stories where the monster vanishes at sunrise.

But that wasn't the case. Just as the morning birdsong was starting, we heard one of the barricades near the gym break.

I was one of the people who got to the barricade first. I saw the thing push the tables away from one of the windows near the main entrance. Again, I didn't see all of it, but I did see three hands clawing at the table, pushing it and splintering it with punches.

I was close enough to see that the hands were bloodied. The skin in tatters, the nails ripped off, bits of glass stuck through the palms.

But I never heard a sound from outside, no breathing, no grunting, no talking. The hands just kept coming at the table.

Someone—a man who I think must have been a teacher—had found a fire extinguisher somewhere in the building, so he tried bashing at the hands. He actually broke some fingers, I could hear the bones breaking from where I was.

It took a few hits, but eventually the hands drew back through the window.

And that's when the smell hit me. I swear to you, it stank like . . . like the world's biggest infected cut. It was horrible, reminded me of maggots and pus and rotting meat.

The thing left us alone after that, but we could still hear it moving around the school, so we were all on edge even after the police came. I'm honestly surprised that none of them got attacked, too.

I haven't gone back home yet. I don't think I can after what happened. I have a friend who still lives there and she says that the whole town feels like a tomb and everyone who still lives there can feel how wrong the whole place is.

She tells me that everyone there looks tired out and afraid. Says she's been having bad dreams, although she won't tell me what they're about. She says that even the policemen who're stationed there are just as uneasy as the people who chose to stay.

I'll have my friend get my things for me. She's going to move away, and I think I'll join her.

Alden isn't safe. I think it needs to just . . . fade away.

Part 3.

This next testimony was given shortly after Sandra Williams's. Not long after her testimony was recorded, several officers stationed in Alden were found in comatose states near wooded areas.

Near them were found several strange clusters of an organic material that was found to emit a noxious gas in large quantities. Most of these clusters were burned, but several were taken for examination.

QO: Please state your name and occupation for the record, sir.

Herbert Halsey (HH): My name is Herbert Halsey, I'm a coroner and microbiologist working at Quantico. I was brought in to study the mounds found in Alden.

QO: All right, my next question was going to be "What were you called in for," but I can see that you've beaten me to that. So what can you tell us about the mounds?

HH: Well, some people came into my office one day and told me that there was something that I needed to take a look at. At first I thought it would be a standard autopsy or something like that, but when they shepherded me to a decontamination shower and a hazmat suit I knew I was in for a day.

QO: (Chuckles) I'm sure it was. Now, can you tell me about the mounds?

HH: Of course. When I first saw them, I wasn't honestly sure whether or not I was being pranked. I mean, they looked like big old piles of offal just plopped into trays.

But then I got closer and, let me tell you, I decided to drop what I was doing to examine them. I mean, I don't want to get my own hopes up, but what I found will probably get me in a few medical papers, maybe some of the big ones like the *New England Journal of Medicine*. I mean how many . . .

QO: Sir, could you please describe the mounds?

HH: Oh, yes, of course. Well, they were large and red and covered with fine white hairs. They were soft to a degree and filled with little holes, like a showerhead. And their bases had a few dozen offshoots that looked like . . . well . . . like veins and arteries.

QO: So the stuff was . . . flesh?

HH: Yes. I ran it through a few dozen tests, took a look at it under the microscope, and I found that it was composed mainly of dog, deer, bobcat, several types of birds, and an unknown substance that I have yet to identify.

I found various animal organs inside of the thing when I cut it open, but all of them had been . . . well . . . I guess the scientific term is "assimilated," they had been assimilated into one mass.

But it wasn't some bizarre case where the organs had rotted and putrefied and turned into a slurry, no, it was whole and it was functional. Everything needed for an organ to work was in place, there was no damage, the different parts had been blended together seamlessly.

QO: What was its function?

HH: I found a strange, very volatile liquid inside of the organ, one that reacted to oxygen in a very odd way.

You see, I took a sample and put it under an electron microscope. When I took a look I discovered that the cells within the liquid were actually multiplying. Within a few hours my petri dish was filled with little red clumps that had a cellular and biological structure like I'd never seen before.

QO: I see, and how fast did they grow?

HH: Fast enough so that they spilled out over the petri dish and started to spread over the counter. And I had just left the office for a few hours. Of course, we had to burn the samples after that happened, but it was for the best.

QO: And the mounds?

HH: We recorded what we could, froze a few samples, and burned the rest. It was excreting spores that probably would have had dangerous effect had we not decontaminated the whole damn place.

QO: Well, thank you for your testimony, Dr. Halsey. You may leave now.

HH: Oh, trying to get rid of me quick, huh? You got another interview coming up?

QO: Yes, he'll be back from his smoke break soon. It was a pleasure speaking with you.

HH: Same here.

Moore's testimony concludes.

QO: Welcome back, Officer Moore.

Moore: Yes, hi, whatever, let's just finish this. You want to know what happened on the 23rd and 24th, right?

QO: Yes.

Moore: Fine, just let me leave after this.

QO: I think that can be arranged.

Moore: Good, this place stinks like a hospital and I don't like to be out after dark anymore.

QO: Could you please . . .

Moore: You know that what was out there wasn't human . . . right?

QO: You've indicated that, Officer Moore, but I don't believe in monsters, at least not the kind you're talking about.

Moore: That thing wasn't human, kid. There's evidence to support my theory. Like what Sandra Williams saw that night in the school, she told me in vivid detail.

QO: She said it was dark . . .

Moore: No, the sun was already up.

QO: She might have been hallucinating . . .

Moore: From what? We tested her, she came out clean of any mind-altering drugs and her fellow townspeople corroborated her story. We tested them all and no one was on anything, so that's out the window. Try another, kid.

QO: Maybe the scientists were contaminated by some kind of mind-altering spore from the coffin and they just . . . went crazy and ran off?

Moore: (Chuckles) That's almost a comforting thought, but, if that were the case, then did the same thing happen to the people in Alden? I asked the people who got ahold of that coffin to check it for anything like that and do you know what they concluded?

QO: That there were no spores.

Moore: That's right. No spores. Not even the slightest trace of mold or fungus. They told me that coffin barely had dust on it. So what would make a building full of respectable, sane people strip and run off into the woods? Were they on drugs, too, eh?

QO: I . . . maybe they were scared?

Moore: Scared? Scared so bad they jumped out of their clothes?

QO: I . . . I . . . I don't know. Let's . . . let's wrap this up.

Moore: All right.

I was called in after a bunch of my fellow officers were found in comas up in Alden.

I don't honestly know what the chief was thinking sending them up there, it's not like whoever took the people was just gonna come waltzing out of the woods and give itself up and I highly doubt that anyone left in Alden had the spirit to riot or start shit with each other.

So the officers—their names were Tony Rhodes, Claudio D'amico, and Curtis Parker if you want to know—ended up in comas near a bunch of meat pods or whatever the hell they were, and that got most of my higher-ups off their asses and they actually tried to do something.

They called me and a bunch of others in to do a search of the woods. They brought the dogs, plenty of firepower, and the helicopter with the big-ass searchlight, the whole nine yards.

We split up into groups of two and spread out with the intent of going in a grid pattern. Me and my partner, a guy named Bill Lincoln, who was as old and experienced as I was, found ourselves alone pretty quick.

We tried the usual things to keep away that uneasy feeling when you're alone in the wilderness. We joked and talked about our favorite movies and our loved ones, but our words ran out after a while, so we walked in silence.

It was the silence, I think, that started getting to me. I've been in the reserve plenty of times and there was always, *always* animal activity.

But not that night. That night all I could hear were our footsteps and the wind moaning through the trees around us. It was like whatever had settled there had driven the animals away.

Bill and I were quite a ways in when we heard something coming at us from the undergrowth to our left.

We readied our guns and aimed them where we thought the attack would come from. I can still feel the tremor in my hand when I think of that moment. I was petrified, waiting for the boogeyman to lunge out from the shadows, wondering if I could fire the gun.

But, as it turned out, I didn't have to.

The thing that bounded out of the undergrowth was a deer. A big buck with one of its antlers snapped off. It was gone just as quickly as it had come, but the fear in its eyes told me that the thing was close.

Another few steps and we passed a canopy and came to a place where the trees had been bent and cracked, and the ground was torn up and covered in tracks. Some of which looked just like the marks of bare feet and hands.

QO: What did you do then?

Moore: I did my job and called it in.

Now, I was content to just stay put and wait until everyone grouped up, but all that went out the window when I heard something ahead of us, not too far away, but far enough so that we had no clue where it was coming from.

It was a girl . . . a little girl . . . and she was screaming. Do you have any younger siblings?

QO: Yes. A brother.

Moore: He ever break a bone when he was little?

QO: Yeah . . . we were at a Walgreens. He slipped on some ice, broke his arm in two places.

Moore: Do you remember how he screamed?

QO: Yes.

Moore: The sound that I heard that night, from out of the darkness, was a thousand times more agonized than that. It was a little girl screaming like every bone in her body was getting ground to paste.

The screaming kept going and both of us were looking around and neither of us knew where the hell it was coming from.

And then Bill screamed.

What happened next happened so fast . . . so damn fast. One minute he was beside me, his gun drawn, the next minute he was on his back, his gun gone and his body being dragged into the darkness with more speed than I thought was humanly possible.

He was gone before I could try to help. But I did see something in those seconds before he was gone.

I saw two hands clutching Bill's ankle. One with painted nails, one with a wedding ring.

It was stupid, but I just stood there after it had happened. I . . . I couldn't wrap my head around what had just happened. I didn't see where the hands ended, or where they had come from or how they could have dragged poor Bill away like that with as much speed as they did.

I felt like someone had sucker-punched me. But I should have reacted faster, maybe I could have gotten a shot off, scared the thing away. Then again, maybe not.

I was only really . . . uh . . . brought back to earth when I heard Bill start screaming from somewhere nearby and, unlike the girl, he kept on screaming and I was able to get a good read on where he was. So I ran after him.

QO: Your fellow officers said that they found you near the main road. Is that where you went?

Moore: No . . . no, I followed the screaming deeper into the woods. Got some nasty cuts from the brambles, stumbled over roots, nearly broke my neck a few times. But I didn't care.

It had just been such a long month. A month of waking up from nightmares. Of listening intently to the local radio, wondering if I'd hear about more disappearances. Of wondering if whatever had taken those scientists had seen me in the lab, if I was going to come home to find it waiting in the darkness for me.

Or maybe coming back home and finding a window broken . . . and a pile of ripped clothes belonging to my wife.

And now I was going to get some answers. At least, that's what I thought.

Bill kept screaming, and the louder it got, the more afraid I became. But I kept on running until I burst through a cluster of trees and found myself in a clearing.

Well . . . it was . . . it used to be a clearing. When I got there it looked more like Hell itself had oozed up from the earth.

Those mounds you guys found? The ones made from animal parts? They were everywhere. They were all growing from animals who'd had their stomachs opened up and their guts stretched out over the ground.

There were so many of them, it must have been most of the reserve's animal population in one place. The ground was completely covered in them. When I got closer I saw that their muscles and tissue, their skin and bones, they'd all been ripped out and . . . woven together . . . like a carpet.

And the mounds were all moving, pulsing like hearts. I could hear them, all of them together at the same time.

And the animals . . . the animals were still alive! I saw them move and twitch. I could hear them trying to breathe, I saw the moonlight reflected off their eyes. They couldn't have been alive but they were!

QO: Officer Moore, please calm . . .

Moore: That's why the woods were so silent! All of the fucking animals were plastered together in that clearing and turned into a living carpet, I can still hear their lungs trying to work and those tiny, little whimpers they made.

QO: Mr. Moore?

Moore: And at the center of the clearing, surrounded by these huge, throbbing mounds, was a pond. A pond that stank like piss and blood and other things. A pond where all the juices from those animals collected.

I heard Bill from across the way and I looked, and there he was, being dragged to the pond by . . . it . . . it looked like a tentacle . . . or a tail. But when I looked closer I saw the two hands that had grabbed him . . . then two more . . . then a dozen more . . . and then I saw arms of every skin color and wet muscle and dripping intestine.

The thing that had hold of him was made of human parts and it was *moving*!

Bill screamed for help, he screamed like a child, like a baby when it gets delivered. He begged and cried and howled as he was dragged closer to the pond and I . . . just stood there and watched.

And then I saw something in the pond move.

Something big. Something that twitched and moved like every part of it was living.

A leg . . . at least, that's what I think it was . . . came out and grabbed ahold of the ground with a thousand fingers. Another followed, then four more. And then the rest of it came out.

Have you ever seen a person go into shock? Of course you have. I have, too. But I never actually experienced it before that night.

But when that . . . that thing surfaced I . . . I just felt my whole body go cold.

It looked like a spider and a crab and an octopus all at the same time. But every part of it was made from human remains. Legs with their feet still attached and arms with their hands intact dangled below it, twitching and grabbing at nothing.

Its back was made from bone—spines, femurs, whole fucking skeletons—all bound by tendon and other stuff.

In between the cracks in its hide, I saw organs and smaller limbs . . .

The thing that had ahold of Bill was . . . I think . . . the thing's tongue.

I don't know. I used what I had left of my strength to run the other way as fast as I could. It ate Bill, I know it did. Officially he's been reported as "missing," but they're never gonna find his body.

They may find his clothes, though, if they ever find that clearing. And, if they do, they're not gonna leave to report back.

I quit after that night. Packed my things and left with Andrea, and didn't say a word to anyone. I'm not guilty about that. I had to get out, had to protect my wife.

I used to think that the world was simple. That bad shit happened and we had to live with it, that the universe was one big clusterfuck of bizarre coincidences. That there was nothing supernatural, no boogeymen, no monsters that didn't look human.

But I know better now.

Listen to me, kid. If you have any say whatsoever, you'll get your bosses to go into that reserve and set the fucking place on fire.

QO: I don't . . . that's just . . . I can't believe that . . .

Moore: Have you seen the news, kid? I have. It seems like the people who live near the reserve have started reporting less animal activity than is normal. Pretty soon whatever remained of the animal population is gonna be gone, fuel for . . . whatever that thing is doing.

And how much you wanna bet that you'll be seeing a few disappearances in the towns that are farther away in the coming months?

Take my advice. Talk to our bosses.

QO: I . . . I think our time is up here, Mr. . . . I mean, Officer Moore. You can go now, we'll have a car waiting when you get out.

Moore: Thank God. You remember what I said, kid. Burn the reserve. Don't let that thing spread.

(A door closes.)

As of now, seventeen disappearances have been reported in towns near and around the reserve. There also seems to have been a sudden rash of nightmares—with elements much like the ones described previously—in many people in the surrounding towns and even outside of them.

These statements have been gathered in order to provide clues as to whom the culprit might be.

No actions, government-sanctioned or otherwise, have been taken.

PERFUME

Michael Whitehouse

The perfume haunted me. It fluttered through the air, teasing me, leading me toward an obscured end. I ran down hallways bathed in red tapestries, my nightgown shuddering in the cold. Moonlight showed me the way as I searched for the perfume's source. Around blind corners, through doorways of solid oak, into rooms once filled with laughter and terrible deeds. With each step the scent grew stronger. Roses. A sting of ginger and citrus. Never quite putting my finger on the familiarity of it all.

And then I entered a chamber. An old room that differed from the rest. One solitary candle sat by a large four-poster bed. The light cascaded out, revealing a room dark and brooding. The floor was cold, the wood warped slightly; my bare feet lost what little heat they once held. A huge fireplace lay opposite the bed, unlit, devoid of life. And above it, a large portrait dominated the room. In the painting a woman sat, wearing a dark green dress of many decades past. Her hair was pulled tightly in a bun, her pale skin like languid pearl, and her eyes cold and cruel with dispassion.

Those eyes seemed to watch, following me as I wandered around the bed until I stood at its foot. A once rich, now faded crimson blanket covered the mattress, and as the candlelight struggled against an unseen draft, it became clear that someone lay in the bed.

I could not see the face of this person; the body was covered from head to foot by the red blanket, shrouded by it. The sight of that cloth outline struck fear into my heart—I dared not remove the blanket, uncertain that my nerves could endure the shock. Again, I was stung by the familiarity of it all, a memory hiding in the shadows just out of sight, refusing to reveal itself. The pungent rose perfume was stronger than it had been before, as I could feel the spiteful gaze of the portrait behind me, watching the proceedings. Then I noticed another scent. Something that had festered in that room for years obscured by the sweetness of the perfume, a foul underbelly.

As I stared at the outline of head and body beneath the blanket, the stench grew. With each breath I was treated to a mixture of roses and something humid, murky, like soil after a downpour. There was something rotten in that room with me. The rancid smell became so thick that I could taste it. The hidden memory threatened to break loose from its chains. I had to flee. Run. Be away from that room, that house, out into the open where I could breathe again.

I walked quickly to the door where I had entered. It was locked. I twisted at the metal handle, its spherical body covered in dark brown paint. The locked mechanism entombed in oak echoed out into distant recesses that taunted me and resisted; I was a prisoner confined to a solitary room, to a place where the sweet air of flowers was mixed with that of death.

I pounded on the door. Shouted. Screamed. But my pleas went unanswered. They simply faded into that lonely house, my family home, which I had not visited since I was seven. A place that hid dark recollections, and wounds that ran deep, covered thinly by the preceding decades. At last I gave in. I stopped my protests, rested my forehead on the cold wooden surface of the locked door, and tried to compose myself.

Then I heard a sound.

One at first, followed by three others. It was a clicking, creaking noise. I turned around slowly to see what was there, but the room was as it had been. The body in the bed lay still, the blanket forming a perfect impression of it. The bedside candle flickered but remained, and as it did so shadows danced around the room. They created the illusion of movement, and for a moment I stared at the portrait, the woman's eyes peering out at me from above the darkened fireplace, and it was as if a flicker of recognition fell across the face.

I shuddered, believing that it was merely a trick of the light, but still, the face looked on. Then I heard the creaking sound again. A series of quick clicks, like an aching door that had not been opened for an age, slowly moving in the night. But I could not see the source. My heart raced as I looked around, and for the first time I noticed in the dim light that there lay an old wooden wardrobe on the other side of the room.

The creaking sounded once more; a frightful unease began to take over as each click sounded that both puzzled and repulsed me. I turned to the door and twisted the handle as hard as I could, but the reality had not changed. I was locked in that room with a body rotting under the sheets and a clicking noise coming from inside a wardrobe. A noise that felt organic, alive somehow, differing itself from the shifting contractions of the wooden floor and beams of the old house. It at once sounded natural and yet felt unnatural.

Another creaking, clicking, and I knew that I had to look at the wardrobe across the room. I was terrified by what I might find, but the anticipation of waiting, just waiting until something threatening emerged from its wooden tomb, was too much to bear. I wanted this torturous night to be over, to return to my adult life. Something had compelled me to visit my ancestral home, but I was sure that if I ever felt the cool breeze of the outside world again, I would curse that place and never return.

Obscured memories flickered in front of my eyes once more. The familiarity of the perfume stinging my senses. The room . . . A dreadful window into my past. I would not be tortured like this, played with; I had to know what was inside that wardrobe.

I stepped forward, moving around and then to the foot of the bed. I was certain that the portrait stared on menacingly, but I dared not catch its eye, and so my gaze remained fixed on the wardrobe as I neared. The clicking, creaking noise sounded intermittently. With each step I listened intently, sometimes being greeted by that horrid sound, other times being welcomed by the silence, an equally unappealing nighttime noise.

As I reached my hand out to the wardrobe door, my blood ran cold. The door moved, if ever so slightly. But it did move. I could see an inch of the darkness inside, a small sliver of black air, and I felt as though a watchful eye was glaring at me from within it.

A creak replied to my proximity, this time louder than before. But it took on a new characteristic, like knuckles being clicked; bone and ligament snapping in place, limbs that had not moved for an age breaking free of time's relentless hold. I reached my hand out slowly and pulled the door open with force. For a moment, I thought I saw two eyes in the dark of the wardrobe peering at me, but as the light from the room's solitary candle reached that dark place, I saw nothing. No clothes, no belongings, no creeping eyes, just the emptiness of a life now vacant.

I sighed with relief, but when I turned to the room I froze to the spot. Something was different. Something had changed. It wasn't the portrait on the wall. The bitter face of the woman in the painting stared onward. It wasn't the fireplace, either, remaining as it did unlit, its mouth bathed in night. It wasn't the door on the other side of the room, my only avenue for escape, standing still closed, no doubt locked by some unseen jailer.

No, none of these things had changed. But what had frightened me, tore at any composure I still had within me, was the figure lying under the covers in the bed. That dead, silent corpse that filled the air with perfume and macabre aura.

It was gone.

The red blanket had been pulled aside revealing white silk sheets, and the only evidence that someone had been lying there was an impression in the mattress, an outline of a now missing body.

I gasped as the creaking sounded once more, this time from the bed, but there was no sight of the body. The room was unoccupied, and yet the air did not feel absent of company. Something was there. I looked around, and it was then that I entertained a thought. One which otherwise would have been preposterous to me. Perhaps it was an invisible specter that had been lying under the red blanket. An apparition with the body of a person, but transparent to the naked eye.

Creak.

The noise drew closer.

Creak.

This time from the foot of the bed. Whatever it was, it was slowly walking toward me, the warped floorboards shifting under its weight the only sign that I wasn't alone.

If only I could see the cadaverous thing before it placed its rotten hands on me. At that thought I leapt to the bed, and as the specter stepped forward, I pulled the sheets off the mattress, throwing them into the air like a net. They fluttered with movement, bringing with them that sweet, rancid perfume. And then they came to rest, but not on the floor—instead they covered the walking corpse, showing me its outline. A shrouded dress of white sheets, resting over something hideous beneath.

Perhaps I should have allowed the thing to walk unseen. For the sight of a long draped sheet stepping toward me almost stopped my heart. Creak. Creak. Each invisible footfall brought with it pangs of dread the likes of which I had never experienced before. And then came the rustling, as something else moved underneath the sheets. A prodding motion, as what I could only assume were two hands outstretched beneath their shroud reaching out toward me.

I stumbled backward. I cried out, and as I did so the room dimmed. My retreat had led me into the wardrobe. The arms of the shrouded figure were now almost upon me, and my only recourse was to pull the wooden door of the wardrobe toward me, to shelter me from that thing.

My newfound sanctuary shook violently as the shrouded specter heaved and pulled at the door. I held on with all my might, my fingers poking out into the room, grasping onto that piece of wood, the only barrier between me and that rotten apparition.

Memories began to flood back, the dark wardrobe a trigger to painful events I had managed to bury deep within me, of a little girl locked in dark places. Cellars, attics, wardrobes . . . A girl put upon. Beaten. Mocked. Emotionally tortured by her one and only caregiver. My body convulsed and shivered as the reality of my early childhood filtered through.

The attack ceased, silence became my world. And then I heard two whispered words:

"Little . . . Sophie . . ."

The words were more breath than voice, and in them I recognized the speaker. My grandmother. That horrid woman who had abused her duty.

"I was only a child!" I screamed at the top of my voice.
"How could you?"

Still, I held on tightly to the door, sure that the spirit of my grandmother stood in front of it. This was confirmed to me when I felt a warm, sticky breath on my fingers. A mouth, seen or unseen, must have hovered over them for a moment, exhaling foul air. Then something wet licked the length of my fingers. A rotten tongue from beyond. But I dared not open the door. There was little I could do. I held onto it tightly, while the ghost of my twisted grandmother licked at my exposed flesh.

Then nothing. Again silence. No breath. No shaking of the doors. Nothing.

Teeth dripping with saliva then bit hard down onto my fingers. I screamed in agony as they delved deep through skin and then crunched into bone. Under my screams of pain I heard a laugh of delight.

History had repeated itself as more memories flooded through the torture. She had done awful things in the past. Malevolent, twisted things. Locking me in the darkness, beating, prodding, and more. The pain of memory mixed with the pain of the moment as those dreaded teeth ground deeper.

No more!

I screamed in rage and pushed the wardrobe door, knocking the shrouded figure to the ground. My fingers gushed blood, but they were free, as was I. Leaping onto the bed, I charged for the locked door once more. I yelled and cried and fought as the door remained tightly closed. It would not budge. I pounded and railed against my imprisonment. Then two hands reached from behind, wrapping sheet-covered fingers around my neck.

We struggled, the grip around my throat tightening, choking the breath from me. And in a moment's rage, a moment of pure survival, I reached for the solitary candle that sat by the bed and cast it to the feet of my grandmother, catching the shroud of sheets. The room burned. The bed. The painting. The wardrobe . . . And my last memory was looking beside me, to see my grandmother's corpse burning on the floor.

I was found standing in the garden of my family home, dazed, watching it collapse in on itself, consumed by flames. I had returned to my childhood home to oversee my grandmother's things after she was done with this mortal world. But it appears she was not done with me. After that night, at long last, I was certainly done with her.

A DARK STRETCH OF ROAD

Barnabas Deimos

Driving . . .

Melanie and Diana had been driving for days together. Recently married, the women had been traveling from Florida to California as a long and surprisingly stress-less honeymoon. Somewhere in Arizona or possibly New Mexico, the two had been driving for quite some time along a dusty stretch of road. Miles and miles of nothing stretched in front of them as they plowed down the deserted highway whose number both of them had forgotten. All they knew was that they were headed northwest along it.

In the day the road stretched on with nothing but dust and rock on either side, while ahead of them was a range of short, squat mountains they intended to cross. Now, after they had driven for so long, the sun had gone and abandoned the dust, rocks, and mountain to be devoured by near total darkness on a moonless night. Only the smallest bit of starlight illuminated their world.

Both talked and let the time pass as they drove. They were in no rush. But slowly they began to wonder when this stretch would end. "Shouldn't we at least start feeling an incline?" But white-line fever often sinks in without you noticing it. Besides, they were enjoying their long overdue and well-deserved time together as wife and wife.

As they drove and drove, their highway hypnosis finally gave way. They both saw it, and a dreadful feeling began to seep in, replacing the happy and carefree feelings they had felt along this trip. Each time they noticed it, Melanie would grab Diana's hand and squeeze it. A comforting motion to assuage the worry and dread nailed into them each time they saw the fuel gauge slowly drop and drop.

They had been driving for so long, they should've gotten there already. Something was wrong . . . did they misjudge the length? Did they not fill up before? Things simply did not add up.

And like the inevitable swing of the reaper's scythe on all our mortal coils, the car began to slow as the gas that had turned to fumes turned to nothing.

With a crunch on the gravel ground, the car stopped.

Checking both their personal phones and Diana's work cell phone, they found—not much to their surprise—that signal was nonexistent. It wasn't really a shock considering they had suffered dead spots often on the drive thus far. So the conversation began as to what to do: Stay in the car or walk forward?

A compromise was reached: They would walk forward a bit to see if, by some stroke of luck, there was a sign of civilization close by or even perhaps a roadside assistance call box.

Granted, it was nearly pitch-black out with but a small bit of ambient light. The road was a black stretch touched by oceans of deep purples and blues dotted with shadows.

It was still rather warm outside and they both felt that the fresh air could be good for them. They did their best to make fun of the situation by joking and being playful in order to ignore the possibilities of their unfortunate situation.

The two trod for but a few minutes before the car was out of sight. They discussed whether they should turn around and go back, and each time they did the discussion ended with "just a little longer," "just a little bit farther."

And so they went on farther and farther, wrapped up in their quest and in each other, not noticing much else, until it snuck up on them. Clouds. Thick rolling clouds spreading across the sky. Blotting out the already feeble starlight with their inky black.

"Go back . . . we have to go back," they both agreed as the last bit of starlight was voided out. But as they walked back toward the car, they realized it was far too late for such a choice. Blackness stretched before them, behind them, above them. The only way they even knew the other was there was by their clasped hands and breathing.

"We'll eventually get to the car," they thought. "Just keep a straight line. And we'll get there."

On they walked but nothing broke up the monotonous pitch-black world.

Worry, panic, fear, and frustration seeped into their voices. Only the fact that they held each other's hand throughout it, and knew the other was there, kept them from devolving into abject loss and hopelessness.

It felt like an eternity . . .

Then light.

A small flicker of light springing to life in short bursts then finally stabilizing to a constant one.

It appeared to be a roadway light, which meant that something was there or at least nearby. At least they hoped so.

The women ran to it, toward the light bobbing up and down in their sprint toward what felt like a light of salvation.

As they got closer they noticed the night was so dark that the light barely illuminated the ground beneath it and it didn't even shine on its own post.

They ran to it regardless. If nothing else at least they could sit below it until daybreak.

They both ran up to it, and underneath the feeble light, they embraced. Not even realizing the ground was wet though it had not rained.

They lost themselves in a celebratory and relieved kiss. So relieved that they didn't even mind the strong smell.

Suddenly, the light bobbed a bit. They both looked up.

Two bulbous cloudy white eyes were revealed by the moving light.

The tongue they were standing on moved.

The light went out.

The wives screamed, holding each other, as the monstrous jaws they had walked into slammed shut.

A TRICK OF PERSPECTIVE

Matt Dymerski

They're very good at hiding in plain sight. The human brain only perceives summaries and expectations, and they use that to their utmost advantage. A man in a gorilla costume can walk across a video of athletes passing basketballs without the viewer noticing; the creatures I'm talking about can skitter right on by when they know you won't be paying attention. Your awareness is their plaything.

Ever thought you saw a face in the shadows? You absolutely did—and it was watching you right back.

They're not magic, and they're not spirits. They are physically present, with bodies you might accidentally brush up against, and probably have. That's the key, though, and their primary strength: you just don't realize it when it happens. Even if you somehow sense you're not alone and you become alert, you'll expect the warm limb of a human assailant or the chill void of a ghost, but neither trigger will come. Truth is, you could be backed up against one right at this moment and you wouldn't know it, because the brain interprets most every sensation as something familiar and benign. You could turn your head and the entity behind you would have already anticipated that and moved to the next place you're not looking.

The damn thing's not even quiet—you just don't know what to listen for.

Imagine this: go back to a memory of a sunny day and recall a bird chirping outside your window. Yes, it's daytime. Did you think light would save you? The creatures in question have no association with shadows and darkness. If they did, I might hazard a guess as to what the hell they are. No, there's no easy safety in light here. Now, the same way that you hear a spoken word and slowly transform it into another word in your mind's eye by analyzing and re-analyzing it, listen to that chirping bird. You didn't even notice it before, did you? De-prioritized by your traitor neurons, it slid right past your awareness.

A foreign stranger speaks a word with a heavy accent. At first, it means nothing. You frown, you concentrate, and you look at his moving mouth for clues. Moment to moment, the word changes shape as you turn it and study it. Suddenly, you have it. You smile in agreement, and, from that point on, the memory of his first speaking has changed. You can't hold on to what you first thought you heard. Your brain has literally edited your understanding of your present and your past. But what if the choice it made was wrong? There's every possibility the chirps you heard outside your window on that summer day can morph the same way—back to what they really were. Don't think too hard on it.

I first became aware of their existence when I was fourteen. As I've laid out, they're extremely good at hiding in plain sight, but every process has a non-zero failure rate. It might be one in a million, or even one in a billion, but it *will* happen. I was that unlucky failure.

There was still half of the backyard left to mow and my interests did not extend beyond finishing my torturous chore and running back to my video games. I was innocent. I was just a kid. I was listening to the birds chirping on a summer day.

My mind wandered. I thought of my future in some unknown college, I thought of my past as a child young enough to avoid chores, and I thought of my present. The birds didn't have any responsibilities. They just hung out all day, flew around as they pleased, and talked all the time in song.

Nobody else would have randomly focused on the lilting sounds the way I did. I didn't stop to listen more closely. I didn't look around and smile at the beautiful weather. I just kept my eyes ahead of the mower and tried to hear what I could here over the roar of its engine. I gave no outward indication whatsoever that my attention had shifted, and that was what led to its mistake.

The longer my mind delved down beneath the blanketing sound of the mower, the more I could hear the birds; the closer I focused on the birds, the more I lost hold of the sound in my mind. It was very close to typical birdsong at first, but then continually lost fractions of its normalcy and beauty second by second until it became distorted, alien, and haunting. I could understand how I'd thought I was listening to birds, but now I struggled to process what sounded like wind moving through a series of twisted holes designed to mimic other noises in the environment. My mind's eye envisioned a strange organic stick of some sort, hollow in many avian ways, but whose bones and hole-ringing muscles were open to the air to allow aural camouflage. This image came to me as if from some half-forgotten nightmare; nausea-inducing, imminently threatening, and vaguely familiar. My moment of unconscious action came when I realized there was no breeze. To make continual noises like that, the unknown bone-and-muscle stick would have to be moving. To be moving, it would have to be a leg.

I erupted from my blank-stared focus without a moment's warning and flung my arm around faster than I could look. My hand closed on what I immediately recognized as a tree branch, and I was already relaxing in that split second that it took to swing my vision around to see what I'd—

No. I'd only thought it was a tree branch. It had presented that texture to me by tensing mottled patches of skin clinging to the black exoskeletal bone I'd gripped. I stared in awe and horror as it rotated interpretations in front of me: an umbrella that last night's storm had thrown in from a neighbor's yard, a large bush that I had somehow forgotten about, and even a stick I'd managed to blindly catch right out of a surprise dust devil.

But I wasn't letting go. Rings of muscle closed around some of my fingers, bringing that horrible nightmare-born image right back to the forefront of my awareness, and I knew the thing was alive and aware. It jerked away twice, escaping on the second, and I stared after it as the shifting shadows of clouds made a weird pattern between the houses and a truck drove by on the road until it was out of sight. Both the pattern and the truck had been tricks of perspective. I grabbed my head and struggled with the memories; my brain wanted to interpret them away, but I knew I had to hold on. I'd just seen something horrible beyond understanding, and I couldn't let that knowledge sink under my stream of consciousness and vanish.

I managed to get inside the house and write down what I could before I became too unsure of myself. How had it so expertly presented stimuli of colors, light, and sound to me that I'd nearly interpreted away my awareness of it? I came to the conclusion that it had been watching me in particular for quite some time and learning my senses, my behavior, and the lay of my nervous system. What else could I believe? If it was just that good at manipulating everyone all the time, what hope did I have of figuring out what it was?

I looked things up on the Internet most of the night, but found no real corroborating stories. The next morning, I came up against its second line of defense: memories, imaginings, and dreams are all indistinguishable. In the safety of my bed, the nightmarish encounter seemed nothing but a fleeting series of random sensations. Had I dreamed it?

The lawnmower remained halfway across the backyard, its job unfinished.

It had happened.

I went out there and completed my chore before my father noticed the unfinished task, but I remained wary at all times. There was no way to know if that creature had been real, but if so, there was a good possibility that it was hostile. Every shadow seemed to hold a threat, and every sound made me jump. For weeks, I was stressed beyond belief, and there was nobody I could tell.

Each day began blurring into the next, as they tend to do, and I was eventually forced to relax my guard. Without proof, there was no other choice. Thinking back on it, I wasn't able to be sure it had been real; the mutable nature of memory continually stole details away from me until all I had was a story I kept telling myself about what had happened. When the only thing you have left to believe is your own insistence that something insane occurred, well, that's when you have to worry about being crazy.

Occasionally, I would still go down unexpected streets or look in random directions, but these actions produced no results. If the creature had been real, it had probably taken my unexpected randomness into account after the first failure. Or, maybe, it was staying away from me to avoid giving me a chance to be certain. Once was an inexplicable and weird experience. Twice would be a prompt for action.

As bad luck would have it, I'd been right about two things: there were more than one of them, and they did adapt to specific people and communities. That was the cause of my second experience. I was twenty and in college by then, and had firmly put the whole thing behind me as a sort of scary story I'd brewed up as a child. My friends and I had gone camping and we were deep in the woods of a state park, sitting around a fire at night. There was nothing around but the flames, the beers, my friends, our tents, and the trees—until a falling meteor lit up the night as it burned out just above the distant horizon.

My friends all reeled and cheered. I just stared across the fire at the darkness in the woods beyond. The meteor had been a totally unpredictable event not predicated on the actions of any earthly being, and, thus, our silent watcher had been slow to adjust. Under the meteor's three seconds of shifting light, I stared directly into the complex multi-orbed eyes of the enemy. Did it know that I knew? Did it see light the way we did? In many unintentional ways, I'd prepared for this moment for years. I kept my heart rate and breathing normal and made no move, not even with my eyes, that might give away my awareness.

And now I was certain. In that single moment, years of self-doubt and cognitive dissonance vanished.

But the creature had not come for me. I drank beers and told stories and laughed with the rest of the group while secretly amazed at how blatantly obvious the thing was now that I had noticed it. It often circled the camp in the darkness, and, with the corner of my sight, I kept track of it until I knew who it was most interested in. One of our friends was the governor's son, a fact that he made known often and loudly, but the person most often studied was actually his girlfriend.

Now I had become the secret observer. I did not intervene as she walked off into the woods to look for the campground's outhouse, and it followed.

She didn't come back. Her boyfriend had passed out by that time, and our group had begun the process of splitting up into different tents. Her absence was not truly noticed until the next morning.

I was not stupid enough to mention what I knew to the police. They figured she'd wandered off into the forest and gotten lost and hurt; I certainly wasn't going to tell them I'd seen a living horror follow her into the darkness. They sent out some search parties, but, as I expected, they found no trace of her. The case was closed and the official story was that she had likely run off on purpose to start a new life.

The biggest concern that tumbled around in my thoughts that year was: why her? And why not me? I'd grabbed one, even seen it face-to-face, and it had retreated. She wasn't a danger to them, while I'd known about them for years.

Or perhaps my previous uncertainty had meant I was not a threat. As I studied to be an engineer, I realized that every system had a failure rate. I couldn't be the only one that had seen them, and they couldn't simply eliminate every single person who did. There were many layers of defense, most of all the lack of proof and fallibility of memory, and I had to guess that many people had seen something strange or inexplicable in their lives but written it off later out of confusion. Above all, normal people didn't *want* to believe that such horrific creatures existed, let alone that they walked freely around the streets of the neighborhoods of mankind.

And walk freely they did. Now that I knew what to look and listen for, I began to sense them almost everywhere. They stood most often in places that were close but untrodden: grass islands in parking lots, walkways between buildings, and high rooftops. They could fold their eight limbs and disjointed bodies into strange shapes and adjust their appearance and texture to blend in. The most astounding ability I observed was the fact that they could adjust to multiple people at once. I talked to a friend on the way to class once while I observed a nearby creature using light and shade from my perspective at one angle and a different pattern inlaid on its folded-up body from my friend's perspective to create a multifaceted optical illusion that words simply can't do justice to. It was these camouflage tactics the creatures used, along with incredibly intimate knowledge of each person's particular senses, to hide in plain sight as a tree, a shadow, a car, or anything else they somehow knew would be instinctively written off and ignored.

But they didn't always hide.

Saying and doing nothing, I watched as they took two more people I vaguely knew over the next four years. These weren't direct acquaintances, but people I subtly chose to be around more often because of the increased activity of the creatures around them. In fact, the more I came to understand these strange beasts, the more I was able to evade and watch them myself in exactly the manner they had once done to me.

About forty-eight hours before a disappearance, three of the creatures would visit the person in question—and that person's handler—to closely examine something about him or her. I managed to get there before the process began for the fourth time in my experience, and I hid two yards over in a dense group of trees and watched with binoculars. While one creature waited and watched in the corner of the bedroom, the visiting triad leaned over the sleeping girl and did something delicate with their long appendages. While most of the segments of their limbs were full of exposed muscle and air-holes for stealthy movements, the end-points were incredibly sharp, almost . . . surgical.

It was at that moment that two questions presented themselves to me. First: what did I really think I could do about this even if I logged enough of their behavior to create proof? They could simply eliminate *me* if I spoke up. Second: how did these creatures know their victims would be somewhere alone forty-eight hours from that moment? Without fail, even though the decision sometimes seemed random, these people ended up somewhere solitary.

It wasn't mind control. It was worse. Everything the creatures did was about data and prediction. As a full-time engineer for several years by that point, I had begun to understand what they were doing. A human being has the capacity for creativity and inspiration, but we are, each of us, largely predictable in our daily lives. Watch someone long enough and you can guess at their future actions. This girl had been watched for a very long time, and they knew she would be alone and vulnerable in forty-eight hours. It was always done in such a way that no mysteries were left behind. If she was asleep in her bed in a locked house, the disappearance would raise questions.

Keeping incognito in a large coat and low hat, I watched her for the next two days, noting her handler's subtle new quivering behavior. Was it *excited?* The thought of that thing growing excited for whatever it was about to do turned my fear into anger.

The hour approached. She was up later than usual because she'd been at a bar with friends, and now she was walking home by herself. Other drunk people were on the street with her. How did they intend to—

Her phone rang. Answering it, she turned left down a quieter street. She spoke to someone she liked on the other end; it was not a trick. How the hell had they predicted that? Just how deep did their data extend? My mind ran endlessly over the insane requirements of it all. They would have to have complete behavior profiles not just for the girl and her caller, but for every drunk on the street, every person who had been at the bar, and every driver in the area.

Of course they had long-term and detailed data on all of those people. It was what they did. It was *all* they did! Day in and day out, slinking around behind us, watching, logging, studying. The bastards knew everything about us!

I shouted a warning.

The girl turned around suddenly and stared right into the face of her attacker—smooth chitinous plates over unidentifiable pulsing fleshy sacs and nodes, all set under complex insectoid eyes. Obviously, she screamed.

It didn't go after her as she ran for her life. Instead, it whipped its head around and stood high on its segmented limbs. The creatures were usually low or folded in some manner, so the sight of it cresting ten feet high broke my resolve and I, too, ran. A strange call went out, much like the horn of a truck, and I knew it was calling others to the hunt.

I had enough wherewithal to realize that running into the chill night would mean death. I dashed onto the street and slowed to a walk among the drunks leaving the bars in loud and laughing groups. My jacket was bulky and the brim of my hat mostly hid my face. Would the creatures know who I was? I altered my gait and focused on the unconscious behaviors of my body in an attempt to avoid fitting any data they had on me. Would my very pattern of breathing give me away?

But drunks were not the defense I thought they were. Their attention was minimal and scattered, and multiple shadows began lurking at the edges of my oasis, moving inexorably closer as they found vectors where nobody was paying attention. They could pick me right out from the middle of the crowd and the drunks would never notice. I needed inspiration.

Another group stumbled out of a nearby bar and merged with ours in a stream. I punched one direction and moved another within the sea of people. Men began shoving and shouting, and I ducked, slipped my jacket and hat off, and left them on the street. I laughed and shouted along with the other human beings around—it was time to see how well my pursuers could pay attention.

My joviality became real as the tightening noose slackened. These were field observers, not the data-handlers, and they didn't have profiles to compare with each of us to root out which one of us had been the deviant. Every single one of us was sweaty, red-faced, loud, and kinetic. A man in a gorilla suit could have walked through us at that moment without the creatures noticing.

All I needed to do was drift away as all the bar-goers eventually did, and, if I wasn't followed, I was home free. Of the two dozen of us out there on the orange-lit sidewalk, the four creatures would have to choose only a sixth of us to follow. Those were better odds than I could have hoped for.

But my luck came up short. One of them slipped after me as I split away from the crowd. I couldn't return home and let it know who I was. Worse, it had freedom now to get creative. It took on the flashing blue and red qualities of an approaching police cruiser at the corner of my vision, just enough to get a normal drunk to turn around in surprise, and it knew it had me when I panicked and ran instead. I ducked under a rusted fence, dashed through a construction area, and took many hard turns in a suburban area, but I eventually found myself knocked to my knees in a dark yard. The shadow of the monstrous creature loomed over me, and I felt the surgically sharp end of one of its limbs trace gently across my throat—just enough to scrape, but not to kill. With that, it departed.

At first, I was terrified and confused, but then I understood: they knew who I was now. They didn't need to kill me. My little rebellion had been cut short because my hidden behavior would now be included in their data. I would never be able to interfere again.

What to do, then? I've waited and watched for a number of years since, now only aware of disappearances through Internet articles and social media posts. I go to my job, I work, I go home, and I watch TV. I've dated. I assume I'll get married and have kids someday. But always they lurk, watching, waiting, and surgically slicing away specific people from the fabric of our communities. I write this now because of an offhand comment from an old acquaintance I ran into this week; it was that governor's son I used to hang out with, and he told me that his father had been considering running for Senate all those years ago but had opted not to because of our friend's disappearance in the woods.

Now that speaks to me of something far greater and far more sinister than even I have guessed at. How far ahead do they see? How long have they been watching us, editing us? We might rise up enraged as a species if glorious world leaders or local kind-hearted souls were to disappear, but we think nothing of the impact the removal of unimportant individuals have on those around them. Before the person who might save us from these creatures can even become a leader, someone close to them and important to them can be excised, and therefore none of us are the wiser that we've lost someone amazing.

I know now why they've let me live, and even why they're letting me write this. First, they seek submission and hopelessness, and I have long submitted and given up hope. Second, they know you won't believe me, and they know that, even if you did, you would submit and give up hope, too. You are like me, bandied about in a world of apathy, distraction, and pointlessness. On the off chance you feel like doing something about it—don't. Don't look behind you. Don't start paying attention. Most of all, don't start thinking about why things are the way they are. If you're the type of person who might wake up and look around, I guarantee there are eyes on you at this very moment, and those ghastly eyes see more than you ever will. They know absolutely everything about you and can punish you before you even begin an attempt to resist. As for how to pass the time in our shared invisible captivity, I can recommend some really great TV shows.

DOWN IN THE LIBRARY BASEMENT

Rona Vaselaar

Running a library is not an easy thing to do.

You'd be surprised at the number of people who think that all librarians do is sit around and read the whole day. They have no concept of all the duties that come with being a librarian. In just one day, my mother will teach a class for senior citizens on how to use the computer, help four different families find the graves of their loved ones, register a thousand new books into the system, reorder all the books that have been returned, hold a story-time session for the children . . . the list goes on and on.

The point of me telling you this is for you to understand that it takes a person with a degree and years of experience to run a library . . . and I am not that person.

My mom has run our small town's library for over twenty years. She's damn good at what she does, and that's the only reason our town still has a library. Unfortunately, this meant that it was difficult to replace her, even for a short amount of time, when she fell down the basement stairs and broke her leg.

I should have suspected something was up when she called me home. I'm a freelance writer, so it's not difficult for me to come back to rural Minnesota at a moment's notice. You'll understand, however, that I don't do it very often—I rarely have any shred of desire to return to my hometown.

"I need you to watch over the library for me until I can go back to work."

When my mom said that, it wasn't a request so much as an order. It was easy to tell from the set look in her eyes that she had already mentally decided I would be taking over for her—regardless of any request of mine.

As the librarian's daughter, I knew better than anyone how difficult her job is. I blanched when she asked me and said, "Mom, there's no way. I don't know how to register books, I don't know how to use the system . . ."

My mom waved her hand dismissively. "That's not a problem, you won't have to register any books. You can just check them out, which you've done before. Another librarian from Rock County will be coming once a week to register any new books and fix anything you might have screwed up." I wanted to scowl at that, but I held back, mostly because it was true. "For the most part, I need you to deal with patrons. Help them find books, help them with research, keep the computers up and running."

"You do realize you're asking me to do the impossible, right?" I deadpanned.

My mom sighed. "Look, I know this isn't ideal. But it's only for a few weeks until my leg is better. I just need you to keep things afloat. You know if there was anyone qualified to do this, I'd ask them. As it is, you're the closest to a qualified librarian this town has, aside from me. You've grown up with the library and you know the basics of how it works. You can do this."

I gave my mom a skeptical look, but she just returned it with an encouraging smile. I sighed as she began to give me a rundown on my duties as her stand-in. There were so many details that I actually had to take notes. By the fourth or fifth page, I was convinced that she was setting me up for failure.

"Just do your best, you'll be fine," she said.

Yeah. Right.

• • •

The first day at the library was utter and complete hell, mixed in with some chaos and a healthy dose of self-loathing.

I followed my mom's instructions to the letter, but even that was a paltry comfort.

> Make sure you have story-time in the morning. It starts promptly at 9:00 A.M.

Usually I love kids, but not when I'm the one who has to try to keep them in line. And they never stop talking. It took me fifteen minutes to get to the fourth page of the stupid picture book I'd picked out, something about a dumb jellyfish that lost his glasses. Jellyfish don't even need glasses, you little shits.

> Try to run a virus scan on each computer before noon. If one computer goes down, the rest are sure to follow, trust me.

Of course, it would be my luck that the computers would all crash on my first day. I called the town's resident IT guy, a man from across the county who proved to be distinctly unhelpful. "I can probably get in to fix them later this week," he said. Oh, perfect. Computerless for a week. I don't remember what exactly I said to him, but apparently my threats were frightening enough to get him in within the hour. He carefully avoided me as he fixed the computers.

> Some patrons might need help with genealogy research—just do the best you can.

Even with the websites my mom provided, it was near impossible to find these people. "My great-great-grandmother's name was Ethel. Can you find her for me?" "I can try. What's her last name?" "Oh, I'm not sure, but I know she lived in a red house." ". . . I see. Any other information?" "She was a witch. I'm trying to find her spell book." ". . . Right."

> Some kids will probably be coming in to find books for school. They have a reading program in school and they have to earn a certain number of points in a semester by reading books in their reading level. Make sure to get them books appropriate for both their age and reading level.

"What do you mean, my son shouldn't read *A Clockwork Orange*?!" screamed the soccer mom, her long manicured nails tapping on the library desk. Her eight-year-old son stood a little ways away, browsing the sports books.

"It's just not age-appropriate, ma'am."

"I'll have you know my son is damned smart and he can read whatever he wants."

"Ma'am. About half of this book is about rape, and the other half is about murder," I said, losing patience.

"WHAT?" she shrieked, throwing the book down on the counter in disgust. "Why on EARTH would the school recommend such filth? And why do you offer it here? Really, I expect more from a public institution like this!"

So, like I said. That first day was exceptionally long and brutal. The days after weren't much better.

• • •

There were a few . . . odd instructions that my mom had given me before sending me on my doomed mission. They were so strange, in fact, that I asked the hospital if they'd checked my mom for a concussion, because she was obviously talking nonsense. She had to be.

"Every night after you lock up, go down to the library basement. Make sure to take along a book of your choice—it can be anything. Then, you'll need to sit down there and read aloud for at least half an hour."

I blinked as I stared at my mom, giving me a stern look from her hospital bed. "Um . . . am I supposed to record this, or . . . ?"

"No, don't worry about that. Just go down there and read."

"Mom, there's nothing down there." It was true; the basement was a decrepit dust-fest, complete with a bare concrete floor and rows of useless crap that had never been thrown away for some odd reason or another.

"It doesn't matter if there is or isn't anything down there. You just do as I said. Understand?"

She was rarely so harsh with me, so I agreed, making a big show of writing it down. She relaxed.

"Make sure you lock the doors before you leave, but leave one light on, the one by the front desk. If you remember, leave some candy behind, too." She must have seen the look I was giving her, because she said, "I know this all seems like an odd thing to ask, but it's very important to me. All right?"

I couldn't say I was sure that my mother was completely sane, or that she hadn't conked her head hard enough to drive logic out the window. But she was looking at me as though this was the most important part of my job, so I gave a resigned nod and said, "All right."

The practice, however, was much harder than the theory. Mostly because I really fucking hated going into that basement.

The first night I went down, I grabbed my copy of *Wuthering Heights*—one of my favorite books—and descended the stairs, flicking on the light as I went. There was only one functioning light in the basement, a bare bulb hung from the ceiling that illuminated a tiny circular spot on the floor. I felt like I was stepping into the spotlight as I sat down in the chair my mother must have placed there.

I sat in the total silence and cleared my throat. It was strange being down here alone. I really didn't like it. But I had a job to do, so I set a timer on my phone for thirty minutes and started reading.

I stumbled a little at the beginning, the words jumbling together on their way out of my mouth, but soon I had found my groove and the narrative flowed just fine, my voice carrying throughout the damp basement. It made me nervous, the way I broke the silence. It seemed wrong. I could feel my pulse hammering hard in my throat and I began to wish that I had just ignored my mother's instructions. I'm stupid. This is stupid. And I'm stupid for doing the stupid thing. Stupid.

As I kept reading, I gradually became aware of the feeling of somebody watching me. Of course I'd feel that way. I mean, I was sitting in this creepy old basement, all alone with barely even a light to keep me company, my voice echoing off the cement walls in total solitude. It's completely normal that I'd begin to feel creeped out, as though I wasn't really alone.

Normal, but that didn't mean that I liked it.

I was startled when my phone roared to life, its jingle signaling the end of my thirty minutes. Swallowing hard, I silenced the offending object and raced up the stairs, suddenly feeling that something was going to slither out and drag me back down if I wasn't careful.

I slammed the basement door shut and ran through the library, finishing everything as quickly as I could. I left the light on over the front desk. I'd bought a candy bar during lunch—a Milky Way, if you're curious—and I left it on the desk. It looked like an offering to something. I couldn't stop shaking.

I ran out the front door and locked it, checking and rechecking to make sure that I hadn't made a mistake. I won't lie; I was relieved after locking it, as though the extra barrier between myself and the basement would save me from . . . something.

It took me a full ten minutes before I was calm enough to climb into my car and drive to my parents' house, where my mom and dad had set up my old room for as long as I'd be running the library. Dad was at the hospital with Mom, who hadn't come home yet, so I had the house to myself. I got drunk that night, prying open my dad's liquor cabinet and drinking whatever I laid my eyes on. I threw on some stupid sitcom and sat in the living room, all the lights on and a blanket drawn around me like a suit of armor.

So ended the absolute worst first day of a job I'd ever had.

• • •

That first week was anything but easy.

On Tuesday, I made a kid cry during story-time. On Wednesday, I caught one of the patrons trying to watch porn on the computer. On Thursday, the town pervert came in specifically to harass me, and I had to threaten to sic the police on him when he started bragging about his "massive cock." On Friday, it rained and the roof leaked, ruining about a dozen good books that would have to be replaced.

The one thing that got easier, at least, was the basement.

At first, I'd been so confused as to why my mother had asked me to do all these strange rituals. It was like she was trying to assuage a spirit or something . . . The moment that thought occurred to me, I realized what was happening. My mother, you see, is a BIG believer in ghosts. The library has always had its share of bad luck—lights going out on their own, computers crashing, etc.—and she must have started to believe that it had its own little haunting. Perhaps she thought that if she read to it, gave it offerings, things would go smoothly.

After that, my nightly rituals actually became . . . kind of fun.

I started to imagine that the "ghost" my mom had been communicating with was another young woman, just like me. I picked out books that I thought she might like (read as: books that I liked) and put more feeling into my readings. Occasionally, I'd find myself talking to her absent-mindedly throughout the day.

In the end, I even started believing she might actually be there.

It started with the candy. As per my mother's request, I'd buy the elusive little spirit something as an offering. I started out with chocolate, and I'd throw it away in the morning. One night, however, I left a bag of Skittles, and the next morning it was gone. I had scoured the library, looking for some sign of the candy, but it was just . . . gone. From then on, I started buying all different kinds of treats, seeing if I could get different results. Chocolates were usually left behind, but hard candies were almost always gone by the next day.

After about three weeks, I'd decided that, yes, there was a ghost, and I was beginning to understand its preferences.

• • •

Maybe it seems that I'm being a little too cavalier about all this.

After all, it's not every day that people decide they're dealing with ghosts and start messing around with them. Of course, you have to remember that I hadn't actually seen any ghosts. I'd just imagined that they must be there. To me, it was something of a game—I got to play make-believe and some forces-that-be played along. It was fun, if a little strange.

That all changed one night just after closing, when I made the mistake of letting down my guard.

Everyone in town knew that the library closed at 8:00 P.M. on Thursdays (and that day was a Thursday). It was already 8:30 and I was choosing a book—I'd just about decided on *Little Women*—when I heard the bells above the door jingle and somebody step inside the library.

Now, I hadn't locked the door yet because . . . well, I didn't think I needed to. I can already hear you guys telling me how stupid I am, but cut me a little slack. After all, it's a small town. And nothing ever happens in small towns, right?

Guess again.

I peered out from the bookshelf I was standing near and saw the town pervert walking toward me. He had this big shit-eating grin on his face and immediately I was on high alert.

Let me give you a quick rundown on how this guy looks. He's massive—and I don't mean fat. He's ridiculously tall with a fair amount of muscle bulging out of his ill-fitting and stained clothes. He lacked the capacity to understand personal hygiene, apparently, because his hair was always greasy and his breath smelled like the inside of a bat cave. He had a bad habit of getting inside a person's personal space and leering at her, his eyes traveling shamelessly over her body. It disgusted me.

My mom had always warned me about this guy—we'll call him Chad, for the sake of anonymity. See, Chad would try to fuck anything that moved, regardless of age or circumstance. He'd been around since I was a kid, and he had often tried to convince both me and my older sister to come into his house and talk with him, just for a moment, he had something nice to give us. He'd gotten kicked out of the library several times in the past for hitting on minors, or on my mother herself. He had wandering hands and no sense of decency.

And, at that moment, I was alone with him.

"You still working here for your ma, Cassie?" he asked easily, his steps not slowing as he approached me. I took a few instinctive steps back, putting the desk between us as a sort of barrier. Not that he couldn't work his way around that. I wondered if I'd be able to grab my mace from my purse.

"You know I am, Chad," I snapped, already annoyed with him. "You know you're not supposed to be here after hours, either. You need to leave. Right now."

He gave me an easy smile. "I just want to talk to you, sweetie. We're friends, aren't we?"

I felt a heave deep in my stomach at those words. I scanned my work area for my purse, but remembered all to late it wasn't there. Fuck, I left it in the car!

"No, we're not friends. If you don't leave right now, I'm going to call the cops."

Not that calling the cops would do much good. The reason people like Chad could still exist in such a small community was that the cops were absolute shit. Still, I reached for the phone anyway, because I don't make threats that I don't intend to keep.

Chad's polite mask slipped off then, as I knew it would. I'd been hoping he was smart enough to high-tail it out of there when I made my threat, but my hope was clearly misplaced, especially since there were no witnesses to his behavior. His eyes darkened and he snarled, "You fucking bitch!"

In a moment, he was halfway over the desk and I shrieked. I stumbled backward just out of reach as he lumbered toward me, sporting a tent in his pants that told me he enjoyed chasing me into a corner. In an absolute panic, I ran down the stairs to the basement, stumbling and falling the last few steps and sprawling out on the concrete.

A deep pain flared up in my arm as I landed on it, and I knew instantly that it was definitely sprained, maybe broken. I could hear Chad pounding down the steps and I crawled into the darkness, my legs shaking too hard to support myself.

I had just about made it past the little circle of light—he must have turned it on before he came down—when his hand shot out and caught me by my ankle. He was freakishly strong, although I shouldn't have been surprised, given his physique. He clamped his hand down so hard I thought he might actually snap my anklebone. I screamed again as I tried to pull myself away from him, but my attempts were futile. I heard him panting hard in arousal as he pulled me back.

"Filthy little slut, been teasing me all these years, now look what it's gotten you . . ." he muttered, falling on top of me and pinning me down. I thrashed and yelped as he fumbled with my blouse, cursing its buttons.

And then, just then, I got that feeling again. That feeling of being watched.

This time it was much stronger than before. I instantly froze, suddenly feeling a great danger surrounding me—a danger other than Chad. The air in the basement seemed to have dropped a good ten degrees and I could see puffs of his rotten breath forming above me. On instinct, I began to strain my eyes, looking past his hulking body into the darkness, even as he undid the last button and reached for my bra.

There, in the darkness—something was moving.

It was as though the darkness in the room had become liquid, and it was shifting and twisting. My breath caught in my throat and I barely felt Chad's hands on me. I had gone silent when I sensed the disturbance, but now I began to make strange wheezing noises as the liquid darkness moved toward us.

Chad didn't ask if I was okay, or what was wrong. I don't think he even noticed. He was too busy trying to get me out of my slacks.

He never saw it. But I did.

It had black fur, which was probably why I had never seen it before. Its body was absolutely massive, pushed along by four long, spindly legs. It looked something like a spider, but for the way it walked. Its body was obviously heavy because the legs did little more than drag it forward, its body scraping along the ground. I noticed that its legs ended in a sharp claw, making each into something of a spear.

I couldn't scream. I wanted to, but I couldn't.

As I lay there under the body of my would-be rapist (I was dimly aware that he hadn't quite succeeded in de-clothing me yet) I saw one of its front legs snap forward. It had been lumbering toward us so slowly that I almost thought it was incapable of speed. Apparently I was wrong, because in the time it took me to blink its leg had managed to spear through Chad's chest, poking through the other side and showering me in blood.

I gagged.

Chad's eyes were wide open, staring at me in utter confusion as though he thought I was the one who did this. In reality, I was just as surprised as he was, especially when the leg began to split apart into smaller appendages, goring him from the inside out.

In absolute horror, I crawled backward, bumping into some boxes behind me.

The creature dragged Chad's still-struggling body backward toward its bulk before extracting its limb. With great effort it pulled itself up on its legs. Now I could see its belly. Well, what should have been its belly. I watched its fur pull back to reveal several rows of jagged, yellow teeth, pointed just slightly outward. Its maw was larger than my torso, and I watched as it lowered itself down on top of Chad.

I'm glad that I couldn't see what exactly those teeth did to him—most of my vision was blocked by the black furry body—but I did manage to see the blood. The amount of red that covered the floor and coated the beast gave me a pretty good idea of what was happening. I seem to recall that Chad's screams went on a great while longer than I expected them to.

Eventually, the thing finished feeding. The sickening crunch of Chad's bones stopped and it settled itself on the floor once more.

Its legs began to drag its body forward as it crawled to me.

Tears were coursing down my cheeks as I thought about what had happened to Chad. I had never really planned out what kind of death I wanted, but I knew that wasn't it. I was shaking so hard the boxes behind me started to rattle as the thing crawled toward me at an agonizingly slow pace.

It stopped just in front of me. I found myself frantically searching for eyes, but I found none. I had an awful moment where I wondered if it could smell me.

And then, something amazing and unbelievable happened.

It lifted itself up just a bit and spit out a wrapper.

A Skittles wrapper.

There was a long moment where neither of us moved. The black creature was waiting for me to do something, and I was waiting to do it. Eventually, I mustered up enough courage to reach forward and pick up the wrapper.

As soon as I did, it turned itself around, dragging its heavy body back to the corner it had been hiding in.

I sat there for a long moment, staring alternately at the wrapper and at the mess of blood that the beast had left on the floor, splattered with the occasional eyeball or tooth. I stared and I thought.

Eventually, I stood up.

I walked on shaking legs up the stairs to the young adult's aisle, plucking *Little Women* from the shelf. I walked back down to the basement, righting the chair that had been tipped over during my struggle with Chad. I sat down and, in a surprisingly steady voice, I began to read.

• • •

It was about two weeks later that my mom was cleared to come back to work.

Well, "cleared" might be a poor term. It's more that she ordered the doctor to give his consent for her to return to work, otherwise she was going to find him and kill him in his sleep. Something to that effect. Hey, the women in my family are scary, what can I say?

I decided to stick around for a few more weeks, helping my mom out as she got back to her daily routine. She observed me carefully, probably trying to decide if I knew what she thought I knew.

One night as we were closing, she asked me, "Did something happen to Chad? He usually comes in at least once a day and I haven't seen him at all since I've been back."

I shrugged, thinking of the hour I'd spent cleaning up the basement so there would be no trace of the . . . incident. "Guess I don't know, maybe he decided to skip town."

"It does look that way, doesn't it?" she said, watching me closely.

After a moment of silence, she said, "Would you like to read tonight, or should I?"

I answered her with a grin that told her everything she needed to know. "I think I'll do it tonight. I still need to finish *Little Women*."

My mom smiled at me, knowing that she'd found a fellow conspirator.

I know I should go back to my writing, but I'm finding it a bit hard to leave the library now.

After all, it's not every day that you meet a new friend!

VOICES IN THE SPIRIT BOX

Michael Marks

When I was seventeen my mother was murdered. But this story isn't about her. My mother's killer is still in prison for his crime. No, this story is about what happened afterward.

About a year after my mother's funeral, my dad started mentioning that she would come visit him at night. He said she glowed in a pure white light and reached out to him with a warm smile on her face. He said she looked just the way she did the last time he saw her, before she left for the store on the last night of her life.

My sister and I both missed our mother very much and we wanted to believe it was true. We did whatever we could think of to try and contact her, but it was only my dad who ever saw her. We just wanted to say goodbye.

Ouija boards, spirit boxes, automatic writing, psychics and mediums; we tried them all and all proved to be little more than distractions.

About three months into our efforts my dad had his first blackout. He claimed it was just stress but my sister and I agreed in confidence that it was more than that. He would forget things all the time, talk about old memories out of the blue, and then he started getting these horrible migraines. We didn't learn the source of it all until he finally agreed to go to the doctor. He had a brain tumor. Inoperable.

His doctor told us it was the likely source of all he'd been experiencing, including the hallucinations of his dead wife. My sister and I lost all hope of ever saying goodbye to our mom and focused on our dad instead.

By then I was nearly nineteen and my sister was twenty-two. She ended up moving back in with Dad and me to help take care of him. Even with treatment he only lasted six months, though, which was three months longer than the prognosis. When our dad finally passed away, we were both devastated. I can still remember that night so vividly in my mind; the loneliness, the realization that both my parents were gone. And it was worse to realize that in all of our attempts to find proof of some kind of afterlife, we'd found nothing.

Dad's last words to the both of us were about Mom:

"She's telling me to come with her, she looks so beautiful . . . so beautiful."

My actual story starts almost a year later, though, when I finally decided to move out of my parents' house and in with my longtime girlfriend.

"Alex!" I could hear my sister yelling for me downstairs. She had moved back in with her boyfriend months ago but she was home to help me pack up the last of our parents' things for sale or donation. "Alex, what do you want to do with all these dishes?"

I poked my head out of my half-packed room and yelled back down to her.

"Donate!"

"What?"

I sighed and went bounding down the stairs, taking the last five in a single jump, landing in the hallway. My sister stood in kitchen doorway and repeated her question.

"What do you want to do with all these dishes?"

"Donate. Clean your ears, Lilly, I could hear you just fine."

"Are you telling *me* to clean something? That's a fucking laugh!" Lilly spun around and went back into the kitchen, talking as she walked. "Are you sure you don't need any of this stuff?"

"Nope. Carla has everything we need in the dishes department." I followed her into the kitchen and saw her staring down at a beige plate decorated with a chicken and two ears of corn that sat below its feet. It was from our usual dining set; I remembered sitting down to dinner every night to those plates in front of me.

"I think I want to keep one of these."

Lilly's eyes had misted over, and I knew how she felt. It was the little things that seemed to catch you. I smiled and walked over to her, placing my hand on her shoulder.

"Yeah, you should. Save one for me too, okay?"

She looked up at me and smiled.

Suddenly, we both felt something whiz between our heads at a high speed and heard it crash against the far wall just below my mom's old cat clock. Lilly nearly dropped the plate she was holding as she jumped back and let out a yelp. We had both been startled right out of our family moment and I could feel my heart beating at a mile a minute.

"What the fuck was that!" Lilly yelled, setting the plate down on the kitchen table and stepping toward the far wall.

She bent down and disappeared behind the tablecloth for a second before re-emerging with a piece of broken plate in her hand. She had a confused look on her face, one I must have mirrored. We were the only two people in the house; no one else could have thrown that plate. On the sliver of porcelain Lilly was holding I could see a chicken's foot raising up from behind an ear of corn. It was from the same set we had been discussing.

"You've gotta be kidding me." I said, turning my head to glance at the cupboard full of dishes and then back at Lilly. She shrugged and gave me the "I dunno" look. That's when I noticed that the familiar ticking from my mother's cat clock, a sound I had been accustomed to hearing for years, had stopped. I looked up at the wall behind Lilly and noticed the cat's tail had stopped swinging and its always shifting eyes had frozen in place.

It was staring directly at me.

I shivered involuntarily and went to help Lilly pick up the pieces of broken dish scattered about the kitchen floor.

The plate incident reminded us of all our efforts to contact our mother. In all our attempts we never saw anything even remotely paranormal happen, yet here we were face-to-face with an event that neither of us could explain. It didn't take long to decide we should pursue it.

The incident had also cast doubt on the theory that my father had been hallucinating prior to his death. In our desperation, we eagerly jumped on the small chance to talk to them one more time. I know now that hope can be as dangerous as it is comforting. Lilly and I went to our significant others and explained what we were going to attempt: we wanted to give the Ouija board and the spirit box one more try. Carla was open to the idea when I told her about it and she actually seemed kind of excited. Lilly had a harder time with David. As she relayed it to me, she had to "drag him along, kicking and screaming." In the end, though, he showed up and I knew that even if he didn't buy into any of it, he would be there for my sister.

Two nights later we all gathered at my parents' house. At the time, we were excited, giddy. We had no idea what we were signing up for. If we had, I would have walked away from that place and never looked back.

"Is everyone ready?" Lilly asked, her fingers already resting on top of the planchette.

Carla looked at me, green eyes that darkened to a near black in the dim orange candlelight. She winked at me and put her hands on the planchette next to Lilly's. Then I placed my fingers on the other side of the plastic toy and did my best to ignore the disapproving look on David's face. He had reluctantly agreed to be our scribe, writing down the words that might be spelled out during our séance.

Lilly started moving the planchette around the board in the infinity shape we had always used before. I could feel the same excitement welling up inside me that I'd had the first time we'd tried this. I could see the same fervor reflected in my sister's expression.

"What now?" Carla whispered over the board.

"Now we ask some questions." Lilly held her head high like she was trying to channel some kind of divine energy. My sister always got a little bit too into the theatrics of the whole thing.

"Is there anyone here with us?" I took the lead.

We all watched the board with bated breath, hoping to feel some movement beneath our fingers. Suddenly the infinity shape motion stopped and we watched the planchette move slowly across the board toward the top left corner before stopping at the word YES.

"Okay . . . you guys aren't fucking with me, right? 'Cause I didn't do that." Carla was looking at me again, I could see out of the corner of my eye. I was stunned; in the million times we had tried this, nothing had ever really happened at all.

"No, we . . . we aren't fucking with you."

"Ask another question!" Lilly's voice had gone up at least two octaves and she was smiling like a crazy person. It was the same look she would get on Christmas morning when we were kids. The joy of discovery and the satisfaction of finally getting what you've been waiting for.

"What is your name?" I asked, diving right in. This was going to be the moment of truth.

I was surprised at just how quickly the planchette started moving around the board. We called out each letter as the planchette briefly stopped and I heard David scribbling away.

I-T-S-D-A-D-D-Y

"It's . . . Daddy." David murmured the words in a voice that contrasted his previously cool demeanor.

Lilly's hands left the planchette and she slapped them across her mouth. I could see her eyes quickly filling with tears. Carla and David both sat there slack-jawed and I'm sure my face had a similar look.

"Lil, put your hand back on the thing," I said weakly, feeling like the wind had been knocked out of me. "Lilly! Please put your hand back on."

She did as I asked and when her hands left her face I noted the smile she had been hiding.

"Daddy, is that really you?" Lilly's question choked out through a mixture of laughter and tears.

YES

The response was immediate.

"We miss you so much, Daddy. It's been so hard since you and Mom have been gone!"

W-E-M-I-S-S-Y-O-U-T-O-O

"Holy shit!" Carla couldn't contain herself any longer and I found myself smile at his use of the word "WE."

"Dad!" I couldn't even hope to disguise the excitement in my voice. "Is Mom there with you?"

YES

My sister—now suffering through full-blown sobs of joy—leaned her head over and rested it on David's shoulder. He stared down at his notepad rereading the words, barely registering that she was there. I didn't know if he was stunned by what he was seeing or horrified at how deluded we all were. David had never been much of a believer.

"Dad, can Mom talk to us?" I wanted to keep the dialogue going.

IM SORRY

I raised an eyebrow at the response.

"What are you sorry about?" I asked, unsure if I was speaking to my mother or my father.

SHES TOO COLD

TOO HARD FOR HER

The smile fell from Lilly's face and the mood of the room became more solemn as David read the last sentences out loud. The planchette continued to move then without any more prompting.

SO COLD HERE

SO LONELY

WE MISS YOU

WE MISS YOU

ITS DADDY

PLEASE HELP

PLEASE

WE NEED YOU

After the last 'U' the planchette suddenly shot out from under our hands, paused just milliseconds over GOODBYE, and then fired across the room and hit the wall at roughly the same speed as the plate that morning.

I jumped up and away from the board in shock. Lilly was now sobbing loudly as David held her but his eyes remained fixed on the board as if it were the most alien object he'd ever seen. Carla touched my hand with shaking fingers and I looked down to see fear in her eyes.

"I don't understand," Carla said and stood up. "I'm so sorry, baby." She wrapped her arms around me and it was only then that

I noticed the wetness on my own cheeks. I hadn't cried since my mom's murder, and I figured something in me had broken that day. Even when Dad passed I didn't cry. Now, though, in this moment, the tears finally came.

We tried to contact my parents all night but the planchette didn't move again.

We'd hoped contact with our parents would make us feel better, give us some sense of closure, but instead it had devastated us, Lilly most of all. Most days she would sit in the living room for hours, listening to the static of the spirit box, hoping to hear a voice.

As the weeks went on Lilly became quieter and more introverted. She retreated into herself, hardly speaking to anyone. The conversation with the Ouija board had made an impression on me too, but Lilly had become obsessed. I gradually became less interested in contacting our parents again and more concerned about my sister's mental state.

And then one night I woke from that nightmare to a more real, more horrifying one.

I answered my ringing phone to hear David's voice yelling through the earpiece.

"Alex! Your sister just took off!"

"Took off? What do you mean?" David's tone was panicked and I rubbed the sleep from eyes and tried to focus.

"Alex, she's been way worse than she lets on. Lilly doesn't sleep anymore. She just sits in the kitchen and listens to that damn little radio."

"The spirit box?"

"Yeah, that fucking thing! She says she can still hear your parents talking to her. I want to believe her, man, but I sat for hours with her one night and didn't hear a single thing."

"Jesus."

"Alex, I'm scared for her. Tonight she was listening to it and talking back to it, her voice woke me up. I couldn't understand exactly what she said but she was crying and then I heard her bolt out the door and slam it behind her."

"She went back to my parents' house."

It wasn't a question; I could feel it in my bones. I may not have known the full extent of what was happening but I did know that something very, very bad had just happened to my sister. She couldn't cope with what the Ouija board had told us and after all these years of suppressing her sadness, she had just cracked.

"You think? That's what I was thinking too. I know you have keys, man, can I meet you there? I think we need to get her help."

I sighed into the phone, knowing he was right. Lilly may never forgive us, but I was quickly becoming convinced that she needed professional care. The weight of the decision to admit her somewhere felt smothering. I looked down at Carla who was awake, staring warily out the window with lines of worry etched on her face.

"Yeah. Yeah, just let me get dressed. I can be at my parents' in about forty-five minutes. Let me see if I can talk to Lilly."

"Thanks, Alex, I'm gonna head over now. I'm a lot closer so I'll let her know you're coming."

We hung up and I relayed the entire conversation to Carla. Despite my best efforts to keep her safe at home, she insisted on going with me. And when I protested she challenged me to try and stop her. Ten minutes later we were in the car heading to my old house.

The argument with Carla had delayed my departure and we actually arrived at the house more than an hour later. Both Lilly's and David's cars were parked in the driveway, so I parked on the street and Carla and I headed to the front door.

I noticed as we climbed the porch steps that no lights were on inside the house. The front door was slightly ajar and I took a deep breath before pushing it all the way open with a creak. Beyond the door was utter blackness, a seeming void instead of a welcoming foyer. I had never seen the house this dark before. As I let my eyes adjust, I listened intently for any sound. All I could hear was the clicking of the spirit box rapidly changing channels through the soft static. I finally stepped inside and made my way down the hall, taking Carla's hand as she followed behind me. "Lilly!" I yelled out and I heard the acute fear in my weak, shaking voice. I couldn't understand why I was suddenly so terrified in my own house. But I couldn't shake the feeling.

I hugged the walls until we rounded the corner into the softly lit living room. A dull blue light was emitting from somewhere and I could see Lilly sitting in front of it. She was cross-legged on the floor; the spirit box was in front of her and her head was hung between her shoulder blades, blonde hair covering her face. "Lilly?" I whispered, squeezing Carla's hand as I let go to walk toward my sister. I was halfway to her when Carla suddenly flipped on the light switch—and screamed.

I was blinded at first, and disoriented by the screaming, but my eyes gradually made the adjustment.

I blinked a few more times and found myself still facing Lilly, who had remained sitting on the floor with the spirit box in front of her. Her forearms were cut wrist to elbow and she was sitting in a pool of blood. David was there, lying next to her, stabbed God knows how many times in the chest, neck, and face. I could only assume it was him, as the body was unrecognizable.

I heard Carla take off down the hallway and slam the front door as she left the house. As I adjusted to my state of absolute shock, I scanned the room calmly before hysteria set in. The walls were covered in writing, the same three phrases over and over again, written in fresh blood.

ITS DADDY
WE MISS YOU
WE NEED YOU

I snapped out of my trance, suddenly, and stumbled over to Lilly. I begged every god I had ever heard of to let her be alive somehow, to let me save her. I choked on my prayers as I rescued Lilly's limp body from the crimson puddle and screamed for Carla to call 911.

Her skin lacked the warmth of life and I pressed my face to hers, begging her to wake up, my whispers falling on dead ears. I cried; the soft static of the spirit box played the score to my pain. How many eternities passed before Carla returned, I do not know. But I saw her there, finally, standing in the doorway, talking to emergency services and staring at us. I cradled Lilly's body and rocked back and forth. I could tell from the look of disgust and pity set upon her face that Carla couldn't hear the sounds coming from the spirit box.

"Alex, it's Mommy . . . we need you."

It was faint, but it was her. My mother's voice was unmistakable.

A year later, when the detectives finally called to let me know they were releasing my sister's things, I brought the spirit box home. I didn't let Carla know that I had it; she had never quite recovered from what she'd seen the night of the murder/suicide. The media had called Lilly's case a "tragic descent into madness." Carla and I couldn't have agreed more. But sometimes late at night, when Carla is asleep, I slip out of bed and sneak into the living room. I pull the spirit box out from behind a stack of books and I turn it on, just for a few seconds. But in those moments, I listen closely to the clicking sounds of the radio quickly scanning through the static. I strain to hear their words, the voices of my family.

And sometimes I hear them.

In the few seconds, I've heard them say many things. They tell me that they need me, that they love me, and that it's lonely without me. They claim that it's cold. They beg me to join them, Lilly says that it's easy, and that I should bring Carla with me.

They say we'll all be happy there.

But there is something behind their voices, something that sometimes bleeds through. Lilly must have either ignored the sound, or blocked it out completely.

Beneath their warm invitations and desperate pleading, I can hear something laughing. Something inhuman.

WHEN DUSK FALLS ON HADLEY TOWNSHIP

T.W. Grim

Sunset over Hadley Township is almost always picture-perfect, no matter what time of year it is—it's doubtful that anyone would disagree with that statement, not if they've ever witnessed the event firsthand. However, most people in these parts would argue that the sunset is at its most stunning in the summertime. In mid-July, Hadley Township is one of the most beautiful places in the world, and when the pink-laced gold of the early evening sky begins to deepen into the dark crimson shades of dusk, it could be mistaken for the Garden of Eden. Soon enough, all the lawns will begin to sizzle and die beneath the oppressive glare of the August sun, but for now, the grass is green and the meadows are dense and lush with the bounty of summer.

Aside from its natural beauty, Hadley is basically a desolate patch of wilderness, a rural municipality with a total population of just under two thousand souls. It's a place without tourist attractions or major urban centers, mostly comprising forest, farmland, and towering blue sky. There are a few scattered hamlets within its borders, but most of them are basically just a collection of houses surrounding a wide spot in the road. They might boast a gas station, a variety store, or maybe even a small bank, but never all three.

Hadley Township is said to be blessed, and after taking in the spectacular sunset, it would be hard to disagree with that statement. A blessing, however, can sometimes also be a curse.

On this particular evening, Roger Mossley is out cutting the grass on his riding lawnmower, a never-ending task when one lives on a farm. He notices that the shadows are starting to lengthen and realizes that it's high time to call it quits on mowing for the evening. He parks the mower in the barn and takes a wander around the barnyard to look for his daughter. Even though it's still relatively early in the evening, it's time for her to get inside. Normally, he'd let her stay out late enough to go chasing after the fireflies, but not tonight.

Tonight, everyone has to be inside before dusk.

Roger has lived on this farm his entire life, and he is grateful for his quiet, honest existence. The farm is successful and has always turned a profit; the modest prosperity of the land stretches back for ten generations. Family roots run deep in Hadley Township. Most of the farmers still plow the same fields that their ancestors cleared with an ax over two hundred years ago, and Roger was no different. He was born a Hadley man, and he would die a Hadley man.

Roger finds Sadie and Rufus at the edge of the cornfield, chasing after butterflies in the slanting sun rays, identical grins plastered on their faces. Both girl and dog have been stained green by the fresh-cut grass. He brings them up to the house and sends them inside for Katie to deal with, answering her annoyance with a meek little shrug. She kneels down to give them both a mock scolding at eye-level, her hands planted firmly on her generous hips and a smile threatening to break out and spread across her face. Sadie and Rufus look down at the carpet and shuffle their feet, enduring Katie's lecture with pouting defiance.

"I'll be in soon," he says. "Gonna have a smoke." Katie gives her husband a small nod over the top of Sadie's sweaty, tousled head. A look passes between them.

"Don't be too long," she tells him, softly. "Tonight's the night."

Roger takes a walk around the house, frowning at the uneven lawn and lighting a hand-rolled cigarette with a match. He notes that the cut looks pretty ragged. The mower blades must be getting dull. He stands in his front yard and watches as the western half of the sky begins to glow with a gentle, golden hue, the bright blue slowly giving way to shades of amber and rose. He looks up at the sky for a long, long time, motionless and tense, and his rollie gradually burns into a forgotten tower of ashes between his fingers.

We leave Roger Mossley standing in his front yard and travel west down County Road 22, chasing after the setting sun. We pass endless acres of rustling cornfields, all of them standing well over eight feet in height. The soil in Hadley Township is renowned throughout the county as being uncommonly rich and fertile. If a Hadley man were to sell his farmstead to an outsider, it would fetch a pretty penny above market value . . . but it's unlikely that will ever happen. There hasn't been a sale of land within township lines in well over two hundred years. The landscape is dominated by the surnames Mossley, VanDoren, Borden, and Weir: they are emblazoned onto mailboxes and road signs all across the township, as well as appearing in the names of public schools, bridges, nature reserves, and a dozen different little hamlets. Even garbage dumps and transfer stations bear the mark of the four original families, the oldest bloodlines in the municipality. The entire historical patchwork of Hadley Township is threaded together with these names, and there's hardly a single acre that hasn't been owned by one of these families during the span of the past two centuries. Interwoven family trees and their equally complicated claims on the land have turned Hadley into a very close-knit corner of the world, which is exactly how they want it. The people here take care of their own. Outsiders are tolerated, but they are never truly welcomed.

Hadley is a place of uncommon beauty, but it is also a place of secrets.

The massive cornfields come to an end at the corner of County Road 22 and Weir Line. From there, there is a three-mile stretch of land on either side of the 22 that has been divided into a number of large private lots. The majority of these lots are occupied by homeowners, but a few small businesses can be found in the mix, Mom-and-Pop operations that are run by local residents. Not everyone in Hadley is a farmer; there is a small but thriving business community here as well, enterprises that vary from pet groomers and candle makers to car mechanics and machine shops. All of them are at least modestly successful.

Here we meet Brian Caldwell, the owner and proprietor of a small supply warehouse for landscaping materials, a one-man operation with the decidedly unimaginative name Caldwell Landscaping Supply. Although it is currently the height of landscaping season, Brian called all of his own suppliers earlier in the day and canceled his pending orders. He then flipped the sign on the door from Open to Closed, turned off the lights, and sat down on the floor in the middle of his showroom. He is still sitting there now, slumped over in the gloom as the sun lowers in the sky and the shadows stretch their skeletal arms to the east.

Brian Caldwell has gone insane, which is not an unusual occurrence in Hadley Township. In fact, it happens all the time.

People around these parts have their secrets, it's true . . . but there are a number of people in the township who are unaware of its old traditions, Brian being one of them. His father had known of them all too well, but Rick Caldwell had always taken great care to shield his sons from certain facts regarding the true nature of their little corner of the world. Even still, Hadley is one of those places where an uncomfortable sort of psychic residue seems to linger in the air; it rasps away at the back of the mind, a low and unpleasant itching of the subconscious that makes people extra irritable during the long, hot days of August and downright mean when the temperatures plummet in the month of January. Unfortunately, some people are naturally more sensitive to this low-key mental assault than others, and Brian Caldwell is unlucky enough to be such an individual.

Over the course of the past few weeks, Brian has become convinced that the moon is actually the staring eye of an ancient beast, an evil presence that dwells in a howling void that exists somewhere just beyond the reaches of outer space. Brian believes that the beast watches our world every night with its jealous eye, hungering for our destruction. His delusion began as a nagging little notion in the back of his mind, a soft, insistent whisper, but it quickly inflated into an all-encompassing paranoia that occupies Brian's every waking thought, every single minute of the day.

Nobody knows about Brian's increasingly volatile mental state or the nature of his delusion. At first, he refrained from telling anyone because he was afraid people would think he was crazy . . . but as his strange new conviction sank its poisonous hooks deeper into his mind, Brian began to fear that his friends and customers might actually be servants of the evil eye, agents who spy on him and report their observations back to their nocturnal master when the sun goes down. Brian decided that it was imperative to hide his newfound awareness from the people around him. He became quiet and watchful, glaring out at the world through bloodshot eyes, squinted and bleary under the weight of his constant suspicion.

Brian has been awake for almost a hundred hours. Sleep is an impossible feat. Recently, the eye developed the ability to see right through the roof of his house, and at night he can actually feel the thing's loathsome gaze crawling across his trembling body, coveting his very existence. Dawn brings temporary relief, but the eye is always lurking just beyond the horizon, waiting for the heavens to grow cold and black in the wake of the waning sun. Waiting for its chance to arise and stare hatefully into Brian's soul.

Brian Caldwell became a time bomb waiting to go off, and this morning the inevitable explosion finally came. As he sat at the kitchen table, staring blankly at the sunlight that was streaming through the east windows, Brian suddenly realized that his own wife was actually an agent of the beast, and so was his teenage daughter. The revelation hit him like a ton of bricks and he let out a keening, whistling little gasp, his pallid face crumpling with grief and rage. All along, it had been his own fucking wife and kid, for Christ's sake, his own flesh and blood.

Emmie asked, "Did you just say something, hun?" without looking up from the dishes, and Brian stared at her back, his fists clenched on the table on either side of his coffee mug. He tore his eyes away from the treacherous demon-bitch and gazed back into the depths of the hazy morning sunbeams, his eyes narrowed into slits. Of course they were serving the eye. They had always served the eye. How had he been blind to this fact for so long?

Brian got up from the table and crept in behind Emmie as she stood at the sink, his lips skinned back from his teeth in a rictus of hate. He took out his folding Buck knife and pulled the blade.

When he was done, Brian placed Emmie's head on the counter and stepped carefully over her body, trying his best to be stealthy and quiet. He tiptoed upstairs and pounced on Mary Beth as she was engaged in some last-minute fussing with her eyebrows in the bathroom mirror, rushing to get ready in time for school. Mary Beth fought him like the demon she really was, screeching and clawing; she managed to fend off her father's initial attack and bolted past him, running down the hallway with her hair streaming behind her and blood blooming like roses on the back of her shirt. Brian scrambled after her, his eyes bulging and his face crisscrossed with deep, oozing scratches. He was simultaneously grinning, crying, and snarling like a rabid dog.

"Didja think I'd never find out? Hah? DID YOU?"

Brian tackled his daughter at the top of the staircase and pinned her to the floor of the hallway. He pushed the side of her head into the carpet and she wailed, "No, Daddy, please! Please don't hurt me!" He ignored the monster's trickery and plunged his knife into her neck, sinking it right up to the hilt. The blade pushed between two of Mary Beth's cervical vertebrae and severed her spinal cord. She abruptly stopped thrashing beneath him and he finished the job in relative peace, sawing through her throat with no more emotion than if he'd been slicing into a particularly tough cut of rare steak. It was gruesome work, but that was how it had to be done. Brian knew this to be true because a sunbeam had told him so in the kitchen. It spoke to him in the patterns it made with the dancing motes of dust in the air, the arrangements of the shapes projected onto the linoleum as it shone through the east windows. Sunlight is golden. Sunlight is salvation. Brian knew this to be the truth.

The whole thing was kind of a big relief, really. After long weeks of fear and confusion, it was finally all crystal-clear. He'd been right all along.

The darkness belongs to the eye of the beast, and sunbeams never tell lies.

We leave Brian sitting there on the cold concrete floor of his showroom with his arms wrapped around his knees and continue on with our journey. The sun is almost touching the horizon now, and the heavens above have been painted with broad strokes of red and gold. We backtrack to Weir Line and head north. It isn't long before an old church appears up on the right-hand side of the road, tucked cozily between a field of soybeans and a field of corn. It's a nondenominational house of worship that goes by the name The Church of Welcoming Dawn, which is where Pastor Jonathon Borden can be found on most Sunday mornings (and on Wednesday evenings, the night he hosts a weekly Alcoholics Anonymous meeting). Pastor Jon is currently sitting at his desk in the small office at the back of the church, reading through a passage in the Good Book and scribbling down notes in a binder full of lined paper. The bible he is studying is unusual in appearance; it is a large, imposing tome that weighs almost ten pounds, bounded in faded leather and likely printed by means of a wooden printing press. This bible has been in use at the church for more than two hundred years, and it has never been handled by anyone except the pastors of Welcoming Dawn, local men who have dedicated their lives to administering to the spiritual needs of the citizens of Hadley Township.

The bible is written in an alphabet that predates Latin by almost three thousand years, a language long dead to the rest of the world. Pastor Jon began his instruction on how to decipher the strange-looking runes when he was still a boy, tutored after school every day by dour old Pastor Will, the man who had preceded him as head of the church. Pastor Will taught young Jonathon how to divine the deeper meaning behind the passages written in their Good Book, and showed him how he could relay God's word to the rest of the congregation with his sermons.

The most important lesson imparted on young Jon during these formative years, however, was to always obey the word of the Lord, always, without question or hesitation. Pastor Will would often say, "The Lord has generously blessed our little community with fertility and good fortune, as He is a kind and loving God. But He can also be an unforgiving God. Never forget that, Jonathon. Never."

Pastor Will stressed to him on a near-daily basis that it is the duty of mankind to praise Him, to satisfy His demands in the manner that has been laid out in detail in the Good Book. He darkly warned that woe will soon befall those who turn their backs on the will of their Lord, woe and suffering beyond imagining.

Pastor Jon is currently struggling to write a sermon for his next service. The theme of the sermon is highly ironic to him—deliverance. He studies on the subject of deliverance quite often, although not in the manner you might expect. Jon Borden yearns for a personal deliverance from the grave responsibilities (and even graver consequences) of his life as the head of the church. Sitting there at his desk with the fading light streaming in through the west window, Jonathon closes his eyes and tries to imagine what life would be like if he had been born completely free and unbeholden to anything or anyone. Free to wander, free to think or feel in any manner he might choose from one hour to the next.

He scrubs his hands across his face and blinks down at his notes. He imagines setting the pages in the binder on fire, then using them as a torch to spread the blaze around the entire damnable church.

He smiles to himself, a bitter twist of his lips. He wouldn't dare do such a thing, not ever. He is trapped by virtue of his bloodline. There will be no deliverance, not for Pastor Jon. He will serve the church until the end of his days. The alternative is too awful for him to even contemplate.

The Lord who watches over Hadley Township is unforgiving. His will must be obeyed.

We still have one more stop to make before nightfall, so we leave the church and continue north on Weir Line until we reach a large patch of old-growth forest, a wild and rambling area that the locals refer to as Mossley Woods. We hang a right onto Blackmore Road, a glorified gravel lumber road that is in decidedly poor condition. Most Hadley residents avoid it like the plague, claiming that it's far too bedeviled by deep potholes and soft, crumbling shoulders to be safe for travel; taking your vehicle onto Blackmore Road is a great way to bust a tie rod or bitch up your alignment if you aren't careful.

Although it's true that the road isn't worth a damn, it's not really the potholes that people wish to avoid, it's Mossley Woods. It is thick and vast and forbidding. People have been known to get lost in there. People have been known to disappear in there entirely.

We follow Blackmore's meandering, northwesterly path through the woods. It's already getting dark down here at ground level, but high above our heads, the treetops glow like ripe summer wheat in the fading daylight. Dusk is almost upon us.

There is a dirt path coming up on the left, peeking out from between a birch tree and a tangle of wild raspberries. You could easily miss it if you didn't know where to look. The path isn't much wider than a single vehicle and it's in even worse shape than Blackmore Road, heavily rutted from years of ice, floodwaters, and erosion. We follow it into the woods and discover that the rough little path is actually someone's driveway. That someone is Kurt Weir, an elderly recluse with a sour and unpleasant disposition. Kurt has just awoken from his afternoon drunk and is feeling a bit under the weather, but there's no time to piss and moan about his aching head. He has work to do.

Kurt is seventy-four years old, a gangly scarecrow of a man who is blind in one eye and mostly deaf on the same side. He suffered these injuries back in the fall of '87, the result of standing a tad too close to a leaky moonshine still that decided to explode. Old Kurt still lives in the same dilapidated shanty that he built almost half a century ago, a tarpaper shack with rusty aluminum siding nailed to the roof. He is the proud owner of several old Chevy trucks, all of which are decaying on cement blocks in the dirt patch that serves as his front yard. He is also something of a scrap metal enthusiast who hordes large quantities of rusty iron rebar, steel beams, crates full of brass doorknobs, and other such metallic detritus. His property is a safety hazard of jagged metal and random piles of rubble.

Kurt has lived in seclusion in his remote little shanty for so long, most of the younger generations don't even know that he exists. The old-timers (those who are still sharp enough to remember that far back) could tell you that old Kurt had purchased the seven-acre woodlot from Roger Mossley Sr. for a song back in '67, just a few scant months after his young wife tragically died in a car accident. Nancy Weir had lost control of her vehicle early on a Sunday morning and hit a telephone pole out on the 22, not more than three miles from the Hadley-Elbin border. Nancy had been doing at least sixty miles an hour when her Oldsmobile careened off the road and smashed into the pole. She was given a closed-casket funeral.

What the old-timers won't tell you is that there had been a short police investigation following Nancy's death. A number of the injuries the coroner found on Nancy's body were inconsistent with what would be expected from a fatal car accident. There were also questions regarding the state of the Oldsmobile's brake lines. Kurt Weir was soon paid a visit by a detective from the Burton County homicide unit, a stone-faced Irishman named Sean O'Connell. Kurt's answers to O'Connell's veiled accusations were sparse and well-rehearsed. Frustrated by his inability to sweat a confession out of his suspect, the detective tried questioning Weir's closest neighbors. His inquiries were met with a brick wall of sullen, hostile silence.

Unable to build a solid case, O'Connell was eventually pressured into throwing in the towel. Nancy's death was ruled an accident.

Despite the County's official stance on the matter, Detective O'Connell never actually stopped working on the case. Nancy

Weir had been murdered, and was likely dead before she was placed behind the wheel of the Oldsmobile. She'd been torn apart, ripped, and mutilated by a curved instrument with a sharp point. O'Connell believed that the murder weapon was a meat hook. There was no doubt in his mind that if he'd been able to obtain a search warrant, he would've found such an instrument hidden somewhere in the farmhouse the Weirs had been renting from Gilbert VanDoren, Kurt's uncle through marriage.

At first, the detective assumed that Kurt's motive was the insurance payout, but after a while, he began to suspect that Nancy's murder was part of some greater, even more sinister conspiracy. He'd seen it in the eyes of the people he'd attempted to interview; they all had the blank, closed-off stare of someone who has grown accustomed to guarding a dangerous secret. O'Connell did some digging around and discovered that the reeve of Hadley Township had personally paid a retaining fee to secure the services of a hotshot trial lawyer from the city. Why would the reeve of the township hire a lawyer for a man who hadn't been officially charged with a crime, let alone the likes of Kurt Weir? He was a white-trash, alcoholic, chronically unemployed ne'er-do-well. It seemed highly unlikely that a man like that would have friends in such high places. It was also doubtful that foggy-headed Kurt could have orchestrated the "accident" on his own. Someone helped him do it. But who, and for God's sake, why?

Detective O'Connell kept searching for the answers to these questions for five long years, right up until the day he died of a massive heart attack at the police station. His colleagues found him sitting upright at his desk, his eyes bulging from their sockets and his mouth opened to let out a scream. A copy of the previous year's census for Hadley Township was clutched in one of his hands. There was an open notebook in front of him, and he'd scrawled the words "connected by blood" on the page so hard that the paper had torn beneath the tip of his pen.

Kurt trudges out back to feed the livestock, a few sheep and goats that he keeps in a dilapidated pen behind his shack. He used to keep a few hens and a rooster, too, back when he could still eat eggs, but these days Kurt sustains himself mostly on a diet of meal replacement drinks, oatmeal, and whiskey, and the coop stands empty.

The livestock are not for meat or milk. They serve a higher purpose.

Kurt watches the snarfling, jostling beasts as they feed and randomly picks out one of the nannies. The number and nature of the beasts that he must put out into the dusk comes to him in his dreams, usually several nights beforehand; tonight, it will be a single goat. The billy goat has been granted perpetual exemption from the process—Kurt has developed a sort of grudging affection for the mean little bastard and doesn't have the heart to put him out into the dusk. He decided a while ago that he'll just let the foul-tempered creature idle the rest of his days away in the pen, eating oats and kicking the living hell out of any creature that dares to venture too close. The billy's demeanor reminds Kurt of himself, to the point where the old man has affectionately christened him Kurt Junior.

Kurt Junior is the first animal that Kurt has bothered to name in a good long while. The ranks of the livestock change too often to care much about who is who. Jimmy VanDoren's half-wit son Dougie comes bumping down Blackmore Road in his father's cattle truck every month or so, bringing out new animals as needed; Kurt makes sure that he always has at least three goats and as many sheep on hand at all times. He knows through personal experience that it's very bad to be caught short, very bad indeed. There are repercussions.

Kurt Weir is the seventh son of a man who was himself a seventh son, the lineage going back over ten generations. He has the dreams, and he brings the animals into the woods to suffer their fate. This is Kurt's inherited duty, and it has cost him dearly.

The livestock are extremely skittish of leaving the safety of their pen. They refuse to approach the gate unless lured by some unfamiliar and exotic-looking treat. Kurt rips a clump of dandelions from the hard-packed soil in the yard and coaxes the nanny goat by waving them around and crooning, "Come over here and git the pritty yella things, goat! Tasty, pritty little yella things! Come on, now." The nanny cautiously creeps in a little closer and Kurt swings open the gate. He bares his scant collection of caramel-corn teeth in what's meant to be a disarming smile and makes kissy noises at her, dandelions in one hand and a rope knotted into a noose in the other.

"That's it, come on out and git them pritty yella things. That's a good girl."

The goat balks at crossing the threshold. She lowers her head and bleats, tensing to flee if the old man tries to grab her. Kurt starts pretending to eat the dandelions, smacking his lips and exclaiming at just how damned good they are, until the goat's curiosity finally outweighs her fear and she delicately tiptoes out of the pen.

The little goat stretches her neck out to chomp down on the bobbing dandelion heads and Kurt throws the noose around it, snapping it tight with a practiced flick of his wrist. The goat lets out a garbled-sounding shriek and tries to back away, but Kurt yanks the panicked creature off her feet, pins her to the ground beneath his rubber boot, and strangles her with the noose. He asphyxiates the poor creature until her struggles weaken and taper off into a few random twitches of her back legs, then eases the tension on the rope. It simply wouldn't do to bring out an animal that was unconscious or dying—it had to be both alive and aware when the sun slipped past the horizon. These are the rules, and to deliberately break the rules was unthinkable.

Kurt gives the goat a few minutes to recover, whistling tunelessly and staring off into space as he waits. When it seems as though the gasping little nanny will be strong enough to stand on her own, he hauls her upright and begins to lead her into the woods, still whistling his tuneless song. You can pick out enough of the melody to recognize that the song is "Last Kiss" by J. Frank Wilson and the Cavaliers, the song that Kurt and Nancy had their first dance to at their wedding. It was supposed to be "Blue Moon" but the elderly gent who was hired to spin the records that night accidentally put on the wrong record—he was more of a Guy Lombardo sort of man and didn't really know the difference. Kurt and Nancy laughed it off and swayed around together in the basement of the Legion in Palls Mills, smiling for the cameras as their guests hooted and clapped and banged their fists on foldout tables. Happy with the positive reaction it got, the old fella spun that little 45 over and over again that night, and Kurt's pretty young wife grew more enchanting in his eyes each time it was played.

Kurt brings the goat to the sacred knoll, a journey that seems to get longer and longer with each successive full moon. He ties her to a post that has been sunk deep into the top of the little hill and leaves her there, bleating mournfully after him in the gathering darkness. When he was a younger man, Kurt used to feel a certain kind of sadness for the animals he left behind for the Lord. Nowadays, he feels nothing for them at all. All the bad feelings are reserved solely for himself and the faded memories of his lost love, who was taken from him by the Good Lord on a foggy, rainy night in 1967.

The Lord is unforgiving, and the Lord is vengeful. Kurt knows this to be true from personal experience. He is the seventh son of a seventh son, and his task is a grim one—but the repercussions of failing in this task are far, far worse.

Kurt trudges back to his leaning little shack, still whistling his sad little tune. We leave him to his bottle and his inner demons. The sun has slipped below the horizon; dusk has fallen on Hadley Township, and the moon now dominates the night sky overhead, full and bloated. It really does resemble an evil eye, a dead, milky eye that glares down on our world with cold, hateful glee.

All across Hadley Township, people have locked themselves in their houses and pulled their curtains shut. They retire to bed early and restlessly wait for sleep to come, yearning for the welcoming dawn that will drive away the dreaded darkness that shrouds the fragile shell of their existence.

The goat bleats and cries in the distance. An hour passes by, then another . . . and then there is the sound of powerful wings beating the air overhead. A stench of brimstone and corruption assails our nostrils. The goat begins to cry out with renewed vigor, fighting to escape the noose around its neck, strangling itself in a state of terrified panic.

The moon is momentarily blotted out by a long, serpentine shape. There is a split-second impression of gigantic bat wings and gaping jaws, and then the goat begins to scream.

The screams abruptly stop. The flapping wings disturb the stillness of the night once more, and then all is silent.

The will of the Lord has been satisfied. The people of Hadley Township will live to welcome the dawn once again.

THEY DIE NAMELESS

Aaron Shotwell

My name is Ad m Ja es . . .

My name is Ada J m s . . .

My name is dam ame . . .

I've been writing these words over and over for the past twelve hours, writing to remind myself. Yet, no matter how many times I try to write it, it never lasts through the final stroke of the pen. I suspect it won't be long before the memory fades as well. I just hope this journal finds its way into someone's hands; anyone's hands. Please. Whoever you are, please remember me.

—June 5th, 1964—

Since before my university years, I have been fascinated by ancient Egypt. The cradle of civilization, where gods and empires rose from untamed sands; these stories of our beginnings lay buried in silent tombs for thousands of years. The Valley of the Kings held answers to many mysteries, and sometimes new mysteries for the finding. A wealth of revelations and surprises, and its allure drew me to the life of a historian many years ago. Above and beyond the profession, unveiling these wonders has been my greatest pleasure.

To that end, today is a momentous day for my career. Until today, my research has been limited to secondary sources. As one might imagine, gaining access to original texts and artifacts can be a challenge. Yet, I have the great fortune of receiving a rare donation concerning my most recent subject of intrigue, courtesy of a generous private collector. Unfortunately, for sake of privacy, he wishes to retain anonymity in all publications. Still, though I cannot credit him for his contribution, I am most grateful.

My current work involves the end of the eighteenth dynasty, family line of Akhenaten and his controversial rejection of the old pantheon. Their reign is generally accepted to have ended with the death of his son, Tutankhamun. However, the contents of the boy king's burial chamber would suggest otherwise, namely the two fetuses buried alongside him, each in its own sarcophagus. One died in what appeared to be its seventh month of prenatal development, the other in its fifth. Their identities and the causes of their miscarriage are as of yet unknown.

My anonymous benefactor will be supplying me with those very same sarcophagi. Per request, he has sent them to my office at the University of Southampton. Hopefully their examination will provide me with a valuable lead in answering these questions once and for all. The package will arrive by month's end, and I am eager to begin.

—June 29th, 1964—

The package arrived this morning. Though in a rather precarious state, I must say—left unattended at my office door rather than at the security desk as requested. The package itself was less than sturdy, hardly adequate protection for such priceless treasures. I'll be sure to voice my concern to the delivery company in the near future.

The artifacts are no worse for the wear, however, and they are beautiful indeed. My benefactor kept them pristine, clearly not in a dusty storage facility as I might have imagined. Two tiny sarcophagi adorned in gold and black, each containing an even smaller sarcophagus like Russian nesting dolls, and their shriveled remains would have rested therein. I had expected them to be brittle, yet they had weathered the ages with surprising integrity.

Unfortunately, the bodies themselves are unavailable to me. They are closely guarded at another facility granting strictly limited access, and rightly so. Regardless, the coffins alone are a promising starting point in my research. I will begin my work at once.

—July 10th, 1964—

The coffins have been in my possession for over a week now, and they provide more questions than answers. The photographs I had seen before their arrival showed no obvious signs of identity, so I suspected a more careful examination would be necessary. Yet, they've yielded nothing. No names, of course. No epithets, no prayers, no symbols of protection. Not even the smallest indication of ritualistic practice concerning such deaths.

That these fetuses were embalmed and entombed in royal fashion, yet put to rest with no marks of distinction, is a confounding enigma. I can only assume that they were Tutankhamun's miscarried children based on how near they were found to his resting place. And even that poorly supported conclusion lends no clue to the circumstances surrounding their deaths.

Clearly these two were of great importance. Their bodies were treated with the same care as any king. Why, then, would they die nameless? Why would it be permitted? This was no folly of incompetence or neglect. No, I can say with confidence that they were deliberately omitted. How very puzzling.

—July 23rd, 1964—

At the height of my frustration, I have made an astonishing discovery. To be honest, I am surprised that I am the first to notice it, or, at least, the first to mention it. At the foot of one of the inner sarcophagi, near the edge of the lip beneath the lid, I found a very fine, nearly undetectable slit in the clay.

It could easily be mistaken for a stress fracture, and I almost dismissed it as such. However, when I adjusted my desk lamp, that's when I saw it: something deep in the slit reflecting the faintest touch of light. After probing with a needle and a pair of tweezers, I was able to extract a small, tightly folded piece of papyrus reed parchment. Of course, it did not age as well as the clay sarcophagus, made thin and weak at its ancient seams.

Keeping it intact whilst unfolding was a delicate and trying task, yet mostly successful. The last bit adheres to itself rather strongly, and with evident purpose. The ink is quite faded, but I have been able to discern the following:

> "Let their names die with them, sealed in earth and forgotten. They were called . . ."

Doubtless, the last bit conceals what would have been their names in life, had they survived. Though risky, I may be able to undo the last few folds with the careful application of a razor blade and a noncorrosive solvent. But I must use caution, as this could very well be the key to solving this riddle, thereby documenting a solid conclusion to an important period in Egypt's history.

—July 24th, 1964—

I've been staring at this blank page for a while now, trying to find words to describe what I experienced last night. It sounds ludicrous no matter how I think to phrase it, so I've been trying to rationalize it. It may be due to lack of sleep, or perhaps mounting frustration. Perhaps oncoming sickness and feverish hallucinations. I am uncertain, but I cannot fathom the alternative. Yet, for all my reasoning, I cannot dismiss the chill crawling over my skin.

The last of the parchment's folds gave more easily than I expected, requiring very little pressure at all, and they revealed what I now struggle to explain. I understood the characters that I saw; I understood their meanings and uses individually. I understood the sounds they should have made. But together, as I saw them in that state, they evoked no thought, only a dense fog of confusion, and any semblance of meaning dissolved from my mind the moment I looked away.

Even as I attempted to copy the characters I saw, to put them to paper, I found that I was unable. I understood the lines that composed them, yet I could not move my hand to recreate them. It is as though these words, these names, refuse to be repeated.

When I unfolded the last bit, I swear that I felt a gust of cold air rush over me. I heard a wordless whisper in my ear, calling me. It is a peculiar feeling. And as I labor to overcome it, I feel something dreadful surrounding these names. Something dark. What in the world have I disturbed?

—August 12th, 1964—

I have ceased my study. I would return the artifacts to my benefactor if they did not frighten me so. To be in the same room, to see them sitting atop my desk as I stand at a distance, is unbearable. The parchment is nowhere to be found, and for that I am grateful. I dare not set eyes upon those characters again, for just the one glance will certainly haunt me for life as it is. I have had horrible, relentless visions since the night I unveiled them, visions of suffering and regret.

I will not set foot in that office again, not while those terrible things remain. I'll be leaving the city tonight. I do not know where I will go, but I am compelled to flee. I cannot abide this place; it's been tainted.

I saw the jackal last night.

He spoke of false gods.

—October 18th, 1964—

I'm running now. Not home or anywhere specific, just away. I have to keep moving, or they'll find me again. The two girls, two little girls with silver crowns, watching from the darkness. Wherever I go, they find me, and the shadows rattle like scarabs beneath their feet. Always the smell of sand in the wind, and they appear before me.

They tell me they bring the wrath of the lion, the justice of Sekhmet. They tell me their names, a sound my mind cannot understand or tolerate, a sound not for the living. I must run. The names torment me.

No gods before Ra. As are his faithful, so is the fate of Aten.

—December 6th, 1964—

I returned to the university today, perhaps in the hopes that I may appease the dead. That I may somehow give their names back to the void, and the unborn daughters might leave me in peace. I returned as a stranger. Colleagues had forgotten my name, old friends had forgotten my face. And my office, where my curse began, had never existed. In its place, I found nothing more than the wall connecting the rooms that once sat to its left and right, a wall yellowed with the same age as the building itself.

I'll find no asylum here. I will move on. But I grow weary, and the lion woman awaits my resignation.

—May 30th, 1965—

The months have crawled by, stripping away my former life little by little. I am without a home. I live in my car and I steal to survive. Nobody seems to notice me anymore; they forget me as quickly as they see me. Nobody listens to my cries for help, and I sometimes believe they may not even hear my voice. I press on through the streets as a broken man, trudging more than walking, and they move past me without a second glance. My parents no longer know me; they never had a son. I have become a ghost, a lost cause with nowhere left to turn.

My car broke down two days ago. No time to find another. No time to stop. I flee on foot. I sleep only where I lose consciousness. I pray they don't take me in my sleep, and I count my blessings when I wake where I collapsed. But I always see them waiting for me in the last moments of dusk before sunrise.

I've taken shelter in a sewage tunnel for the night, but this is where I will likely find my final rest. I've grown too tired to stand. I cannot go on. I await my judgment.

—May 31st, 1965—

When the sun last set, Aten's gaze turned from me as it did from them. The boy king came to me, adorned in his burial garb, and he spoke with the hiss of the cobra. He gave me the names of his daughters, and with them an understanding. To know faith in Aten is to know the anger of Ra. To know Aten's faithful is to know the wrath of Sekhmet. To remember the banished ones is to face the void. And so, in exchange for their names, he took my own.

This will be my last entry. Here, on this page, I leave my last words to the world, though they may never be known. Each letter's ink lifts from the page like ash on a breeze. And as I lay here dying, slowly collapsing to dust without the essence of a self, I cannot help but reach out to another in vain. I cannot help but try to leave a memory.

Please remember me. My name is

THE NICE GUY

WellHey Productions

Frank, Thomas, and Kirby enter the office break room at approximately 12:25 P.M. on a Tuesday afternoon. Each man has various containers designed for holding food and drink, and as they lazily slump into the fiberglass chairs that were haphazardly pushed under the table after their previous uses, the room echoes of violent thwop-pops and elongated scraw-jips as Tupperware lids fly open and Velcroed bags release their treasures.

"God dammit!" Thomas rolls his eyes.

Frank, with a mouth full of cold pizza, mumbles in empathy, "Wife packed ya tuna salad again, huh?"

Thomas tosses the soggy sandwich down onto the table with a resounding glop.

"She knows I hate this stuff! I swear, I've almost reached my breaking point with this shit!"

"Why don't you just pack your own lunch." Kirby attempts to speak through teeth caked with salad. A drip of ranch dressing falls from Kirby's lip and collides with the table. Thomas just glares at Kirby in disdain.

"You don't get it, man. I've told her, like, fifty times, 'I don't like tuna salad,' but does she listen? Nooooooo!" Thomas raises his right hand to his forehead. "I swear, I'm up to here with this!"

"Well, at least you're not like that one guy." Frank wipes his mouth of the residual pepperoni grease with a cheap paper napkin.

"What one guy?" Thomas looks at Frank in slight confusion.

"You talking about that guy from CompuTools? I heard about it on the news last week." Kirby chimes in; he has already begun digging into his pudding cup.

Thomas spins around to Kirby. "What the hell are you guys talking about?"

Frank wipes off his hands with another napkin, folds his hands in front of him, and leans in quietly. Thomas and Kirby follow suit.

"Y'see, there was this guy over at CompuTools. Nice guy, I hear. What was his name?" Frank concentrates on the ceiling, searching for a name. Suddenly he snaps his fingers. "Phil Kerbson. Anyway, he was one of those diligent workers, never complained, always got his work done before deadline. Hell, he would even stay late to make sure that his perfect record was never tarnished."

Thomas chimes in, "Ugh, I hate those guys!"

"Well, supposedly, CompuTools hired this new hotshot manager. Basically ROTC'd up from Corporate, y'know, never lifted a finger in his life and got to skip right to the front?"

Thomas shakes his head in disgust.

"Exactly. So this guy was brought in to"—Frank raises his fingers to make quotations—"help. And since this douche really didn't know anything about CompuTools products, he would just bark orders and micromanage everyone. Everyone in the office was buzzing, 'We're gonna quit,' 'Let's get HR involved,' 'This guy is completely heartless,' the usual empty water cooler promises. Everyone was in a tiff except Phil.

"Phil would mind his own business and do his work with a silent smile. He would even go as far as asking this new manager, 'Anything else I can do to help?' Well, I don't know if that manager deliberately planned to be this malicious or if it was just common nature for him, but he got this notion in his head to see how far he could bend Phil, until he broke.

"Starting the very next day, the manager threw the biggest workflow onto Phil's desk and barked out, 'I need this done by five o'clock today or you can just pack your shit now!' or something to that effect. Phil quietly turned to face the manager, smiled his calm innocent smile, and said, 'Sure thing, boss.'

"Five o'clock rolls around and Phil walks into the manager's office and proudly places the completed report onto the man's desk. 'Here ya go, boss.'

"The manager looked up from polishing and buffing his prized six-hundred-pound marble desk to the completed pile of papers with a look of complete shock. How could one man complete that report in only seven and a half short hours? His eyes then shifted from the report to glare viciously at Phil's calm, lucid face. 'Anything else I can do to help?' smiled Phil. The manager simply shook his head in disbelief. 'Okay, well I'm going to head out for the day, sir. You have yourself a great evening.'

"The manager was flabbergasted. He steeled his motives and vowed that he would try harder to break this man's spirit by the end of the week.

"Well, the end of the week came and went and still Phil was as cheerful as ever. Always responding to every outrageous task with a happy, 'Sure thing.' And then turning in the completed work to the manager at the end of the day with a pleasant, 'Anything else I can do to help?' Well, this went on for a few weeks and the manager, now seeing that current efforts were fruitless, decided that maybe he needed to up the ante. The manager would now bombard Phil with major accounts and lengthy business trips and tedious conferences, all to quell his passion that Phil must be broken. But with every new and more difficult task, Phil would embrace it with a 'Sure thing, boss' and come back for more with a sunny, 'Anything else I can do to help?'

"The manager, now at his wits' end, had one more trick up his sleeve. Although his lack of concentration on the job he was hired for was beginning to come under fire, he wanted to give it one more shot before he himself had to face the firing squad. He got it in his head that it was the breaks in between each eight-hour day that were allowing Phil to wind down, regain his bearings, get a good night's sleep, and come back the next day ready for more. So, with that in mind, he gave Phil the budget report for the following year and told him, 'I don't care how long it takes, but you cannot leave your desk until we trim at least five million dollars off of next year's budget.' As always, Phil replied with his trademark 'Sure thing, boss.' The manager turned away knowing that this task would be Phil's breaking point. And, like clockwork, Phil came into the manager's office with the completed budget and handed it to him. 'Anything else I can do to help?' The manager looked over the budget and said, 'Eh, I really don't like these numbers.' The manager threw the report back at Phil. 'Do it all over, and this time do it right!' Phil's smile sagged a little, but he soon rebounded and turned around and headed back to his desk.

"The manager saw Phil's smile buckle for just a moment and he chuckled to himself that his plan was finally working. Eight o'clock rolled around and Phil returned back to the manager's office. But Phil looked a bit different. His hair was a bit disheveled. His horn-rimmed glasses were now on his forehead. One corner of his shirt had become untucked from his pants. Phil's stride wasn't as carefree. Phil handed the report to the manager and exasperatedly uttered, 'Anything else I can do to help, sir?' The manager, now seeing victory close at hand, looked at the report. 'Uh, Phil. I think you made some miscalculations here.' He gave the report back to Phil and said, 'Do it again, and remember what I said! You stay until it's complete!'

"Phil, dejected, defeated, disappointed, looked at the report in his hands, wiped the sweat from his brow, and scratched the back of his neck. The nearly broken man headed back to his desk to correct his errors. As soon as Phil left his office, the manager closed the door and danced a twisted victory dance. Phil was nearly gone. The manager was going to sleep good that night.

"At eleven o'clock, Phil trudged back into the manager's office and handed him the completed and corrected report. Exhausted, Phil asked, 'Is there anything else I can do to help, sir?' The manager, now a shining example of pure arrogance, threw the report on the floor and exclaimed, 'Why did you do the budget for next year? I asked you to do the budget for *this* year. Can't you even follow simple instructions? I want you to march back to your pathetic little cube and you are going to stay all night if you have to until you do exactly what I ask you to do, or so help me God, I will find someone else who *can* do it!'

"Now, no one knows exactly what happened next. But some of the late-night stragglers who heard the manager's tirade claim that as soon as he was finished. Phil took off his glasses, cleaned them off with the corner of his shirt that was still untucked, put his glasses back on, and closed all of the blinds in the manager's office. What came from the room next was a thunderous crash and a high-pitched shriek. The door flew open and the manager bolted out of the room with glass shards in his hair, bleeding profusely from his face, screaming, 'CALL SECURITY! CALL SECURITY!' Witnesses then claim that they saw Phil calmly walk out of the office, blood-spattered about his shirt and hands. He held a letter opener in his right hand, now stained with blood. Phil's calm and happy expression was lost to a visage one person could only describe as berserk. Phil's brow furrowed, scrunching his eyebrows into wide arches. His teeth gnashed and, according to one person, appeared sharp and pointed. His skin, once pale and fair, was now red and scaly. His slick hair now flailed wildly about his head and danced of its own accord. Phil marched toward the cowering manager. 'Sure thing, *sure thing, SURE THING!*' Phil continued to chant these two words over and over and the volume of his voice continued to climb until he was shrieking. Phil destroyed everything in his path to get to the manager, who was now scrambling for the elevator. He turned over cubicle walls, hurled the office printer, and overturned desks but was still marching at a steady pace. Not once did Phil's gait increase in speed. The elevator doors finally opened and the manager quickly darted inside. And as he was frantically pounding on the Door Close button, Phil's arm thrust inside the cabin as the doors began to shut. The manager let out a girlish cry for help, and then . . ."

Thomas, now sitting on the edge of his seat, blinks. "Yeah?"

"Well," Frank continues, "Security hauled him away. The folks that stuck around for the whole ordeal say that they've never heard Phil use any profanity, ever. But on that day, they heard curse words so vile that they almost sounded like they were in some form of ancient tongue, some demonic language. Only by the grace of God was Security able to restrain Phil. As the paddy wagon rolled up into the office building drive, witnesses noticed three things. First, that Phil was kicking and screaming the entire time, and was hardly recognizable. Second, that the manager couldn't stop crying. And third, and the most bizarre, was they realized what made the thunderous crash in the manager's office. The six-hundred-pound marble desk, the manager's prize possession, now lay in pieces outside the office window."

"So that's it? What happened after that? There had to have been a trial!" Thomas exclaims.

"Oh, Phil was deemed too mentally unstable to stand trial, so he was committed to the State Hospital over in Brookfield. And everything died down and returned to normal. The manager was brought in to see Corporate and he was actually let go because not only did the security cameras record what Phil did to the manager and the office, but they also recorded the manager's outburst on Phil that caused him to snap in the first place."

"Just desserts, I say!" Thomas comments. Kirby just shakes his head as he starts to clean up his empty containers.

"Well here's the real punch line. And this I got from Sally Boyd over there at CompuTools, she used to be the manager's admin. After the manager was let go, he was cleaning out his temporary desk, and to pass the time he had the radio on. The manager left his office for a moment to get some more boxes. As he returned back to his office, she heard on the radio announce 'Phil Kerbson, committed to Brookfield State Hospital on Monday, was discovered missing from his cell earlier today.' The manager froze in horror. And as Sally turned around to see the manager's expression, the door violently slammed in her face, knocking her backward onto the ground. As she recovered from her fall, she told me that she could clearly hear the manager pleading for his life. She distinctly heard 'Please! Don't! I'll do anything you want!' And then, a familiar calm and soothing voice came from behind the door, 'Anything I can do to help!' Sally pounced for the door, but it was locked; she tried to look through the window, but the blinds were mostly drawn so she could only see the flailing of arms and legs. Sally kicked at the door repeatedly and shouted, 'SOMEBODY PLEASE HELP!' But it was too late. As soon as the commotion ceased from inside the office, Sally heard the knob click, which signaled that it had been unlocked. With tears in her eyes she slowly reached for the knob and opened the door to reveal a gruesome scene.

"The manager was splayed open from his throat to his pelvis, rib cage and organs exposed. His hands were twisted into contorted knots of flesh and knuckle. His face was warped into an expression of unrelenting anguish and fear, eyes wide, jaw locked, nose broken and twisted. In his left hand, its last cadence drawing to a close, was the manager's own heart. Sally and some of the onlookers who had finally gained access to the room then looked up to see the following message scrawled on the bare dingily yellow office wall: 'We were wrong. He had a heart after all.'"

"Jesus!" Thomas has to hold back the vomit by covering his mouth.

"After that, CompuTools shut down that office. I think they turned it into a . . . MegaBuy." Frank finishes his tale with a solemn sip of coffee.

Thomas rubs his eyes. "Whoa! Wait a minute. What ever happened to Phil?"

"This is when I'm supposed to say, 'That's the strange thing . . .' but it's not really that strange. When they finally opened up the office, the only person in there was the manager. Sally even said she never actually saw Phil, she only heard his voice . . . or at least what sounded like his voice. And he hasn't been seen since."

"That story's completely bullshit!" Kirby exclaims.

Frank and Thomas spin around to glare at Kirby for breaking the mood.

"What?" Thomas inquires. "Like you know exactly what happened."

"I just know that that's not how it happened," Kirby calmly states as he adjusts his horn-rimmed glasses.

"Okay, hotshot. How do you know?" Frank jests.

"Because . . ." Kirby leans in close. Frank and Thomas match Kirby's movement. "The hospital doesn't know I'm gone yet."

Just then, Kirby's manager leans into the break room. "Hey Kirb, I need you to do something for me."

"Sure thing, boss."

As Kirby stands up to leave the now-still break room, Frank and Thomas glance up at his security badge and see his full name—Kirby Phillips.

THE YELLOW RAINCOAT

Sarah Cairns

This is a bad way to start anything but I guess I have to be honest . . . I don't do anything anymore. That's a heavy statement to make but it's pretty true. Not that this is a recent thing; it's gotten worse. I recently finished college and like most grads I can't find a job. You know how it goes—can't get experience without getting a job and can't get a job because you don't have experience. It's a shitty cycle, and it starts to get to you. You can only keep yourself motivated for so long before that drive just disappears.

As I was saying, it got worse recently. Most of my friends have found employment or moved away. It's wasn't their fault my social life took a nosedive; I kind of stopped trying. It was like I was too nervous to even ask people to hang out. I had this unshakable fear that somehow during the process of talking to them, they'd realize what a shitty person I'd become, and that they had absolutely no reason to associate with me anymore. Even when I got the courage to ask someone out I never actually wanted to go anywhere. I didn't have the energy to do anything. The times I did somehow manage to leave my house I became absolutely drained emotionally. So I stopped leaving my parents' home. Sometimes I didn't even turn on the lights in my room. Just sat in the dark checking the Internet, waiting for the day to end so I could sleep again.

I've always been a dreamer; maybe it's from having a creative mind or something. Sleeping was my way of getting out; it was the only part of the day where I didn't feel like I was a complete failure. I had no responsibilities; I could close my eyes, rest, and not give a single shit about anything going on. It was a natural progression that over time I starting sleeping more and more. The dreams I had while unconscious were interesting, and no matter what I did I couldn't achieve a single thing in the waking world . . . It got so bad, I couldn't even be awake for longer than four hours at a time.

When you're sleeping that much it becomes harder and harder to keep track of what is a dream and what actually happens. This consistent napping went on for almost two months without interruption—aside from the various shouting matches with family members over how I'd become a burden. I knew I should have spent more time looking for a job, but every time I tried, my mind would lock up and I'd just get too exhausted to do anything. Maybe part of me had accepted it was pointless to even try anymore. I suppose it was a matter of time before the stress of being alive got to me as I slept.

In my dreams, everything was so crystal-clear and the images my mind played out were almost perfect representations of the real world. I could feel the texture of objects, touch anything and my brain would process it with such unbelievable clarity. Even my dreams started to feel linked together somehow, as if I was watching one story play out . . .

There were always gigantic buildings, like skyscrapers that twisted and turned in impossible ways. Sometimes they'd coil around each other, and it almost seemed like they were forming spider webs. Just looking at them gave you this dreadful feeling that they were going to collapse at any second. Around the inconceivable formations you could always hear metal being ground, stretched, and pounded on. The buildings themselves seemed completely impossible to enter. As I looked at the buildings I noticed a reflection in the glass. There was a figure dressed in a yellow jacket behind me though I could never seem to find it when I looked around for the source. Even in the reflection all it did was stand there and watch me from a distance . . . I wasn't sure if it was even capable of moving . . . It seemed to be completely bound to the reflection of the glass . . .

The dreams always had other people in them. I'd remember talking to them, but at no point would I ever call them anything; it was almost like they didn't have names. I don't even remember knowing anyone who looked like these men and women that populated the world my mind had constructed. I'd spend most of these dreams doing normal things, eating, ranting, and gambling on occasion. My dream friends seemed real in their own ways. They each had their own way of reacting to things. They'd talk about family members I'd never meet or go on about their hobbies. It was the closest thing I'd had to real conversation in weeks; it just happened to be in my own little dream world. It was like the time I still had friends, back when I made the effort to leave my house . . . Well, except for one strange moment that occurred in every dream. Without fail, in every dream one of the people would always ask, "Is it watching you?" in this sort of panicked way.

Once while I was in a dream about a drunken game of tag, it happened between rounds, when everyone had stopped to get a drink. One of the people involved grabbed me and dug his fingernails into my shoulders and shouted the question at me. Even in a dream the list of possible responses to that aren't much more than a stupid unfitting "What?" After that the guy looked at me, seemingly just as confused as I was . . . and then suddenly for a single second it was as if something was watching me. Slightly out of sight, but my eyes still picked up that yellow color . . .

Things like that went on for a couple of weeks. Sure, it was slightly unsettling but it still seemed better than being awake. It was easy enough to ignore that one moment of disorientation;

still, maybe I should have paid more attention to what was going on around me . . . The buildings were changing slowly, it was almost as if they were growing out. They became more complex in the way that they twisted and formed, and the sounds from inside rumbled louder and louder. Once I had noticed the changes it was only a few days before they had completely blocked out the sky . . .

That's when my friends changed on me. They didn't ask me "Is it watching you?" like they had every other single night. No, now the panicked words that fell out of people's mouths simply became "I should go now . . . it's here now." I didn't understand what was going on to make everything change. Sure, I'd been sleeping a little more than normal to see how the dreams were going to change . . . but how was I supposed to respond when these delusions that built themselves as one thing suddenly changed completely?

After a while, there stopped being people around altogether and the air carried an uncomfortable weight to it. When I looked up I could see that the buildings that entrapped the sky were slowly constricting. The idea of it all falling down stopped seeming like a slight concern and became an undeniable reality. The sound that was produced as everything shook and moved around in the world was unlike anything I've ever heard before. It was a loud pounding that made the inside of my skull feel as if it had been ripped open. Like something was slowly grinding away at my brain. Every dream after this point was just wandering through this slowly decaying land and trying desperately to keep my head atop my body. Some nights I swear I could see that yellow thing move just barely out of my line of sight. It was getting brave and almost letting me see it then . . . Still, any attempts to find it on my terms ended up fruitless.

It started to mess with me when I was awake. In fact, it stopped feeling like I'd slept at all. My head would wake up pounding like it had done in the dream. At that point I tried to do anything to avoid sleeping. At least while I was awake I could numb the sting inside my skull with painkillers. The only problem is that when you're downing three pills every two hours it makes keeping your eyes open difficult.

Despite my efforts I finally did fall asleep, and this time the dream world was nothing more than twisted metal forming claustrophobic hallways. The pounding sounds rang out all around; God, it seemed as if it was the very fucking heartbeat of whatever beast had consumed my dreams! I had to run; there had to be some way out of this place. The sound grew louder and louder, as if it was testing my will. It wanted me to quit, sit down, and give up just like I had on every other aspect of my life. It was in my crazed moment of utter madness that I saw it: At first I thought what I had found was a large opening, almost like the inside of a chapel. The metal twisted and formed in strange patterns that seemed to symbolize something that was beyond my grasp of understanding.

In the middle of the room was where I first saw it. It looked like a man in a yellow raincoat. In a moment of complete fucking stupidity, I yelled "Hey!" at it. A profound feeling of regret instantly filled my stomach as the thing twitched and struggled to turn around. It was almost as if after each and every movement it fell apart . . . One moment it would look like some sort of human, the next it would be closer to an animal. Each and every single breath this monster took caused my brain to scream. It was as if my eyes couldn't process what was in front of me and the yellow thing was grabbing every memory, every thought, every single day of my life and trying to make it have a shape. It must have known what was going on in my mind because there was a second among all the clashing occurring in my skull that I swore I heard it laugh.

The wailing within my mind grew louder and louder; it must have gotten closer. My brain wouldn't work, it couldn't tell my eyes to shut, or my legs to move. I couldn't run, my eyes were locked on to it . . . they were still desperately trying to pin some sort of form to the monster. Through the pain I saw the texture of its skin, and something about it caused my mind to connect it to the first thing it could think of . . . a goddamn raincoat.

It was so close now . . . It hid inside its hood, the outline of eyes stood barely buried behind the black tar-like liquid that leaked from its "face." I could feel its breath as it got closer . . . and I was just trapped there, as if my feet were hammered to the floor. I knew this was where I was going to die, this would be how it all fucking ended. I was going to watch whatever it was devour me alive with the jaws my mind was unable to fully process. I felt it rip at my skin, I saw my organs sprawled out over jagged shapes still impossible to describe. No tears, no screams . . . I watched, my mind lost itself to both the sight of it and the pain of every single movement. The last sounds I heard were the grinding of teeth as it devoured my flesh.

And then I woke up . . . covered in a horrible cold sweat. I sobbed and screamed before I finally realized that somehow I was actually awake. Part of me wanted to cry tears of joy after that. None of it was real; I was perfectly fine and everything was all right. It was all just a dream . . . It was going to all be normal again . . . it was all a simple nightmare and nothing more.

It was freeing in a way; it felt like it was all over then. No matter what happened next, it seemed like I'd faced the worst. Whatever that monster was, it was gone forever. I could get back to being normal . . . maybe even start leaving my house again. Everything felt like it was going to be fine. Up until that horrible sense of exhaustion snuck up on me . . .

My eyes got heavy and before I knew it I was back in its chapel, my arms and legs bolted to the walls, no matter how much I struggled there was no way to free myself. And then I realized . . . all around me were the people I'd seen in my dreams just as trapped as I was—and in the middle of it all was the beast in that fucking raincoat. It approached each person pinned to the wall and slowly eviscerated their forms, pulling, biting, and twitching in illogical ways as it did so. Every movement it made sent my mind into a dizzying frenzy. The crushing motions of every single step it took triggered a chorus of screams, slowly building and building until the second it reached me . . . Its neck snapped and twisted in an indescribable way as it struggled to turn its head toward me. Somehow during all of the screaming and rampant panic it allowed my brain one moment of peace. A single second to see its teeth curl into a grin before its hidden eyes flashed an unholy red light. Finally I felt it—its nails dug into my legs. I felt my muscles and skin slowly split and rip apart . . .

I was trapped inside this thing's heart . . . It ruled here, a horrid god within a chamber of metal. Compared to that I was nothing more than a pathetic scrap of rotting meat. Destined to face its jaws over and over . . . it would never let go of something once it had sunk its teeth into it. Its claws and jagged fangs dragged across the metal walls behind me. Through what remained of my shredded form, I learned one thing in those last moments . . . Finally I knew what had caused the sounds I'd heard since this started . . .

Every time I close my eyes to sleep I find myself in its chapel. Torn apart each and every night I dare sleep . . . While I'm awake it's difficult to focus for even a second knowing what monster awaits me in my dreams. It's getting to me; I've been trying to tell myself over and over again it's a dream . . . but it all feels so real . . . I don't do anything anymore, I can't . . . It stops me, it has me terrified of even closing my eyes . . . I'm not sure how much longer I can last. Even now it's becoming uncomfortably tempting. It would be so easy . . . I would just have to down all of those pain-killers . . . that would stop everything, then I could rest . . .

DEPRESSION IS A DEMON

Goldc01n

No one should have to walk in on a suicide. Especially not a teenage kid.

Dad had always warned me about depression. "Depression is a demon," he would say. Looking back, I could see why it was that he wanted to grind that topic into my head so often. When I was younger, I was very absorbed in my own life. That is what teenagers do.

Teenage problems. Teenage drama. Teenage angst.

You miss some of the larger issues that are right in front of you. I missed that Dad switched jobs not for better money or for something he liked better, but because he was let go. I didn't understand the yelling that happened late into the night that I would drown out with music. I overlooked the nights I came home after curfew and Dad was always "waiting up" to make sure I was okay.

Dad would say that depression would loom around. It would hang on your shoulders, and even when you think it's gone, it'll be there waiting for that low point.

I don't think I noticed what he was trying to tell me.

I remember we would go on family trips and Dad would always smile but he would look off into the distance. Almost like he wasn't really there. He was thinking about something else that only he knew about. I think Mom noticed it too. It tore her to the point that she moved out. She said she couldn't handle him anymore.

When I found the note . . . I didn't know what to do.

I had no idea that the word "Goodbye" could be as powerful as it was on that yellow notepad.

I ran through the house screaming for him: "Dad?! DAD!"

My feet thumped around the first floor and up the stairs toward his bedroom. A thin line of light showed under the bathroom door. I pounded on it yelling for him again. "Dad?" Sobbing. All I could hear was my dad's sobbing coming from the other side. "Dad—please," I said more to myself than to him, unsure if he could even hear me with such a whisper. The doorknob was cold to the touch. My hand wrapped around it, but I couldn't will myself to turn it. I knew what the note meant. Dad was behind this door and I wasn't sure if I wanted to see him as he might be. Had he already gone through with it . . . ? What should I do if he had? Should I wait and just call 911? But if I didn't go in now, would he go through with it before anyone else was here to help me?

Thoughts raced through me, but finally instinct took over. My body moved before my mind could find a conclusion. The door swung open slowly. There he was. Razor to wrist and sitting in the bathtub. A small trickle of blood ran over his arm. He was shaking. The blade had just barely pierced his skin. He hadn't gone through with it yet. I could still help him.

I didn't know what to say. "Dad, please. Don't. Please." It was all I could think of. But he didn't listen. He stared like he always did. Away at something like he wasn't there with me.

I followed his line of sight.

Out of the corner of my eye I could see it—or I couldn't see it until I really wanted to. The shadowed figure. An outlined figure of a man with no form. The form knelt beside Dad. He was touching him. No, he was holding him. Holding his arms. Holding his hands. Dad wasn't cutting his wrists. The shadow—the thing I could see, but couldn't see—was cutting him. The long smoky finger of the thing held the razor over Dad's wrist and its head would shift from the blade to meet Dad's gaze and then back again. It played with him, almost asking, "Should I?" When I could finally break my eyes away, they locked with my father's. He stopped looking at the shadow. He was looking at me. Right into my eyes.

"Help me." The blade slid effortlessly down his arm. Dad's eyes were watering and I was frozen. I had no idea what I had walked in on or what I was witnessing, Worst of all, I had no idea how to help . . . Dad went limp. The shadow turned its head to me.

His funeral was a few days ago.

I haven't really left my room much since then. Mom calls me down for dinner and I try. I really do, but I don't think I can ever tell her about the shadow that I saw with Dad. I don't think I can ever tell her that it hasn't left my side since that day.

LICKS FROM A BEAR

Max Lobdell

August 1, 2015, 9:00 A.M.

It's been exactly one year since Jen left. That means it's been one year and one day since I was fired. I haven't worked since. I used to like the idea of being on disability—free money and all the time in the world to spend with her. I guess she didn't think of it that way. She was always ambitious. I shouldn't say "was." Every day I see Facebook updates detailing her constant successes. The most recent one was her engagement. I'd never seen her look so happy.

I guess I knew things with us were going downhill when I looked forward to our fights. She'd always say something about how I'm so smart—that I was smarter than she, in fact—but that I had no ambition. It felt so good to hear that someone as brilliant as Jen thought I was smart, even though she yelled it at me in frustration. She claimed she understood my depression and my anxiety and how they were terrible roadblocks on the path to my happiness. I thought that meant she could empathize and still wanted to be with me anyway. Apparently I was wrong.

Getting disability benefits for my depression wasn't too hard. The money isn't great, but it pays the rent and keeps me fed. The only pain is that I have to go to therapy every week. I also need to go to monthly appointments to pick up prescriptions to help combat my depression, ADHD, and anxiety. It's all so procedural and detached from anything resembling real care. So I'm a lonely, unemployable loser who apparently has this "great mind" that's utterly useless. But I won't stay like this forever. I've discovered something new. Well, something old, actually.

Today begins my new life. The medication never worked, the therapy never worked, the behavior changes never worked. Medicine failed me. Or maybe I failed medicine. Either way, I'm taking control of myself again. I'm not going to be a victim of the barriers my body's put up for me. No more attention problems. No more depression. No more anxiety. For the first time in what may be decades, I'm filled with hope.

August 1, 2015, 3:00 P.M.

All my tools are cleaned and ready. In about an hour, I'll start. I need to keep a pretty comprehensive journal of the procedure to make sure I'm not harming myself. I figure a running account of my experiences will give evidence of the positive (or negative) changes in both my mood and cognitive abilities.

August 1, 2015, 4:05 P.M.

After I traced a dime-sized circle on the upper-right part of my forehead, I used an X-Acto knife to carve through the skin. I wasn't prepared for how much this was going to hurt. I stopped a couple times to wipe away the tears so I could see well enough to continue. The skin lifted off from the bone without too much trouble once I'd finished cutting. I flushed it down the toilet. Now I'm waiting for the bleeding to stop—it seems to be slowing already. It's so weird to see my skull exposed like this.

I'm going to write a sentence or two before and after each of the next steps so I can get as good a description as possible if this all works as well as I'm hoping.

I opted to use a tiny drill bit over a single large one. A ring of tiny holes is going to take a hell of a lot longer, but I think the need for precision dwarfs time consumption in this case. I'm about to do the first hole.

The first hole is done. Imagine the feeling of biting down on a fist-sized piece of tinfoil as hard as you possibly can while your head hums like it's filled with buzzing hornets. The vibration was so excruciating that I'm only now feeling the pain of the drill site itself. I'm going to do the next ten or so holes now before I lose my nerve.

The vibrations became less intense with each hole. The bone pain got much worse, though. I've never had migraines, but I assume they must feel something like this.

I'm shining a light at the ring of tiny bores and doing my best to inspect what's behind them in the mirror. It's not very useful. The remaining structural elements between the holes are extremely thin and brittle looking. I'm going to cut them away with the wire cutters.

I just dropped a circle of my skull into the sink. Now I'm looking at the bright red membrane that's covering my brain. I'm a little surprised by how many blood vessels are in there. I'm going to put out a couple more towels. Cutting away the membrane is the part I'm most scared of.

It's done and the hole is bleeding a lot. I'm taking extra care to not put too much pressure on the organ itself when I'm working to soak up the blood. I'm feeling a little dizzy, so while I hold the towel to the hole, I'm sitting and eating the piece of steak and drinking the orange juice I'd put out just in case this happened. The wound is slowly starting to clot while I wait here. The whole area hurts, but the pain is second to the strong pulsing sensation around the hole. It's almost like I have a second heart beating there.

The blood stopped pouring out and I'm cleaning the area with water and rubbing alcohol. Now I can see my brain. It's gray. It doesn't look like it even belongs to me; I don't know why it all feels so surreal. It's almost like I'm watching all this happen to someone else. On the plus side, I'm not dizzy anymore, but I'm exhausted. I'm going to bandage everything and go to bed. I'll clean up tomorrow.

August 2, 2015, 6:30 A.M.

I woke up this morning with more energy and drive than I've ever felt. Even sitting here writing this feels like a joy; I'm not struggling to find words, I'm not dreading how I'll reread what I've written and think it's stupid and pointless—everything just . . . works. The accounts I'd read about people who shared their experiences with trepanation made similar claims, but even as I drilled the holes I never allowed myself to truly believe it would work for me. Even now, I'm worried it's all just a placebo effect. The pulsating feeling is real, though, and it's as strong as ever. That was something else my fellow trepanned mentioned. They said it was because the body is letting the brain grow again; something the skull had prevented after it hardened following infancy. I don't know if I buy the explanation, but I can't deny what's happening here.

August 2, 2015, 2:00 P.M.

My day's been spent cleaning the apartment. Over the last year, I'd let things pile up and grow increasingly filthy as my depression festered. Today, it's like a veil has been lifted and light is pouring over everything I lay my eyes on. The place needed to be cleaned, so I just set to work and cleaned it. It looks better now than it did when Jen and I moved in. My therapist recommended that I clean quite a while ago, suggesting that a nice, open area would really help me see my home as a place for potential, rather than stagnation. Now I know what he meant. This is what potential feels like.

The hole in my head still hurts and it looks terrible, but I expected as much. If I go out, I can wear a hat and no one will notice anything amiss. I'm not ready to do that, though. I'm mildly concerned about how badly the site is beginning to itch as it heals. I'm being extremely assiduous in cleaning and caring for the wound as it heals, but I guess part of that process is that damn itch. I'm doing my best not to think about it.

August 2, 2015, 11:30 P.M.
The first full day of my experiment is about to end. I'm about to go to sleep, and I feel like I've accomplished a lot today. My home is spotless, I've finished a short story I'd been working on for the last couple months, I've gotten up to date with my Internet and utility bills, and I even did a couple sets of pushups. I had to remind myself to eat, though. For whatever reason, I wasn't hungry at all until I realized it was nearly 9 P.M. and I hadn't eaten all day. I'm chalking it up to my excitement. It's been hard to contain. But, now I'm all showered and pajamaed and ready to end my day. I can't wait for tomorrow.

August 3, 2015, 5:45 A.M.
I was up before my alarm this morning to watch the sun rise from the roof of the apartment. Last night I slept like a log and didn't wake up once. I noticed some blood on my pillow and under my fingernails, though, and I think I may have scratched underneath the bandage while I slept. I made a beeline to the bathroom to inspect the hole and, thankfully, I didn't seem to do any damage. Everything appears to be healing well.

August 3, 2015, 1:15 P.M.
I don't know if it's endorphins wearing off or just an artifact of my depression, but my euphoric feeling has diminished quite a bit

since this morning. I'm thinking it might be both; maybe I need to have a good meal. There should be something in the fridge.

August 3, 2015, 9:00 P.M.

Whatever I felt this afternoon doesn't seem to have been a fluke. While my mood elevated for a little while after lunch, I was back to near-baseline for the rest of the day and evening. The pulsing in the hole waxes and wanes with my mood, interestingly enough. When I'm happy and ambitious, it pulses a lot. When I'm depressed, it may pulse once every ten seconds. It may have something to do with my blood pressure, so I'll keep an eye on that. Before bed, I'll do some jumping jacks and see if the pulsing returns. I'm fairly certain a higher pulse rate correlates with a better mindset.

Just did the exercise. The pulsing is the same. My heart rate is up, but my mood is still low. I'm going to bed.

August 4, 2015, 11:00 A.M.

I just woke up and I feel terrible. I was scratching the hole again. The pillow is soaked with blood and there are remnants of scabs under my fingernails. Tonight I'll wear gloves. That aside, my mood is still right near where it was before I started this process. I'm worried the surface area of my brain that's exposed isn't large enough to allow long-lasting effects. I don't trust myself to widen the hole that's already there, but I'm prepared to do another one an inch or so away.

August 4, 2015, 12:30 P.M.

There was a problem with the second hole. I did everything just like the last time, but on the last tiny borehole a crack formed in the skull between the original hole and the new site. I had to peel back the skin I'd left to make sure, but it was definitely there. I was forced to decide whether or not I should leave the broken piece, and I opted against it. Now I have an oval that's about 3 inches long and 1 inch wide. Removing the membrane from this part was difficult and I had a minor issue with the blade slipping deeper than I'd wanted. Thankfully, the brain has no pain receptors. It couldn't have gone more than half an inch inside and nothing weird happened to my body so I must have lucked out and hit part of the 90 percent they say we don't use. I know people are saying that's a myth, but with what just happened to me there must be some truth to it.

August 5, 2015, 8:00 A.M.

No scratching overnight. The pulsing is there but it's nowhere near as strong as it was the first time. My mood is still low. I have to be honest with myself here: I feel like a failure. This whole experiment is another example of me setting out to do something with good intentions and having it all blow up in my face. But I'm not going to be defeated by it. In the past, I would've stopped, Jen would've started a fight with me, and I'd just add it to the never-ending cascade of fuck-ups that form my identity. Not this time, though. The increase in my ambition from this treatment must still be going strong, because I'm determined to see it all through.

August 5, 2015, 8:00 P.M.

There are four more holes in my head. I didn't think I'd be able to do it. Toward the end of the last one, I almost passed out. I'm glad I had the foresight to keep a few sugar packets nearby so I could regain the strength to finish up.

Besides the issue with my dizziness, these four went better than the prior two. I used the left and right sides of my head this time, right above my ears. The skull was far thinner than on my forehead, so the vibration of the drill wasn't as excruciating. The blood loss was significantly greater, though, which explains the desire to pass out. I have hand towels wrapped around my head so I won't get blood all over the place. Lucky for me, I'm a pretty quick clotter. That's a funny word. Clotter.

August 6, 2015, 6:10 A.M.

I slept sitting up and awoke to major pulsing not just in the new holes, but in the old ones as well. A small problem's developed with the second hole, though. I think it might be getting infected. The itching is unbearable and I think it might be starting to smell. I poured rubbing alcohol on all the sides and pressed it in with clean towels, so hopefully that'll stop whatever's breeding in there.

My mood was pretty high. Still not as good as the first day, but much better than the days after. I've been thinking about Jen a lot. We had so many things in common. We loved talking about animals and used to go off on tangents where we'd discuss all the exotic ones we'd have when we were rich. Her favorite ones were rhinos. Mine were hippos. I used to tell her about the lake we'd have in our backyard where my pygmy hippo would play with her baby rhino. After they'd gotten tired out, we'd invite them up to the patio where they'd curl up next to one another while we gazed adoringly at them and at each other. I wonder how she'd feel knowing I've been doing all this work to better myself. She'd probably tell me to do more.

August 7, 2015, 12:35 P.M.

I did more. All day yesterday, I drilled. I drilled and cut and pulled and peeled. I feel like I can take on the world; it's almost like that one time I did cocaine in college, but the effect has lasted far longer. I'll update again today if I have to, but for now, I'm going to work on some of my stories.

August 9, 2015, 9:00 A.M.

Where have I been? Writing. Since the other day, I've gotten down 100 pages of a story I never even knew I had in me. Reading it over is like I'm looking at the work of someone else. Someone far, far better. A stranger, I guess.

On a slightly less pleasant note, there's definitely an infection in a few holes. One of them is weeping a gray liquid that smells terrible and all of them itch. When I rub them with the towel to try to scratch, they break open and start either bleeding or leaking clear fluid. I figure it's like a cold that has to run its course, but I'll be damned if it isn't becoming a problem nearly as bad as the depression was.

August 10, 2015, 7:40 A.M.

I scratched in my sleep. I don't know what else to say other than it was bad. It's hard to tell from what I see in the mirror, but I might have damaged some of my brain in the holes of my forehead and left side. A small piece is hanging by a thread that looks like a tiny blood vessel. I tried to tuck it back under the lip of skull, but I had to press pretty hard to do it and I'm worried I messed it up even worse.

At least I saw a bear today.

August 15, 2015, 4:15 P.M.

More holes for me. Shaved my head. No more hair, lots more holes. Remember those Wiffle balls from when we were kids? One day I'll tell Jen how I thought my head looked like a Wiffle ball. She always liked baseball and playing with my hair. My head infection was getting real bad before the bear came. Now he licks my head while I sleep and keeps the gross stuff out. Jen loves bears. Bears and rhinos.

Every morning I have to clean under my fingernails a lot. Petting the bear gets them real dirty. It's nice the bear shaved when I did so I didn't have to feel like the odd man out. Those pulses in my head are nice and strong all the time. It feels good. The bear licks me a lot when I sleep.

Augs 16, 2015 5000

Scratch the bear by his ears and he licks lots and lots. Lots of licks means a lot less itching. Jen would scratch my back when it was itchy. One time she saw me triing to scratch between my shoulders using the door frame. She called me a bear because that's what bears do when there back itches. 60 holes, going to cut out the spaces in between. Make my bear proud if Jen cant be.

PSYCHOSIS

Matt Dymerski

Sunday

I'm not sure why I'm writing this down on paper and not on my computer. I guess I've just noticed some odd things. It's not that I don't trust the computer . . . I just . . . need to organize my thoughts. I need to get down all the details somewhere objective, somewhere I know that what I write can't be deleted or . . . changed . . . not that that's happened. It's just . . . everything blurs together here, and the fog of memory lends a strange cast to things . . .

I'm starting to feel cramped in this small apartment. Maybe that's the problem. I just had to go and choose the cheapest apartment, the only one in the basement. The lack of windows down here makes day and night seem to slip by seamlessly. I haven't been out in a few days, because I've been working on this programming project so intensively. I suppose I just wanted to get it done. Hours of sitting and staring at a monitor can make anyone feel strange, I know, but I don't think that's it.

I'm not sure when I first started to feel like something was odd. I can't even define what it is. Maybe I just haven't talked to anyone in a while. That's the first thing that crept up on me. Everyone I normally talk to online while I program has been idle, or they've simply not logged on at all. My instant messages go unanswered. The last e-mail I got from anybody was a friend, saying he'd talk to me when he got back from the store, and that was yesterday. I'd call with my cell phone, but reception's terrible down here. Yeah, that's it. I just need to call someone. I'm going to go outside.

• • •

Well, that didn't work so well. As the tingle of fear fades, I'm feeling a little ridiculous for being scared at all. I looked in the mirror before I went out, but I didn't shave the two-day stubble I've grown. I figured I was just going out for a quick cell phone call. I did change my shirt, though, because it was lunchtime, and I guessed that I'd run into at least one person I knew. That didn't end up happening. I wish it did.

When I went out, I opened the door to my apartment slowly. A small feeling of apprehension had somehow already lodged itself in me, for some indefinable reason. I chalked it up to having not spoken to anyone but myself for a day or two. I peered down the dingy gray hallway, made dingier by the fact that it was a basement hallway. On one end, a large metal door led to the building's furnace room. It was locked, of course. Two dreary soda machines stood by it; I bought a soda from one the first day I moved in, but it had a two-year-old expiration date. I'm fairly sure nobody knows those machines are even down here, or my cheap landlady just doesn't care to get them restocked.

I closed my door softly and walked the other direction, taking care not to make a sound. I have no idea why I chose to do that, but it was fun giving in to the strange impulse not to break the droning hum of the soda machines, at least for the moment. I got to the stairwell and took the stairs up to the building's front door. I looked through the heavy door's small square window, and received quite the shock: it was definitely not lunchtime. City-gloom hung over the dark street outside, and the traffic lights at the intersection in the distance blinked yellow. Dim clouds, purple and black from the glow of the city, hung overhead. Nothing moved, save the few sidewalk trees that shifted in the wind. I remember shivering, though I wasn't cold. Maybe it was the wind outside. I could vaguely hear it through the heavy metal door, and I knew it was that unique kind of late-night wind, the kind that was constant, cold, and quiet, save for the rhythmic music it made as it passed through countless unseen tree leaves.

I decided not to go outside.

Instead, I lifted my cell phone to the door's little window, and checked the signal meter. The bars filled up the meter, and I smiled. *Time to hear someone else's voice*, I remember thinking, relieved. It was such a strange thing, to be afraid of nothing. I shook my head, laughing at myself silently. I hit speed-dial for my best friend Amy's number, and held the phone up to my ear. It rang once . . . but then it stopped. Nothing happened. I listened to silence for a good twenty seconds, then hung up. I frowned, and looked at the signal meter again—still full. I went to dial her number again, but then my phone rang in my hand, startling me. I put it up to my ear.

"Hello?" I asked, immediately fighting down a small shock at hearing the first spoken voice in days, even if it was my own. I had gotten used to the droning hum of the building's inner workings, my computer, and the soda machines in the hallway. There was no response to my greeting at first, but then, finally, a voice came.

"Hey," said a clear male voice, obviously of college age, like me. "Who's this?"

"John," I replied, confused.

"Oh, sorry, wrong number," he replied, then hung up.

I lowered the phone slowly and leaned against the thick brick wall of the stairwell. That was strange. I looked at my received calls list, but the number was unfamiliar. Before I could think on it further, the phone rang loudly, shocking me yet again. This time,

I looked at the caller before I answered. It was another unfamiliar number. I held the phone up to my ear, but said nothing. I heard nothing but the general background noise of a phone. Then, a familiar voice broke my tension.

"John?" was the single word, in Amy's voice.

I breathed a sigh of relief.

"Hey, it's you," I replied.

"Who else would it be?" she responded. "Oh, the number. I'm at a party on Seventh Street, and my phone died just as you called me. This is someone else's phone, obviously."

"Oh, okay," I said.

"Where are you?" she asked.

My eyes glanced over the drab white-washed cylinder block walls and the heavy metal door with its small window.

"At my building," I sighed. "Just feeling cooped up. I didn't realize it was so late."

"You should come here," she said, laughing.

"Nah, I don't feel like looking for some strange place by myself in the middle of the night," I said, looking out the window at the silent windy street that secretly scared me just a tiny bit. "I think I'm just going to keep working or go to bed."

"Nonsense!" she replied. "I can come get you! Your building is close to Seventh Street, right?"

"How drunk are you?" I asked lightheartedly. "You know where I live."

"Oh, of course," she said abruptly. "I guess I can't get there by walking, huh?"

"You could if you wanted to waste half an hour," I told her.

"Right," she said. "Okay, have to go, good luck with your work!"

I lowered the phone once more, looking at the numbers flash as the call ended. Then, the droning silence suddenly reasserted itself in my ears. The two strange calls and the eerie street outside just drove home my aloneness in this empty stairwell. Perhaps from having seen too many scary movies, I had the sudden inexplicable idea that something could look in the door's window and see me, some sort of horrible entity that hovered at the edge of aloneness, just waiting to creep up on unsuspecting people that strayed too far from other human beings. I knew the fear was irrational, but nobody else was around, so . . . I jumped down the stairs, ran down the hallway into my room, and closed the door as swiftly as I could while still staying silent. Like I said, I feel a little ridiculous for being scared of nothing, and the fear has already faded. Writing this down helps a lot—it makes me realize that nothing is wrong. It filters out half-formed thoughts and fears and leaves only cold, hard facts. It's late, I got a call from a wrong number, and Amy's phone died, so she called me back from another number. Nothing strange is happening.

Still, there was something a little off about that conversation. I know it could have just been the alcohol she'd had . . . or was it even her that seemed off to me? Or was it . . . yes, that was it! I didn't realize it until this moment, writing these things down. I knew writing things down would help. She said she was at a party, but I only heard silence in the background! Of course, that doesn't mean anything in particular, as she could have just gone outside to make the call. No . . . that couldn't be it either. I didn't hear the wind! I need to see if the wind is still blowing!

Monday

I forgot to finish writing last night. I'm not sure what I expected to see when I ran up the stairwell and looked out the heavy metal door's window. I'm feeling ridiculous. Last night's fear seems hazy and unreasonable to me now. I can't wait to go out into the sunlight. I'm going to check my e-mail, shave, shower, and finally get out of here! Wait . . . I think I heard something.

• • •

It was thunder. That whole sunlight and fresh air thing didn't happen. I went out into the stairwell and up the stairs, only to find disappointment. The heavy metal door's little window showed only flowing water, as torrential rain slammed against it. Only a very dim, gloomy light filtered in through the rain, but at least I knew it was daytime, even if it was a gray, sickly, wet day. I tried looking out the window and waiting for lightning to illuminate the gloom, but the rain was too heavy and I couldn't make out anything more than vague weird shapes moving at odd angles in the waves washing down the window. Disappointed, I turned around, but I didn't want to go back to my room. Instead, I wandered farther up the stairs, past the first floor, then the second. The stairs ended at the third floor, the highest floor in the building. I looked through the glass that ran up the outer wall of the stairwell, but it was that warped, thick kind that scatters the light, not that there was much to see through the rain to begin with.

I opened the stairwell door and wandered down the hallway. The ten or so thick wooden doors, painted blue a long time ago, were all closed. I listened as I walked, but it was the middle of the day, so I wasn't surprised that I heard nothing but the rain outside. As I stood there in the dim hallway, listening to the rain, I had the strange fleeting impression that the doors were standing like silent granite monoliths erected by some ancient forgotten civilization for some unfathomable guardian purpose. Lightning flashed, and I could have sworn that, for just a moment, the old grainy blue wood looked just like rough stone. I laughed at myself for letting my imagination get the best of me, but then it occurred to me that the dim gloom and lightning must mean there was a window somewhere in the hallway. A vague memory surfaced, and I suddenly recalled that the third floor had an alcove and an inset window halfway down the floor's hallway.

Excited to look out into the rain and possibly see another human being, I quickly walked over to the alcove, finding the large thin glass window. Rain washed down it, as with the front door's window, but I could open this one. I reached a hand out to slide it open, but hesitated. I had the strangest feeling that if I opened that window, I would see something absolutely horrifying on the other side. Everything's been so odd lately . . . so I came up with a plan, and I came back here to get what I needed. I don't seriously think anything will come of it, but I'm bored, it's raining, and I'm going stir-crazy. I came back to get my webcam. The cord isn't long enough to reach the third floor by any means, so instead I'm going to hide it between the two soda machines in the dark end of my basement hallway, run the wire along the wall and under my door, and put black duct tape over the wire to blend it in with the black plastic strip that runs along the base of the hallway's walls. I know this is silly, but I don't have anything better to do . . .

Well, nothing happened. I propped open the hallway-to-stairwell door, steeled myself, then flung the heavy front door wide open and ran like hell down the stairs to my room and slammed the door. I watched the webcam on my computer intently, seeing the hallway outside my door and most of the stairwell. I'm watching it right now, and I don't see anything interesting. I just wish the camera's position was different, so that I could see out the front door. Hey! Somebody's online!

• • •

I got out an older, less functional webcam that I had in my closet to video chat with my friend online. I couldn't really explain to him why I wanted to video chat, but it felt good to see another person's face. He couldn't talk very long, and we didn't talk about anything meaningful, but I feel much better. My strange fear has almost passed. I would feel completely better, but there was something . . . odd . . . about our conversation. I know that I've said that everything has seemed odd, but . . . still, he was very vague in his responses. I can't recall one specific thing that he said . . . no particular name, or place, or event . . . but he did ask for my e-mail address to keep in touch. Wait, I just got an e-mail.

I'm about to go out. I just got an e-mail from Amy that asked me to meet her for dinner at "the place we usually go to." I do love pizza, and I've just been eating random food from my poorly stocked fridge for days, so I can't wait. Again, I feel ridiculous about the odd couple of days I've been having. I should destroy this journal when I get back. Oh, another e-mail.

• • •

Oh my God. I almost left the e-mail and opened the door. I almost opened the door. I almost opened the door, but I read the e-mail first! It was from a friend I hadn't heard from in a long time, and it was sent to a huge number of e-mails that must have been every person he had saved in his address list. It had no subject, and it said, simply:

"Seen with your own eyes don't trust them they"

What the hell is that supposed to mean? The words shock me, and I keep going over and over them. Is it a desperate e-mail sent just as . . . something happened? The words are obviously cut off without finishing! On any other day I would have dismissed this as spam from a computer virus or something, but the words . . . seen with your own eyes! I can't help but read over this journal and think back on the last few days and realize that I have not seen another person with my own eyes or talked to another person face-to-face. The webcam conversation with my friend was so strange, so vague, so . . . eerie, now that I think about it. Was it eerie? Or is the fear clouding my memory? My mind toys with the progression of events I've written here, pointing out that I have not been presented with one single fact that I did not specifically give out unsuspectingly. The random "wrong number" that got my name and the subsequent strange return call from Amy, the friend that asked for my e-mail address . . . I messaged him first when I saw him online! And then I got my first e-mail a few minutes after that conversation! Oh my God! That phone call with Amy! I said over the phone—I said that I was within half an hour's walk of Seventh Street! They know I'm near there! What if they're trying to find me?! Where is everyone else? Why haven't I seen or heard anyone else in days?

No, no, this is crazy. This is absolutely crazy. I need to calm down. This madness needs to end.

• • •

I don't know what to think. I ran about my apartment furiously, holding my cell phone up to every corner to see if it got a signal through the heavy walls. Finally, in the tiny bathroom, near one ceiling corner, I got a single bar. Holding my phone there, I sent a text message to every number in my list. Not wanting to betray anything about my unfounded fears, I simply sent:

"You seen anyone face-to-face lately?"

At that point, I just wanted any reply back. I didn't care what the reply was, or if I embarrassed myself. I tried to call someone a few times, but I couldn't get my head up high enough, and if I brought my cell phone down even an inch, it lost signal. Then I remembered the computer, and rushed over to it, instant messaging everyone online. Most were idle or away from their computer. Nobody responded. My messages grew more frantic, and I started telling people where I was and to stop by in person for a host of barely passable reasons. I didn't care about anything by that point. I just needed to see another person!

I also tore apart my apartment looking for something that I might have missed—some way to contact another human being without opening the door. I know it's crazy, I know it's unfounded, but what if? WHAT IF? I just need to be sure! I taped the phone to the ceiling in case.

Tuesday

THE PHONE RANG! Exhausted from last night's rampage, I must have fallen asleep. I woke up to the phone ringing, and ran into the bathroom, stood on the toilet, and flipped open the phone taped to the ceiling. It was Amy, and now I feel so much better. She was really worried about me, and apparently had been trying to contact me since the last time I talked to her. She's coming over now, and, yes, she knows where I am without me telling her. I feel so embarrassed. I am definitely throwing this journal away before anyone sees it. I don't even know why I'm writing in it now. Maybe it's just because it's the only communication I've had at all since . . . God knows when. I look like hell, too. I looked in the mirror before I came back in here. My eyes are sunken, my stubble is thicker, and I just look generally unhealthy.

My apartment is trashed, but I'm not going to clean it up. I think I need someone else to see what I've been through. These past few days have NOT been normal. I am not one to imagine things. I know I have been the victim of extreme probability. I probably missed seeing another person a dozen times. I just happened to go out when it was late at night, or the middle of the day when everyone was gone. Everything's perfectly fine, I know this now. Plus, I found something in the closet last night that has helped me tremendously: a television! I set it up just before I wrote this, and it's on in the background. Television has always been an escape for me, and it reminds me that there's a world beyond these dingy brick walls.

I'm glad Amy's the only one that responded to me after last night's frantic pestering of everyone I could contact. She's been my best friend for years. She doesn't know it, but I count the day that I met her among one of the few moments of true happiness in my life. I remember that warm summer day fondly. It seems a different reality from this dark, rainy, lonely place. I feel like I spent days sitting in that playground, much too old to play, just talking with her and hanging around doing nothing at all. I still feel like I can go back to that moment sometimes, and it reminds me that this damn place is not all that there is . . . Finally, a knock on the door!

• • •

I thought it was odd that I couldn't see her through the camera I hid between the two soda machines. I figured that it was bad positioning, like when I couldn't see out the front door. I should have known. I should have known! After the knock, I yelled through the door jokingly that I had a camera between the soda machines, because I was embarrassed myself that I had taken this paranoia so far. After I did that, I saw her image walk over to the camera and look down at it. She smiled and waved.

"Hey!" she said to the camera brightly, giving it a wry look.

"It's weird, I know," I said into the mic attached to my computer. "I've had a weird few days."

"Must have," she replied. "Open the door, John."

I hesitated. How could I be sure?

"Hey, humor me a second here," I told her through the mic. "Tell me one thing about us. Just prove to me you're you."

She gave the camera a weird look.

"Um, all right," she said slowly, thinking. "We met randomly at a playground when we were both way too old to be there?"

I sighed deeply as reality returned and fear faded. God, I'd been so ridiculous. Of course it was Amy! That day wasn't anywhere in the world except in my memory. I'd never even mentioned it to anyone, not out of embarrassment, but out of a strange secret nostalgia and a longing for those days to return. If there was some unknown force at work trying to trick me, as I feared, there was no way they could know about that day.

"Haha, all right, I'll explain everything," I told her. "Be right there."

I ran to my small bathroom and fixed my hair as best I could. I looked like hell, but she would understand. Snickering at my own unbelievable behavior and the mess I'd made of the place, I walked to the door. I put my hand on the doorknob and gave the mess one last look. So ridiculous, I thought. My eyes traced over the half-eaten food lying on the ground, the overflowing trash bin, and the bed I'd tipped to the side looking for . . . God knows what. I almost turned to the door and opened it, but my eyes fell on one last thing: the old webcam, the one I used for that eerily vacant chat with my friend.

Its silent black sphere lay haphazardly tossed to the side, its lens pointed at the table where this journal lay. An overwhelming terror took me as I realized that if something could see through that camera, it would have seen what I just wrote about that day. I asked her for any one thing about us, and she chose the only thing in the world that I thought they or it did not know . . . but IT

DID! IT DID KNOW! IT COULD HAVE BEEN WATCHING ME THE WHOLE TIME!

I didn't open the door. I screamed. I screamed in uncontrollable terror. I stomped on the old webcam on the floor. The door shook, and the doorknob tried to turn, but I didn't hear Amy's voice through the door. Was the basement door, made to keep out drafts, too thick? Or was Amy not outside? What could have been trying to get in, if not her? What the hell is out there?! I saw her on my computer through the camera outside, I heard her on the speakers through the camera outside, but was it real?! How can I know?! She's gone now—I screamed and shouted for help! I piled up everything in my apartment against the front door—

Friday

At least I think that it's Friday. I broke everything electronic. I smashed my computer to pieces. Every single thing on there could have been accessed by network access, or worse, altered. I'm a programmer; I know. Every little piece of information I gave out since this started—my name, my e-mail, my location—none of it came back from outside until I gave it out. I've been going over and over what I wrote. I've been pacing back and forth, alternating between stark terror and overpowering disbelief. Sometimes I'm absolutely certain some phantom entity is dead set on the simple goal of getting me to go outside. Back to the beginning, with the phone call from Amy, she was effectively asking me to open the door and go outside.

I keep running through it in my head. One point of view says I've acted like a madman, and all of this is the extreme convergence of probability—never going outside at the right times by pure luck, never seeing another person by pure chance, getting a random nonsense e-mail from some computer virus at just the right time. The other point of view says that extreme convergence of probability is the reason that whatever's out there hasn't gotten me already. I keep thinking: I never opened the window on the third floor. I never opened the front door, until that incredibly stupid stunt with the hidden camera after which I ran straight to my room and slammed the door. I haven't opened my own solid door since I flung open the front door of the building. Whatever's out there—if anything's out there—never made an "appearance" in the building before I opened the front door. Maybe the reason it wasn't in the building already was that it was elsewhere getting everyone else . . . and then it waited, until I betrayed my existence by trying to call Amy . . . a call which didn't work, until it called me and asked me my name . . .

Terror literally overwhelms me every time I try to fit the pieces of this nightmare together. That e-mail—short, cut off—was it from someone trying to get word out? Some friendly voice desperately trying to warn me before it came? Seen with my own eyes, don't trust them—exactly what I've been so suspicious of. It could have masterful control of all things electronic, practicing its insidious deception to trick me into coming outside. Why can't it get in? It knocked on the door—it must have some solid presence . . . the door . . . the image of those doors in the upper hallway as guardian monoliths flashes back in my mind every time I trace this path of thoughts. If there is some phantom entity trying to get me to go outside, maybe it can't get through doors. I keep thinking back over all the books I've read or movies I've seen, trying to generate some explanation for this. Doors have always been such intense foci of human imagination, always seen as wards or portals of special importance. Or perhaps the door is just too thick? I know that I couldn't bash through any of the doors in this building, let alone the heavy basement ones. Aside from that, the real question is, why does it even want me? If it just wanted to kill me, it could do it any number of ways, including just waiting until I starve to death. What if it doesn't want to kill me? What if it has some far more horrific fate in store for me? God, what can I do to escape this nightmare?

A knock on the door . . .

• • •

I told the people on the other side of the door I need a minute to think and I'll come out. I'm really just writing this down so I can figure out what to do. At least this time I heard their voices. My paranoia—and yes, I recognize I'm being paranoid—has me thinking of all sorts of ways that their voices could be faked electronically. There could be nothing but speakers outside, simulating human voices. Did it really take them three days to come talk to me? Amy is supposedly out there, along with two policemen and a psychiatrist. Maybe it took them three days to think of what to say to me—the psychiatrist's claim could be pretty convincing, if I decided to think this has all been a crazy misunderstanding, and not some entity trying to trick me into opening the door.

The psychiatrist had an older voice, authoritarian but still caring. I liked it. I'm desperate just to see someone with my own eyes! He said I have something called cyber-psychosis, and I'm just one of a nationwide epidemic of thousands of people having breakdowns triggered by a suggestive e-mail that "got through somehow." I swear he said "got through somehow." I think he means spread throughout the country inexplicably, but I'm incredibly suspicious that the entity slipped up and revealed something. He said I am part of a wave of "emergent behavior," that a lot of other people are having the same problem with the same fears, even though we've never communicated.

That neatly explains the strange e-mail about eyes that I got. I didn't get the original triggering e-mail. I got a descendant of it—my friend could have broken down too, and tried to warn everyone he knew against his paranoid fears. That's how the problem spreads, the psychiatrist claims. I could have spread it, too, with my texts and instant messages online to everybody I know. One of those people might be melting down right now, after being triggered by something I sent them, something they might interpret any way that they want, something like a text saying "seen anyone face-to-face lately?" The psychiatrist told me that he didn't want to "lose another one," that people like me are intelligent, and that's our downfall. We draw connections so well that we draw them even when they shouldn't be there. He said it's easy to get caught up in paranoia in our fast-paced world, a constantly changing place where more and more of our interaction is simulated . . .

I have to give him one thing. It's a great explanation. It neatly explains everything. It perfectly explains everything, in fact. I have every reason to shake off this nightmarish fear that some thing or consciousness or being out there wants me to open the door so it can capture me for some horrible fate worse than death. It would be foolish, after hearing that explanation, to stay in here until I starve to death just to spite the entity that might have got everyone else. It would be foolish to think that, after hearing that explanation, I might be one of the last people left alive in an empty world, hiding in my secure basement room, spiting some unthinkable deceptive entity just by refusing to be captured. It's a perfect explanation for every single strange thing I've seen or heard, and I have every reason in the world to let all of my fears go, and open the door.

That's exactly why I'm not going to.

How can I be sure?! How can I know what's real and what's deception? All of these damn things with their wires and their signals that originate from some unseen origin! They're not real,

I can't be sure! Signals through a camera, faked video, deceptive phone calls, e-mails! Even the television, lying broken on the floor—how can I possibly know it's real? It's just signals, waves, light . . . the door! It's bashing on the door! It's trying to get in! What insane mechanical contrivance could it be using to simulate the sound of men attacking the heavy wood so well?! At least I'll finally see it with my own eyes . . . there's nothing left in here for it to deceive me with, I've ripped apart everything else! It can't deceive my eyes, can it? Seen with your own eyes don't trust them they . . . wait . . . was that desperate message telling me to trust my eyes, or warning me about my eyes too?! Oh my God, what's the difference between a camera and my eyes? They both turn light into electrical signals—they're the same! I can't be deceived! I have to be sure! I have to be sure!

Date Unknown

I calmly asked for paper and a pen, day in and day out, until it finally gave them to me. Not that it matters. What am I going to do? Poke my eyes out? The bandages feel like part of me now. The pain is gone. I figure this will be one of my last chances to write legibly, as, without my sight to correct mistakes, my hands will slowly forget the motions involved. This is a sort of self-indulgence, this writing . . . it's a relic of another time, because I'm certain everyone left in the world is dead . . . or something far worse.

I sit against the padded wall day in and day out. The entity brings me food and water. It masks itself as a kind nurse, as an unsympathetic doctor. I think it knows that my hearing has sharpened considerably now that I live in darkness. It fakes conversations in the hallways, on the off chance that I might overhear. One of the nurses talks about having a baby soon. One of the doctors lost his wife in a car accident. None of it matters, none of it is real. None of it gets to me, not like she does.

That's the worst part, the part I almost can't handle. The thing comes to me, masquerading as Amy. Its re-creation is perfect. It sounds exactly like Amy, feels exactly like her. It even produces a reasonable facsimile of tears that it makes me feel on its lifelike cheeks. When it first dragged me here, it told me all the things I wanted to hear. It told me that she loved me, that she had always loved me, that it didn't understand why I did this, that we could still have a life together, if only I would stop insisting that I was being deceived. It wanted me to believe . . . no, it needed me to believe that she was real.

I almost fell for it. I really did. I doubted myself for the longest time. In the end, though, it was all too perfect, too flawless, and too real. The false Amy used to come every day, and then every week, and finally stopped coming altogether . . . but I don't think the entity will give up. I think the waiting game is just another one of its gambits. I will resist it for the rest of my life, if I have to. I don't know what happened to the rest of the world, but I do know that this thing needs me to fall for its deceptions. If it needs that, then maybe, just maybe, I am a thorn in its agenda. Maybe Amy is still alive out there somewhere, kept alive only by my will to resist the deceiver. I hold on to that hope, rocking back and forth in my cell to pass the time. I will never give in. I will never break. I am . . . a hero!

• • •

The doctor read the paper the patient had scribbled on. It was barely readable, written in the shaky script of one who could not see. He wanted to smile at the man's steadfast resolve, a reminder of the human will to survive, but he knew that the patient was completely delusional.

After all, a sane man would have fallen for the deception long ago.

The doctor wanted to smile. He wanted to whisper words of encouragement to the delusional man. He wanted to scream, but the nerve filaments wrapped around his head and into his eyes made him do otherwise. His body walked into the cell like a puppet, and told the patient, once more, that he was wrong, and that there was nobody trying to deceive him.

SHE BENEATH THE TREE

Michael Marks

The first time I remember feeling true fear was in front of that tree, an old decaying thing standing right in the center of an otherwise flat field on my grandparents' land. Its long trunk twisted and knotted around itself; its branches reached out like gnarled hands toward gray skies as if it were in prayer. It was just a tree and nothing more, at least that's what my father told me. I knew though, I knew better than that. It was not just a tree . . . it was evil.

Even back then I noticed that something wasn't right about it. It was as if the grass refused to grow in a five-foot-wide circle around it. It was like none of the animals would approach it—you never saw a squirrel or a bird nestled among its black dead branches. I can remember standing in front of it at the age of six, my father and grandfather standing behind me talking as I stared up in frightened awe.

"That thing is an eyesore, Pop," my father said, taking a few steps toward me. "Why don't you just cut the damned thing down?"

My grandfather, a man still quite fit at that age and still sporting some of the original dark color of his hair, balked at this. "Thing's been there as long as I can remember, 'sides, it ain't doin' no one no harm anyhow."

That was the last word on the subject. Grandpa said "no" so there it remained. There it has remained for twenty years since. It lasted through my grandfather's sudden heart attack, my grandmother's passing shortly thereafter of cancer, my father and mother's divorce, and my father's eventual death from drinking. It's been there, and it's been cursing my family's name. I knew it then, and I know it now.

I inherited the property after my father passed away. He hadn't done anything with it during the time he had it—as he had been far too absorbed in drinking and wallowing at the time—so when I got to the place it had fallen into total disrepair. It would take some work to make it livable again, but since my girlfriend, Crystal, and I had been looking for a bigger place for our family it was something of a godsend. Our son Jeffrey was four years old and I thought it would be great to give him a bigger room and a huge backyard to play in. We could finally even get a dog—something I'd always wanted to do but the crummy apartments I'd lived in hadn't allowed.

I remember walking the grounds and planning everything out in my head. Every color of paint and scrap of wood I would need to get this place back in shape and looking like the place I remembered from my childhood. Then I remember seeing that tree, off in the distance, like a blight on the horizon, its clawed branches still reaching up toward the sky in prayer, its body still rotting and twisted. I leaned up against the house and lit a cigarette while I stared at it off in the distance like it was an intruder. I closed an eye and covered the tree with my thumb. The world looked better without it. I decided in that moment that while Grandpa may have wanted to just let it be, I was cutting that fucker down.

My girlfriend and I decided that I could spend the weekends up at my grandparents' place to get it fixed up for us to move in. My brother, Eddie, offered to help out on weekends that he wasn't busy, but he said that wouldn't be for at least two weeks. I considered the idea of waiting to cut the tree down until my brother could get up there to give me a hand, but the second I laid eyes on that thing again I wanted it gone.

I backed my truck into the field to make it easier to haul out all the pieces and I set to work. As my chainsaw roared to life, in my head I could almost see the twisted thing cringe. It had stood for longer than I'd been alive; today was its last time at prayer to the sky. I covered my face with a dust mask and felt a great satisfaction as the whirling teeth of the saw sunk into its surface. Chips of blackened bark and rotten-smelling sawdust flew free from its knotted, twisting trunk. Some sort of black sap leaked out onto my saw blade as I worked; I could even feel bits of it fly up and hit me in the face. Even through the dust mask I could smell it. Its stench was horrid. I feared for a second it would gum up the works of my saw, but the raw power of the engine kept it moving forward and the teeth of the chainsaw chewed their prey with little worry.

It took most of the day working to get the tree down and chopped into pieces, but as the sun was setting and the bed of my truck was filled with the black, rotting wood, it felt worth the trouble. Left in the tree's place was nothing but a knotted-up stump. The thing writhed with insects and some kind of mold. I would tear it out later when I had some help; who knew how deep that thing had been rooted. I climbed into the cab of my truck filthy and tired, yet satisfied with my work. That night I slept a dreamless sleep of the dead knowing my horizon was free of that twisted shadow. I spent the whole next day working on the main house. There was a lot to do and I didn't want to waste any time.

It wasn't till the following weekend that things started to get strange.

I had been clearing out the attic of the house. It was filled with boxes of junk and old furniture. Most of the stuff was going straight to the dump, a few things to the Goodwill, and a last little handful I was keeping. While I was moving one of the keeper boxes (a box filled with old photo albums), one of the albums fell off the top and sent a couple of loose pictures sprawling across the floor. I set the box down in the guest bedroom—where I was planning to store it for the time being—and walked over to pick up the photos. They were old black-and-white pictures of my grandfather when he was younger. He was standing in front of that horrid-looking tree smiling. My grandmother sat beside him at the base.

"FALL OF '47" was written on the back, but below it was something much stranger: "Le cala, le cala, we seek no end."

The phrase struck a strangely familiar chord with me, although I had no idea what it meant. The photo in and of itself made me feel uncomfortable though. There was something a little too manic in my grandfather's smile and something a little too nervous in my grandmother's. I flipped to the next photo and it took a second to realize what I was looking at. When I did, my stomach turned.

It was my grandfather. This time, though, my grandmother was not in the frame and instead my grandfather was holding a rope that was slung up over the tree and pulled taut. On the other end of the rope was a dog; it had been hung by the neck—presumably by my grandfather—and it appeared to be dead. My grandpa still had the manic smile on his face. You could see it beaming from beneath his wide-brimmed hat.

I dropped the photo, recoiling from what I had just seen. It was sick and I could hardly believe it. My grandparents had always been such kind people and the sight of my grandfather taking such pleasure in killing a defenseless animal made me sick. I steadied myself on my knees and saw the photo lying face down on the ground in front of me. It too had writing on the back:

"Le cala, le cala, accept the end of another."

I snatched the photo up off the ground, not wanting to look at it again, and walked at a steady pace over to the trash pile I had been building up. I shoved the pictures inside one of the boxes and then returned to where I had left the other photo albums and started tearing through them. I came across at least ten other sets of photos from different years. Each time my grandfather and grandmother were in one picture posed next to the tree, then each other time my grandfather was hanging some kind of animal by its neck from one of the branches; it wasn't always dogs, there were also cats and goats. Each one was labeled as fall of whatever year it had been taken, and each one had the same chant written in two parts.

> "Le cala, le cala, we seek no end. Le cala, le cala, accept the end of another."

I tore each photo from the albums and crumpled them up, stuffing them in the same box as the original ones I found. I must have paced in silent shock for at least an hour afterward. What had my grandparents been doing? Was it some kind of cult thing? Why did my grandfather always look like he was taking so much pleasure in killing those animals? It started to make sense to me why that tree had felt so wrong, so evil. They had done something there that tainted that place.

That night I threw the boxes in the back of my truck and dropped them at the dump on my way home. For all I cared they could rot with the tree; I wanted nothing to do with any of it. I thought that would be the end. I would walk away and leave it alone, just keep it to myself and move on with my life. It's never that simple, though; I know that now.

That whole week I was plagued by nightmares about that tree. I could hear my grandfather's hearty laugh as he yanked down on a rope and pulled those animals up into the trees. I could hear them squeal and whine as they were strangled to death. I'd wake up in cold sweats, short of breath and confused as to where I was. The phrase repeated in my head: "Le cala, le cala, we seek no end. Le cala, le cala, accept the end of another." I told my girlfriend that they were just nightmares, probably brought on by stress, but I never told her what it was about.

I was hesitant to return to the house, but I told myself to just forget about it. It was disturbing to learn that my grandparents weren't the people I thought they were—that they were capable of such disgusting acts of cruelty—but any answers as to why had been buried with them years ago. The tree was gone, the pictures gone with it, and the house was mine now. I could make it a home again and fill it with new, happier memories. I met Eddie at the house the following weekend as planned.

My brother and I worked the two following weekends without incident. It was good to spend some time with him, and with his help we were able to get the house into shape in no time. The third weekend I got there on Saturday morning to find my brother staring off into the field. I walked up behind him and touched his shoulder. He jumped back, startled.

"Jesus Christ, Danny! You nearly scared the shit out of me!" he said, seeming to snap out of his trance.

"Sorry about that. It looked like you were straight-up zoned-out, though."

"Oh yeah, just staring off into space." He laughed. "Guess I'm getting senile in my old age."

"Yeah, thirty years old and all. We should probably get you ready for the retirement home." He snorted a quick laugh and gave me a playful punch to the shoulder before turning his attention back to the field.

"Hey . . . didn't there used to be a tree out there?" he asked. "Gnarled old thing, really creepy looking?"

My heart sunk in my chest. I'd had so much fun working on the place with him that I had not thought about the tree or the photos in the past week. "Yeah, I cut it down." My tone became somber. I hoped that he wouldn't ask anything else and I think he could see it on my face.

"Eh, good riddance. Thing was hideous." He smiled at me. "Let's get back to work."

We spent the rest of the day rebuilding the back deck that we had torn down the previous weekend. It had been overtaken with rot and was falling apart. During one of our smoke breaks Eddie cracked a beer and handed it to me. I returned the favor by lighting a cigarette and passing it over to him. He took a drag and coughed a bit before taking a swig off his beer.

"Don't you dare tell my wife I've been smoking," he said, sucking down another drag. "Marla would kill me."

"My lips are sealed, brother." I laughed and lit one for myself.

"So Crystal and my nephew are coming up tomorrow?"

"Yup! She wants to check the place out, and I'm tired of spending whole weekends away from my boy. It'll be good to show them around." I wasn't actually sure how much I meant that. The whole place still gave me a weird vibe I was doing my best to ignore, yet in the back of my mind it gnawed at me.

"This place always had a fucked-up vibe when we were kids," Eddie said, seemingly out of nowhere. He was staring at the backyard fence as if he were looking through it out toward the field.

"What are you talking about?" I said before taking another swig off my beer and giving him a raised eyebrow over the bottom of the bottle.

"Just . . . I don't know." He trailed off a bit before turning his attention toward me. "I'm glad you're fixing it up, Danny."

We both sat silently for a bit till we were almost done with our beers. My brother took down the final swallow out of his bottle and smacked his lips.

"Le cala, le cala. The end of another," he said before turning to me with a smile. I leapt out of my lawn chair and backed away from him as if he had just pulled a knife on me.

"Whoa brother! A bee fly up your shorts?" he said with a laugh.

"Why the fuck did you say that?" I was now standing behind the chair and using it as a barrier between me and him.

"'Cause you jumped up like a maniac," he answered, taking a step toward me. "You okay?"

"Not the thing about the bee, you asshole. What did you say before that?" I stepped back, holding my beer bottle by the neck with a reverse grip.

"I said—that's the end of another break. What the fuck has gotten into you?"

I eased my stance and leaned myself on the back of the chair. Could I have been hearing things? It was possible; it felt as if that phrase had drilled itself into my mind. I decided I may have just misheard and flipped out over nothing and felt stupid. As far as I knew, my brother didn't know anything about what went on here and I wanted him to remain in ignorance.

"Nothing . . ." I looked up at him and forced a smile. "I think I've just been working too hard, my mind is starting to play tricks on me."

"One hell of a trick." His face was flush with worry. I could tell he was genuinely confused. My heart slowed down and I finished the rest of my beer before walking over next to him and clapping him on the shoulder.

"Don't worry about it." My smile came easier now. "Your little brother is an idiot. Let's just get back to work."

That's exactly what we did. We managed to get the whole back deck built over the course of the rest of the day. All the other breaks we took had an uneasy silence to them most of the time. I really just wanted to see Crystal and my son. I hoped it would make me feel less uneasy after my little delusion. Eddie blacked out on the couch shortly after we finished for the day, and fell asleep in the upstairs bedroom.

I think I would have dreamed about the tree that night. In fact I'm sure of it. That is, if my sleep hadn't been interrupted a little before 4 A.M.

I woke to a figure standing over the bed just staring down at me. I was about to freak out and go scrambling for my grandfather's old 12-gauge in the closet, but my eyes quickly adjusted. It was Eddie. The look on his face made it seem as if all the life had been drained out of him.

"Eddie?" I asked rubbing the sleep from eyes. "What the hell is going on? Is everything all right?"

"She beneath the tree demands retribution for what you did."

I raised an eyebrow at him. I felt utterly confused and still half asleep. Before I could ask what the fuck he meant, he spoke again.

"Le cala, le cala, we should seek no end. I don't want her to have you brother, I'm sorry."

My stomach twisted knots in my chest and I threw back my covers to jump out of bed. Before my feet touched the ground, though, Eddie was on me with a strength I didn't know he had. He coiled around me like a snake and I felt his forearm press into my neck like a vise. I gasped and threw elbows in an attempt to get free, but the more I struggled the harder he squeezed. In no time at all, the world went dark.

When I woke again I smelled earth, and damp mold. Dim light crossed my fuzzy vision as I coughed and weakly attempted to rise to my knees. I could hear muffled sounds in the distance—Eddie's voice, and then Crystal's. I tried to call out to them but all I could do was choke out a cough. I pushed myself to my feet, feeling as if I'd been crushed under a ton of bricks. My eyes started to adjust and clear, revealing that I was in the basement of the house.

Suddenly I heard Crystal scream an all-too-short scream before it was cut off by the sound of something thudding against the floor. This was followed by the sound of my son crying. My strength came back to me in that moment and my legs carried me up the basement stairs as fast as they could. I could already hear my son's cries dimming as they moved out the front door of the house and out toward the field.

I crashed into the basement door with all my weight as I shouted Eddie's name in raspy breaths. It felt like an eternity and I wondered how the old door was withstanding my hits better than my shoulder. I finally heard the wood splinter after what felt like ten straight minutes of crashing all my weight into it, and the sliding lock broke into pieces, letting the door swing free. With no hesitation I threw myself around the corner and into the living room where I saw Crystal lying unconscious on the floor. Her head was bleeding but she was alive, and I needed to get to my son. Eddie's words rang out in my mind:

> "She beneath the tree demands retribution for what you did."

Images of my brother hoisting my son up by his neck and smiling manically as he did it overtook my thoughts. Somehow I knew that's exactly what was going to happen, too, which made no sense because I had cut that tree into tiny fucking pieces. I reluctantly left Crystal and sprinted up the stairs to get the shotgun from the closet. I wasn't going to take any chances, not when it came to my son.

I passed the window that overlooked the field and I could see Eddie carrying Jeffrey out into the field, but I also saw something else. Something that froze my blood in its veins. I saw the tree.

A silhouette of black against the overcast sky. Its gnarled body and twisted branches reaching up in prayer . . . the same as it had always been. I didn't have time to wonder how—none of this made any sense, but I knew what was about to happen to my son. I hurriedly grabbed the shotgun, made sure it was loaded, and sprinted from the house.

They had reached the tree before I got to them. Eddie had slung a rope over one of the thicker branches and looped it around Jeffrey's neck. Before I could even level the gun in Eddie's direction, he had thrown the rope over his shoulder and began lifting Jeffrey up by his neck. I lifted the double barrel and pointed it directly at my brother.

"Let him down now, Eddie!" I screamed, my voice still raspy and paining my throat with each word.

"I'm doing this for you, brother! Le cala, le cala, I don't want your end." He wasn't smiling like I'd seen in my head, tears streamed down his face. "She demands your blood. This is the only way!"

"I'm not going to say it again!" I stepped closer to him; there was no chance of missing. I pulled the hammers for both barrels back. I could see Jeffrey's feet kicking wildly in the air. One of his little shoes went tumbling to the ground. "LET HIM DOWN!"

Now the tears were mine. It felt like some compulsion to pull the trigger had taken me over. I could hear a woman's voice in my head. "Le cala, le cala, do it." It was little more than a whisper, but it was there behind my thoughts. I stared up at the tree feeling exactly like the first time, in the grip of true fear.

"SHE NEEDS SACRIFICE FROM YOU!" my brother screamed, his face and voice twisted in madness. "LE CALA, LE CALA, ACCEPT THE . . ."

His voice was cut off by the thunderous sound of the shotgun as I squeezed the triggers.

I don't remember much after that, not much more than bits and pieces. I remember scooping my screaming child up off the ground and carrying him back toward the house. I remember Crystal running toward me and tearing him from my arms with a confused look in her eye. I remember collapsing before the police and ambulances got there. Crystal said they couldn't question me because apparently I kept saying that "IT" shouldn't be there, that I cut it to pieces.

I couldn't bring myself to tell her the truth about the tree. As far as she or anyone else knows, my brother went crazy. I wish I could believe that was true; it would make me feel like less of a piece of shit for dragging his name through the mud after I murdered him. Make no mistake, either—that's exactly what I did. There were other ways I could have stopped him, I've thought through all of them a hundred times. I tell myself the reason I pulled the trigger was because I was in a panic, not in my right mind. I know, though . . . it was "She beneath the tree," as Eddie had called her. She got her sacrifice from me, in both blood and humanity.

I never bothered to cut the tree down again. In fact, I decided to let the old place rot. I refuse to even sell it and I sure as hell will never go near it again. I keep hoping it'll burn down in some freak accident. I know it won't, though.

Hell, even if it did . . . that fucking tree would still be there. Gnarled and twisted branches reaching up toward the sky in praise to whatever power it serves.

SMILE.MONTANA

Aaron Shotwell

I'm tired of running. I'm tired of playing damage control. No one should suffer this. That wicked, human-like grin. Those menacing eyes. That beckoning hand. Night after night, the same image, the same demon demanding me to "spread the word." I tried to protect you all, I really tried. But it has finally gotten the best of me. It's too much. I'm just too tired to go on.

I had hoped the account of Mary E. would be the last I'd ever hear. When I deleted that e-mail and the attached image file, I hoped to leave it all behind me. My curiosity went unsatisfied, but it was for the best. If the monster behind the picture was real, if Smile Dog truly existed, I wouldn't be able to bear the temptation. I would sacrifice some other poor, unsuspecting soul to that thing to save my own skin. I knew that, and so I washed my hands of it then and there. I never imagined that it would follow me.

After graduation, I left my home town to further my career in journalism, just me and my hand-held camera, looking to film something that would catch the attention of the news station of my choice. I needed something to get my foot in the door, something that would lead to greater things in the future. Around a year into the search for my destiny, roaming from city to city, it found me in the most traumatic way possible. It nearly killed me.

On a stretch of I-90 between South Dakota and Montana, I watched in horror as an eighteen-wheeler drifted over the rails of an overpass and plummeted into oncoming traffic. It crashed into the ground in an upside-down heap of twisted metal, mere feet from my car. Had I not slammed on my brakes at that precise moment, I wouldn't be alive to tell this story. In hindsight, that might have been best.

As blessed as I was, however, a few others weren't so fortunate. As the trailer screeched into the southbound lane, two oncoming SUVs plowed into the wreckage at over ninety miles per hour, one after the other. They didn't even have time to react. It was over in an instant, no survivors.

I sat there for what felt like hours in a daze, not completely sure if I'd survived. I could hear sirens approaching, and they brought me back to reality from my stupor. I'm not proud of it, but I saw an opportunity, and I took it. The sight made my gorge rise more than once, but I spent the next few minutes walking the perimeter of the accident, filming everything I could. Twisted and bloody corpses behind the steering wheels, plumes of black smoke rising from crumpled hoods, the hot haze of rising flames . . . and then I saw it.

The semi's driver-side door had been ripped from its hinges, and the driver lay on his back in the overturned cab, his arm outstretched into the street. And there it lay, just beyond his fingertips, signed at one of the corners and splashed with blood. An old floppy disk with three words scrawled on its label: "Spread the word." I stared at it, stunned, and Mary's final words came flooding back to memory.

I still didn't know what I believed, or even if that disk contained the monster that haunted her dreams for so long. For all I knew, it could have been a coincidence, but I wouldn't risk it. I crushed it under foot, stomped it into a scattering of plastic shards, and threw the remains into the fire rising from the first SUV's engine. If Smile Dog was behind this tragedy, I wouldn't let it take any more victims.

That footage proved to be the breakthrough I was waiting for. The director of a local news studio received it with great enthusiasm, and he paid me more than I could have hoped. Gore brings in the ratings, after all. He invited me to keep in touch, said I was going places. It was a bittersweet feeling, especially when the story aired.

As it turned out, the semi driver had not been intoxicated. There had been no mechanical failures with his vehicle. He had no history of suicidal tendencies. His death was a mystery. It was clear that he let it happen, but nobody could discern the reason. But I knew. The lack of another, more reasonable explanation cleared any doubt in my mind. It was his only escape from the nightmares.

Unfortunately, it wouldn't be my last encounter with Smile Dog's curse. It seemed blood and guts were my gateway to a real career, and I was going to give the director what he wanted. If I could prove myself as a freelancer, I thought, maybe I could land a spot in-house. And from there, who knows? Reporter? Anchor? The sky was the limit. So I bought myself a police scanner and got to work.

I had served for six months before it found me again, this time in the back pocket of a jumper in Billings. Then, a week later, lying near the purse of a woman who ran into traffic in Whitefish. Then, a few days later, on the counter of a convenience store where the owner put a shotgun in his mouth. I destroyed every copy I found, but they just kept turning up.

It was following me, and I knew that for sure a few weeks later when a package arrived at my doorstep. I didn't recognize the return address, but I knew what it was. I could hear it rattling around inside, just waiting to claim me like it had claimed all the others. I wouldn't give it the chance. I tore it from the box and tossed it into a heated frying pan, watched the plastic curl and melt, and it screamed. It hissed with the agony of a dying animal, just as it had for Mary's widower, Terrence. The sound chilled my blood.

Things went quiet for a while after that, long enough that I almost thought it had actually given up and taken no for an answer, long enough for me to build some real rapport with the news station and lay down some roots. Life finally seemed to be shaping up, and then I received a call from my mother back home. She said she was just calling to check up, bored me to death with tales of her bridge club and Dad's bodily functions—a typical Mom call. Then she asked me a question that shook me to the core.

"Honey, do the words 'spread the word' mean anything to you?"

My heart leapt into my throat. "W-what? What are you talking about?"

"Yeah, someone left this little, square, plastic thing in our mailbox this morning," she said. "No package or anything. I don't even know what it is. And those words were written on it. Any idea what this is all about?"

I paused, terrified. "I . . . I dunno, Mom. It's probably just a prank. Just throw it away."

"But what is it?"

"Just throw it away, Mom!" I shouted. She heard the panic in my voice.

"Honey, is something the matter?"

I took a breath and wiped the cold sweat from my brow. "Yeah . . . yeah, Mom, I'm fine. Just toss it, okay? Don't worry about it."

She didn't press the issue any further, just moved on to some story about my brother's new girlfriend, and I'm grateful. This monster, this Smile Dog, was now threatening my loved ones thousands of miles away. It was angry, and it was trying to get to me through them. I thank God that it decided to attack the most computer-illiterate person in my family first, but maybe that was the point. Maybe it was a warning, I don't know. But I wasn't about to wait and find out who was next. I had to end it.

Thankfully, the box that held the last disk was still in the dumpster outside my apartment complex. I traced the return address to an abandoned storage facility in Livingston. I drove there with a pair of bolt cutters and five gallons of gasoline, unsure what I would find but determined not to let anybody else die. I would burn the whole place to the ground if it meant saving even one more person from Mary's fate.

I had only just pulled in past the front gate when, sure enough, Smile Dog showed me the way. A single disk lying just outside the door of a unit at the end of the first row, unit 15A. Even as I approached, I could feel the air grow colder, and I could hear the faint sound of white noise just beyond the door. Whatever it was, whatever was responsible for all these tragic suicides, lay just beyond. I could feel it. I cut the lock, and with no small measure of hesitation, I lifted the door. A mistake that I sorely regret.

At last, Smile Dog had claimed me, its ghastly image piercing the darkness from a small, ancient monitor on a desk against the far wall. I stared it right in the eyes, felt its malice boiling from the surface of the screen, felt the red hand grasp my mind as my legs buckled beneath me. Then came the convulsions, wracking my body as white noise roared from its broken speakers. I blacked out.

When I came to, the monitor was gone. In its place and all across the floor, hundreds, maybe thousands of floppy disks, all marked with the same grim instruction, "spread the word." I don't remember much after that. I just snapped, blinded by rage. But I remember the flames and the stench of burning gasoline, and I remember the eyebrow I lost as I stood too close, watching them burn.

But of course, it wasn't over. I knew that. I tried to put off sleep as long as possible. When the coffee stopped working, I turned to cocaine. But it found me eventually, and Smile Dog bore into my mind with the searing heat of a branding iron. And throughout the night, just as it had done to Mary, just as it had done to that semi driver, it demanded that I spread the word.

This monster, it's insatiable. And it will not be reasoned with. I must spread the word, or it will torment me until the day I die. And then it will come for my family. My friends. It will not stop. It will never stop, until I do as it asks.

I broke into the news studio tonight. I used their editing software, just a few frames in some heartfelt piece about soldiers returning home to their families. It should be enough. I don't know what will happen, but I don't intend to be around to find out. By the time it airs, I'll have left the country. Please don't look for me. For what it's worth, I never meant for it to end this way. I'm sorry.

BEDTIME

Michael Whitehouse

Bedtime is supposed to be a happy event for a tired child; for me it was terrifying. While some children might complain about being put to bed before they have finished watching a film or playing their favorite video game, when I was a child, nighttime was something to truly fear. Somewhere in the back of my mind it still is.

As someone who is trained in the sciences, I cannot prove that what happened to me was objectively real, but I can swear that what I experienced was genuine horror. A fear that in my life, I'm glad to say, has never been equaled. I will relate it to you all now as best I can. Make of it what you will, but I'll be glad to just get it off of my chest.

I can't remember exactly when it started, but my apprehension toward falling asleep seemed to correspond with my being moved into a room of my own. I was eight years old at the time and until then I had shared a room, quite happily, with my older brother. As is perfectly understandable for a boy five years my senior, my brother eventually wished for a room of his own, and as a result I was given the room at the back of the house.

It was a small, narrow, yet oddly elongated room, large enough for a bed and a chest of drawers, but not much else. I couldn't really complain because, even at that age, I understood that we did not have a large house and I had no real cause to be disappointed, as my family was both loving and caring. It was a happy childhood, during the day.

A solitary window looked out onto our back garden, nothing out of the ordinary, but even during the day the light that crept into that room seemed almost hesitant.

As my brother was given a new bed, I was given the bunk beds that we used to share. While I was upset about sleeping on my own, I was excited at the thought of being able to sleep in the top bunk, which seemed far more adventurous to me.

From the very first night I remember a strange feeling of unease creeping slowly from the back of my mind. I lay on the top bunk, staring down at my action figures and cars strewn across the green-blue carpet. As imaginary battles and adventures took place between the toys on the floor, I couldn't help but feel that my eyes were being slowly drawn toward the bottom bunk, as if I could see something moving out of the corner of my eye. Something that did not wish to be seen.

The bunk was empty, impeccably made with a dark blue blanket tucked in neatly, partially covering two rather bland white pillows. I didn't think anything of it at the time; I was a child, and the noise slipping under my door from my parent's television bathed me in a warm sense of safety and well-being.

I fell asleep.

When you awaken from a deep sleep to something moving, or stirring, it can take a few moments for you to truly understand what is happening. The fog of sleep hangs over your eyes and ears even when lucid.

Something was moving, there was no doubt about that.

At first I wasn't sure what it was. Everything was dark, almost pitch-black, but there was enough light creeping in from outside to outline that narrowly suffocating room. Two thoughts appeared in my mind almost simultaneously. The first was that my parents were in bed because the rest of the house lay both in darkness and silence. The second thought turned to the noise. A noise that had obviously woken me.

As the last cobwebs of sleep withered from my mind, the noise took on a more familiar form. Sometimes the simplest of sounds can be the most unnerving: a cold wind whistling through a tree outside, a neighbor's footsteps uncomfortably close, or, in this case, the simple sound of bed sheets rustling in the dark.

That was it; bed sheets rustling in the dark as if some disturbed sleeper was attempting to get all too comfortable in the bottom bunk. I lay there in disbelief thinking that the noise was either my imagination or perhaps just my pet cat finding somewhere comfortable to spend the night. It was then that I noticed my door, still shut as it had been as I'd fallen asleep.

Perhaps my mum had checked in on me and the cat had sneaked in to my room then.

Yes, that must have been it. I turned to face the wall, closing my eyes in the vain hope that I could fall back to sleep. As I moved, the rustling noise from underneath me ceased. I thought that I must have disturbed my cat, but quickly I realized that the visitor in the bottom bunk was much less mundane than my pet trying to sleep, and much more sinister.

As if alerted to—and disgruntled by—my presence, the disturbed sleeper began to toss and turn violently, like a child having a tantrum in his bed. I could hear the sheets twist and turn with increasing ferocity. Fear then gripped me, not like the subtle sense of unease I had experienced earlier, but now potent and terrifying. My heart raced as my eyes panicked, scanning the almost impenetrable darkness.

I let out a cry.

As most young boys do, I instinctively shouted for my mother. I could hear something stir on the other side of the house, but as I began to breathe a sigh of relief that my parents were coming to save me, the bunk beds suddenly started to shake violently as if gripped by an earthquake, scraping against the wall. I could hear the sheets below me thrashing around as if tormented by malice. I did not want to jump down to safety, as I feared the thing in the bottom bunk would reach out and grab me, pulling me into the darkness, so I stayed there, white knuckles clenching my own blanket like a shroud of protection. The wait seemed like an eternity.

The door finally, and thankfully, burst open, and I lay bathed in light while the bottom bunk, the resting place of my unwanted visitor, lay empty and peaceful.

I cried and my mother consoled me. Tears of fear, followed by relief, streamed down my face. Yet, through all of the horror and relief, I did not tell her why I was so upset. I cannot explain it, but it was as though whatever had been in that bunk would return if I even so much as spoke of it, or uttered a single syllable of its existence. Whether that was the truth, I do not know, but as a child I felt as if that unseen menace remained close, listening.

My mother lay in the empty bunk, promising to stay there until morning. Eventually my anxiety diminished, tiredness pushed me back toward sleep, but I remained restless, waking several times momentarily to the sound of rustling bed sheets.

I remember the next day wanting to go anywhere, be anywhere, but in that narrow suffocating room. It was a Saturday and I played outside, quite happily, with my friends. Although our house was not large we were lucky to have a long sloping garden in the back. We played there often, as much of it was overgrown and we could hide in the bushes, climb in the huge sycamore tree that towered above all else, and easily imagine ourselves in the throes of a grand adventure in some untamed exotic land.

As fun as it all was, occasionally my eye would turn to that small window—ordinary, slight, and innocuous. But for me, that thin boundary was a looking glass into a strange, cold pocket of dread. Outside, the lush green surroundings of our garden filled with the smiling faces of my friends could not extinguish the creeping feeling clawing its way up my spine, causing every hair on my body to stand on end. The feeling of something in that room, watching me play, waiting for the night when I would be alone, eagerly filled with hate.

It may sound strange to you, but by the time my parents ushered me back into that room for the night, I said nothing. I didn't protest; I didn't even make an excuse as to why I couldn't sleep there. I simply and sullenly walked into that room, climbed the few steps into the top bunk, and then waited. As an adult I would be telling everyone about my experience, but even at that age I felt almost silly to be talking about something that I really had no evidence for. I would be lying, however, if I said this was my primary reason; I still felt that this thing would be enraged if I so much as spoke of it.

It's funny how certain words can remain hidden from your mind, no matter how blatant or obvious they are. One word came to me that second night, lying there in the darkness alone, frightened, aware of a rotten change in the atmosphere—a thickening of the air as if something had displaced it. As I heard the first casual twists of the bed sheets below, felt the first anxious increase of my heartbeat at the realization that something was once again in the bottom bunk, that word, a word that had been sent into exile, filtered up through my consciousness, breaking free of all repression, gasping for air screaming, etching, and carving itself into my mind:

"Ghost."

As this thought came to me, I noticed that my unwelcome visitor had ceased moving. The bed sheets lay calm and dormant, but they had been replaced by something far more hideous. A slow, rhythmic, rasping breath heaved and escaped from the thing below. I could imagine its chest rising and falling with each sordid, wheezing, and garbled breath. I shuddered, and hoped beyond all hope that it would leave without occurrence.

The house lay, as it had the previous night, in a thick blanket of darkness. Silence prevailed, all but for the perverted breath of my, as yet unseen, bunkmate. I lay there terrified. I just wanted this thing to go, to leave me alone.

What did it want?

Then something unmistakably chilling transpired; it moved. It moved in a way different from before. When it threw itself around in the bottom bunk the night before it seemed unrestrained, without purpose, almost animalistic. This movement, however, was driven by awareness, with purpose, with a goal in mind. For that thing lying there in the darkness, that thing that seemed intent on terrorizing a young boy, calmly and nonchalantly sat up. Its labored breathing became louder as now only a mattress and a few flimsy wooden slats separated my body from the unearthly breath below.

I lay there, my eyes filled with tears. A fear that mere words cannot relate to you coursed through my veins. I would not have believed that this fear could have been heightened, but I was so wrong. I imagined what this thing would look like, sitting there listening from below my mattress, hoping to catch the slightest hint that I was awake. Imagination then turned to an unnerving reality. It began to touch the wooden slats that my mattress sat on. It seemed to caress them carefully, running what I imagined to be fingers and hands across the surface of the wood.

Then, with great force, it prodded angrily between two slats, into the mattress. Even through the padding, it felt as though someone had viciously stuck his fingers into my side. I let out an almighty cry and the wheezing, shaking, and moving thing in the bunk below replied in kind by violently vibrating the bunk as it had done the night before. Small flakes of paint powdered onto my blanket from the wall as the frame of the bed scraped along it, backward and forward.

Once again I was bathed in light, and there stood my mother, loving, caring as she always was, with a comforting hug and calming words that eventually subdued my hysteria. Of course she asked what was wrong, but I could not say, I dared not say. I simply said one word over and over and over again:

"Nightmare."

This pattern of events continued for weeks, if not months. Night after night I would awaken to the sound of rustling sheets. Each time I would scream so as to not provide this abomination with time to prod and "feel" for me. With each cry the bed would shake violently, stopping with the arrival of my mother who would spend the rest of the night in the bottom bunk, seemingly unaware of the sinister force torturing her son nightly.

Along the way I managed to feign illness a few times and come up with other less-than-truthful reasons for sleeping in my parents' bed, but more often than not I would be alone for the first few hours of each night in that place. Alone with that thing.

With time you can become desensitized to almost anything, no matter how horrific. I had come to realize that, for whatever reason, this thing could not harm me when my mother was present. I am sure the same would have been said for my father, but as loving as he was, waking him from sleep was almost impossible.

After a few months I had grown accustomed to my nightly visitor. Do not mistake this for some unearthly friendship; I detested the thing. I still feared it greatly, as I could almost sense its desires and its personality, if you could call it that—one filled with a perverted and twisted hatred yet longing for me, of perhaps all things.

My greatest fears were realized in the winter. The days grew short, and the longer nights merely provided this wretch with more opportunities. It was a difficult time for my family. My grandmother, a wonderfully kind and gentle woman, had deteriorated greatly since the death of my grandfather. My mother was trying her best to keep her in the community as long as possible; however, dementia is a cruel and degenerative illness, robbing its victims of their memories one day at a time. Soon my grandmother recognized none of us, and it became clear that she would need to be moved from her house to a nursing home.

Before she could be moved, my grandmother had a particularly difficult few nights and my mother decided that she would stay with her. As much as I loved my grandmother and felt nothing but anguish at her illness, to this day I feel guilty that my first thoughts were not of her, but of what my nightly visitor might do should it become aware of my mother's absence—her presence being the one thing that I was sure was protecting me from the full horror of this thing's reach.

I rushed home from school that day and immediately wrenched the bed sheets and mattress from the lower bunk, removing all of the slats and placing an old desk, a chest of drawers, and some chairs that we kept in a cupboard where the bottom bunk used to be. I told my father I was "making an office," which he found adorable, but I would be damned if I'd give that thing a place to sleep for one more night.

As darkness approached, I lay there knowing my mother was not in the house. I did not know what to do. My only impulse was to sneak into her jewelry box and take a small family crucifix that I had seen there before. While my family was not very religious, at that age I still believed in God and hoped that somehow this would protect me. Although fearful and anxious, I gripped the crucifix under my pillow tightly in one hand, and sleep eventually came. As I drifted off to dream, I hoped that I would awaken in the morning without incidence. Unfortunately, that night was the most terrifying of all.

I woke gradually. The room was once again dark. As my eyes adjusted I could gradually make out the window and the door, and the walls, some toys on a shelf, and . . . even to this day I shudder to think of it, for there was no noise. No rustling of sheets. No movement at all. The room felt lifeless. Lifeless, yet not empty.

The nightly visitor, that unwelcome, wheezing, hate-filled thing that had terrorized me night after night, was not in the bottom bunk—it was in my bed! I opened my mouth to scream, but nothing came out. Utter terror had shaken the very sound from my voice. I lay motionless. If I could not scream, I did not want to let it know I was awake.

I had not yet seen it; I could only feel it. It was obscured under my blanket. I could see its outline, and I could feel its presence, but I dared not look. The weight of it pressed down on top of me, a sensation I will never forget. When I say that hours passed, I do not exaggerate. Lying there motionless, in the darkness, I was every bit a scared and frightened young boy.

If it had been during the summer months it would have been light by then, but the grasp of winter is long and unrelenting, and I knew it would be hours before sunrise, a sunrise that I yearned for. I was a timid child by nature, but I reached a breaking point, a moment where I could wait no more, where I could survive under this intimately deviant abomination no longer.

Fear can sometimes wear you out, make you threadbare, a shell of nerves leaving only the slightest trace of you behind. I had to get out of that bed! Then I remembered the crucifix. My hand still lay underneath the pillow—but it was empty! I slowly moved my wrist around to find it, minimizing as best I could the sound and vibrations I caused, but it could not be found. I had either knocked it off of the top bunk, or it had . . . I could not even bear to think of it . . . been taken from my hand.

Without the crucifix I lost all sense of hope. Even at such a young age, you can be acutely aware of what death is, and intensely frightened of it. I knew I was going to die in that bed if I lay there, dormant, passive, doing nothing. I had to leave that room behind, but how? Should I leap from the bed and hope that I made it to the door? What if it is faster than me? Or should I slowly slip out of that top bunk, hoping to not disturb my uncanny bedfellow?

Realizing that it had not stirred when I moved, trying to find the crucifix, I began to have the strangest of thoughts.

What if it was asleep?

It hadn't so much as breathed since I had woken up. Perhaps it was resting, believing that it had finally got me, that I was finally in its grasp. Or perhaps it was toying with me; after all, it had been doing just that for countless nights, and now with me under it, pinned against my mattress with no mother to protect me, maybe it was holding off, savoring its victory until the last possible moment. Like a wild animal savoring its prey.

I tried to breathe as shallowly as possible, and mustering every ounce of courage I could, I reached over slowly with my right hand and began to peel the blanket off of me. What I found under those covers almost stopped my heart. I did not see it, but as my hand moved the blanket, it brushed against something. Something smooth and cold. Something that felt unmistakably like a gaunt hand.

I held my breath in terror, as I was sure it must now have known that I was awake.

Nothing.

It did not stir; it felt dead. After a few moments I placed my hand carefully further down the blanket and felt a thin, poorly formed forearm. My confidence and almost twisted sense of curiosity grew as I moved down further to a disproportionately larger bicep muscle. The arm was outstretched lying across my chest, with the hand resting on my left shoulder as if it had grabbed me in my sleep. I realized that I would have to move this cadaverous appendage if I even so much as hoped to escape its grasp.

For some reason, the feeling of torn, ragged clothing on the shoulder of this nighttime invader stopped me in my tracks. Fear once again swelled in my stomach and in my chest as I recoiled my hand in disgust at the touch of straggled, oily hair.

I could not bring myself to touch its face, although I wonder to this very day what it would have felt like.

Dear God, it moved.

It moved. It was subtle, but its grip on my shoulder and across my body strengthened. No tears came, but God how I wanted to cry. As its hand and arm slowly coiled around me, my right leg brushed along the cool wall that the bed lay against. Of all that happened to me in that room, this was the strangest. I realized that this clutching, rancid thing that drew great delight from violating a young boy's bed was not entirely on top of me. It was sticking out from the wall, like a spider striking from its lair.

Suddenly its grip moved from a slow tightening to a sudden squeeze, and it pulled and clawed at my clothes as if frightened that the opportunity would soon pass. I fought against it, but its emaciated arm was too strong for me. Its head rose up writhing and contorting under the blanket. I now realized where it was taking me—into the wall! I fought for my dear life; I cried and suddenly my voice returned to me, yelling, screaming . . . but no one came.

Then I realized why it was so eager to suddenly strike, why this thing had to have me now. Through my window, that window which seemed to represent so much malice from outside, streaked hope—the first rays of sunshine. I struggled further knowing that if I could just hold on, it would soon be gone. As I fought for my life, the unearthly parasite shifted, slowly pulling itself up my chest, its head now poking out from under the blanket, wheezing, coughing, rasping. I do not remember its features; I simply remember its breath against my face, foul and as cold as ice.

As the sun broke over the horizon, that dark place, that suffocating room of contempt was washed, bathed in sunlight.

I passed out as its scrawny fingers encircled my neck, squeezing the very life from me.

I awoke to my father offering to make me some breakfast, a wonderful sight indeed! I had survived the most horrible experience of my life until then, and now. I moved the bed away from the wall, leaving behind the furniture I had believed would stop that thing from taking a bed. Little did I think that it would try to take mine . . . and me.

Weeks passed without incident, yet on one cold, frostbitten night I awoke to the sound of the furniture where the bunk beds used to be vibrating violently. In a moment it passed; I lay there, sure I could hear a distant wheezing coming from deep within the wall, finally fading into the distance.

I have never told anyone this story before. To this day I still break out in a cold sweat at the sound of bed sheets rustling in the night, or a wheeze brought on by a common cold, and I certainly never sleep with my bed against a wall. Call it superstition if you will, but as I said, I cannot discount conventional explanations such as sleep paralysis, hallucination, or an overactive imagination. What I can say is this: The following year I was given a larger room on the other side of the house and my parents took that strangely suffocating, elongated place as their bedroom. They said they didn't need a large room, just one big enough for a bed and a few things.

They lasted ten days. We moved on the eleventh.

The Aftermath

After writing my account of the horrific experience I had as an eight-year-old child, many have encouraged me to speak about the aftermath. I've been hesitant to do so, as I have felt unsettled since I broke my silence. Sleep has not come easily to me these last few nights. My skepticism, however, remains resilient and as such I will tell of what I experienced in the other room.

This won't be as long, as what occurred took place over only a few days, but that was more than enough for me.

If you recall, after that unwelcome nightly visitor left me, I was moved into another bedroom a year later. This room was much larger than the previous one and had a warm and welcoming atmosphere to it. Some places feel bad. The room before felt foul, but this one did not.

Thankfully I was given a normal bed. The previous one was taken apart and thrown out (a welcome sight, I might add). I loved my new room, I enjoyed the space for all of my toys, I was happy that the place was large enough to have my friends drop by, but most of all I was relieved just to be out of that uneasy, foreboding part of the house.

On the first night I slept more soundly than I had done for a long, long time. Of course I still moved my bed several feet from the wall. I told my mother that my friends and I liked to use the gap between the bed and wall as a hiding place when we were playing.

I awoke the next day feeling refreshed and relaxed. As I lay there watching some of my favorite cartoons on a small portable television, I noticed something odd. An old dark brown armchair that had always been there sat at the foot of my bed, large and looming. It was frayed and worn, having been given to us as part of a suite by my cousin, but it had been used many times even by then. The chair itself was not unusual, but what unsettled me was that I could have sworn that before I had gone to sleep, the chair had been facing away from the bed. Now, in the cold light of day, the chair was facing me. I assumed one of my parents had moved it while I slept, probably looking for something that had been left there before we switched rooms.

The second night was not as restful. It was around 11 P.M. and I could hear my parents' television from the other side of the house. The room was largely in darkness, the only illumination an orange hue drifting through my window from the street lights outside. I lay there content. Content, that is, until I heard something quiet, yet unmistakable.

At first I thought it was the sound of my own breath exhaling and inhaling as I rested, but when I stopped for a moment, the quiet, almost inaudible, sound of someone else in the room breathing in and out did not cease. It continued, rhythmically and without pause.

I lay there in the darkness, but while I was still recovering from the terror instilled in me from my experiences in my previous bedroom, I was not entirely afraid. The breathing was so distant and unlike the wheezing I had heard during my encounter with that thing in the wall that I remained calm, and even at that early age I believed that it was so subtle that it was probably my imagination playing tricks on me.

Still, I took no chances; I stepped out of bed, walked across the room, and turned the light on. The sound had gone. I stared at that old worn armchair facing the foot of my bed, within reaching distance of where I slept, and turned it around to face the other way. I had no real reason to do so, but something about it sitting there filled me with dread.

The third night I was not so fearless. Again, I awoke in darkness. Lying on my back I stared up at the ceiling, which seemed to happily absorb the dim orange light from the street. The tree outside my window swayed in a calm breeze, casting a strange collection of improbable moving shadows across the room.

I could hear nothing but the long and distant hum of the city's night traffic. Just as I began to drift back into sleep, I heard something else: a creak from the bottom of my bed, as if something had moved or shifted its weight on the floor.

I raised my head, peering through the darkness, but saw nothing strange. Everything sat as it had throughout the day; nothing was out of place. I cast my gaze across the room: some comics on the floor, a few boxes that still had to be unpacked, the armchair unmoved still facing away from the bottom of my bed. There was nothing sinister here.

I was now fully awake, glancing over at my television and considering whether or not to enjoy some late-night TV. I'd have to keep the volume low, of course, as my older brother would hear it in the next room and no doubt tell me to switch it off.

Just as I sat up fully in bed, I heard it again. A low creak accompanied by another sound, the sound of the slightest of movements. I looked at the room again. The dim orange shadows cast by the leaves hanging by my window now took on a more menacing form.

I still saw no reason to be afraid. I stared at the chair at the end of my bed and saw nothing unusual about it. It's quite common for the mind to take a moment to fully come to terms with what it is seeing. It takes time to put the full horror of what is in front of you together, into a moment of cold, bitter realization.

> Yes, I was staring at that old worn armchair in the dark, but what I was also staring at was the person sitting in it!

In the dim light I could only see the outline of the back of its head; the rest was obscured by the spine of the chair. I sat motionless, staring, praying, hoping that my eyes were being misled by their surroundings. The slow creak of movement as it shifted in its battered throne chilled me to my very core; this was no mere trick of the dark.

Then it shifted onto its right side. I knew what it was doing—it was turning to look at me. It was difficult to make out, for even in that room it seemed darker than everything around it. I saw what looked like a collection of long fingers slip over the crest of the chair, and then another. The room was silent but for the sound of this thing shuffling in its seat, and the crash of my racing heart.

At first I could only make out the outline of its forehead, but then it began to rise up, revealing two pinpoints of light in the dark recesses of its deeply set eye sockets.

It was staring at me.

I screamed, and within a moment my brother and mother came into the room, switching the light on, asking if I'd had another bad dream. I sat speechless, barely acknowledging them, staring intently at the now empty armchair.

I was only in that room for another few days before we suddenly moved. I saw nothing for the remaining nights, except for my last sleep in that room when I awoke to the warm air of something breathing into my ear. I jumped out of bed, turning the light on. The slow rhythmic breath of something unseen remained, louder than before. I spent the rest of that night on the couch in the living room.

For two years after that I slept soundly in my bed, in our new house. There had been no other incidences, and I was sure I had left behind whatever strangeness had plagued me in that little average suburban home.

I was, however, left one parting gift. My tormentors (and in my opinion the watcher in that armchair was a different entity than the thing in the elongated room) had one final surprise in store for me. Like an animal claiming its territory, I was not entirely out of their grasp.

For one last, terrifying moment I felt the presence of those things. I lay there sound asleep, two years since those horrifying experiences. I was in the throes of a nightmare and suddenly, happily found myself awake, safe and sound in my bed. The room was darker than usual. I breathed a sigh of relief as one does when waking from a nightmare.

But the room was so dark.

I could see nothing at all, as if something had snuffed out the light. I chuckled to myself, realizing that I must have pulled my blanket up and over my face while sleeping. The cotton blanket felt cool against me, but the air was a little too warm, almost stifling. Just as I was about to remove the blanket for some air, I heard it:

The rhythmic breathing of the watcher at the end of my bed.

Fear gripped me, followed by anger and despair. Why could I not be left alone? I then did something most peculiar. I decided to speak to it. Perhaps this thing did not mean to harm me, perhaps it was unaware of the terror it had caused. Surely a young boy deserved some mercy?

As the breathing grew louder and closer, I began to cry. I could feel its presence on the other side of the blanket, its breath hanging over me like a stagnant wind.

Through the tears I uttered two words, words that surely would put an end to all of this:

"Please stop."

The breathing began to change; it became more animated, quicker somehow. I could hear something shuffling next to me, standing close by. The breathing then moved, first back to the foot of my bed, and then slowly across the room, through the door, into the hallway, and then gone.

Half crying, half elated, I lay in the silent darkness, my face still covered by the blanket. You may consider this a victory of some sort, but I do not. If those things were real, I know now beyond a shadow of a doubt that their intentions were not misconstrued; they were twisted, filled with malice. I would normally never use such a word to describe anything, but it's as close to evil as I hope I ever come.

How do I know that? I'll tell you how. Moments after that thing seemed to have left the house, something pressed forcefully down on top of me, pushing the blanket with great strength against my face. I could feel a large hand with long thin fingers wrapping the covers around my skull, its nails imprinted upon me like razor-sharp ridges. I managed to slide down into the gap between the bed and the wall, quickly making my escape, clambering and screaming out of my room waking my family.

Make no mistake, that thing in the darkness tried to smother me, smother me to death.

My Fears Realized

A few days ago I submitted two nightmarish accounts from my childhood. For years I had been compelled to silence, gripped by the irrational fear that somehow, even after all these years, if I spoke of it, those things would seek me out and once again wreak havoc on my life.

In the name of science and reason I confronted those fears and set out to vanquish the tormented memories once and for all by sharing them with others, exposing them for what I believed they were: the delusions of a troubled child. I have held on to my skepticism and rationality for dear life, I have allowed them to define me, but this morning I was presented with verifiable, physical evidence. Evidence of what I do not know, but it cannot be ignored, and it seems strange to me that the last few days have been so tainted by apprehension and misfortune after I finally broke my silence that I can no longer rely upon entirely conventional explanations.

In the wake of sharing those traumatic experiences I had as a child, I have been plagued by an overwhelming sense of unease. Initially, I attributed this to the fear I had experienced in simply recounting and reliving those terrible events in my mind, but as the days passed it felt like so much more; a feeling of impending doom consumed my every thought.

While sleep came to me, rest did not. Each morning I awoke, my nerves on edge, as if deprived of sleep for an age. Nothing overtly frightening happened during the first few nights—no visitation, no unwelcome bedfellows, no wheezing breaths reaching out from deep within my bedroom walls—but I had that distantly familiar feeling of not being alone.

Do not misunderstand; I did not sense someone in the room with me. I did not hear, smell, or feel anything remotely supernatural, but throughout my days and nights I have sensed something subtle, almost on the periphery of my awareness: the feeling that something is on its way, something is coming, like the first few stagnant blasts of air from a subway tunnel, heralding the arrival of a lurching, unstoppable monstrosity; surprising, yet expected.

My sense of unease grew with each passing day, pushing its way under my skin, deep into my mind like some form of cancerous infection. I tried to focus my attention on various writing projects in a vain attempt to fill my mind up to the brim with other thoughts, hopefully leaving no room for those contaminated memories, but those memories came to me nonetheless.

My anxiety gained momentum until I could think of nothing else. I had to do something! I had studied psychology for years at university and knew that anxiety is often the result of a loss of control, and that one of the most effective ways to combat it is to empower oneself; this is what I intended to do. Call it foolhardy, but I was going to go back to that place, that house where those terrible events took place. I was going to confront those memories and expose them for what they were: nonsense.

It was an hour's drive to my old home, but it was one filled with elation. I was confident, at ease, happy; I was in control now and nothing was going to get in my way from showing that the place I had feared my entire life was nothing but an average, humdrum, harmless little suburban house.

Gleefully negotiating the country roads and then motorway, finally I made it to the city. Gradually the streets began to take on a familiar appearance. Memories of playing in that neighborhood came flooding back to me: a playground with my favorite slide, an ash pitch where we used to play football, my schoolyard filled with hide-and-seek and friendships long since abandoned, but never forgotten.

My mind wandered through those memories like a prodigal son walking home; it wandered so much that before I realized it, I was pulling into the street where I had once lived. The road was long and disappeared far into the distance, finally entering into a sharp, blind turn. It was an old neighborhood, and had been planned and built long before the advent of the car; this was evident by the narrowness of its roads, which created a strangely claustrophobic feeling, as if the houses on each side rose up leering at passersby.

I slowed my speed and cast my eye over each house that I passed. It was a uniform place, with every house looking not dissimilar. My heart suddenly began to beat faster as a cold chill crawled up my spine; there it was, there was the house! It was late afternoon and the street was quiet, almost lonely. I stared at that little place, wondering how such an ordinary home could have instilled so much fear in me.

I had initially intended to only look at the house from afar, confirming it to me as a material construction, entirely explicable, and removed from anything uncanny. But as I parked I took a deep breath, and before I knew it I was out of my car, walking toward that old, metallic gate, its once bright floral shapes now darkened by aged, flaking deep green paint, revealing nothing but rust beneath. I ran my fingers over its uneven top, and with a subtle gasp, I pushed it open.

Walking along the path, I was shocked at how disused the garden was. I thought to myself how much of a waste of a good lawn it was, all but obscured by a thick mosaic of weeds and other invasive species. But as I neared the house, I realized why: It was unoccupied. Once again a shudder crept through me, but as my anxiety rose up, I crushed it with my rational mantra:

"The simplest of explanations is usually the correct one."

I assumed that due to the current economic climate the house had probably just been on the market for some time, and that the owner wasn't too aware of the old sentiment, "the first bite is with the eye," but as I looked around I could see no "For Sale" sign, nor one "To Let." It genuinely seemed as though this house had been forgotten, abandoned, and left to rot.

The windows at the front of the house were filthy and, as such, almost impossible to see through, but as I wandered around to the back of the building, I could see more clearly inside. I would have imagined that a house such as this one would be empty, but on the contrary, it was entirely occupied, occupied by the trappings of a modern life. I could see a television sitting in the living room corner, a coffee table with magazines strewn across it, various pieces of furniture sitting as if ready to be used, and a couple of coffee cups sitting on the windowsill still full, covered in mold. I would have thought the house was lived in if it was not for a thick layer of dust lying over everything, accompanied by the occasional spider's web.

It seemed as though the most recent occupants had left in a hurry, and never returned.

Clambering through a sea of waist-high grass and bushes, I eventually arrived at that innocuous little window at the back of the house. The very sight of it frightened me, but this was mere memory and not the strange feeling of being watched from within as I had experienced as a child. Peering in, the room looked eerily familiar. I suppose there is little that can be done with a room so small, so oddly narrow, but through the dirt-covered glass the room looked almost unchanged from when I had slept in it. A bed, a set of drawers, and what looked like an assortment of toys on the floor.

A profound sense of anger washed over me momentarily, but I shook it quickly from my mind. The room was clearly that of a child's and the thought of that thing harming another innocent filled me with contempt for such a thought, and within me swelled the desire to protect any child from such an abomination.

As I gazed at that wall, alongside which lay a bed, the hairs on the back of my neck stood up. For a moment (and it was for only the slightest) I thought I saw the blanket on top of the bed move. More than that, through that windowpane I could have sworn I heard a wheezing gasp. Closing my eyes tightly I repeated another scientific mantra:

"Science does not owe its debts to imagination."

Opening my eyes I saw nothing but an empty bedroom. No foul spirits, no unearthly things; just a room, no more, no less. I breathed a sigh of relief that all was well with the world for the first time in many days. You may think that it was wishful thinking, but I genuinely felt that I had shown myself that there was nothing to be scared of, other than my overactive imagination.

It was starting to get dark and I wanted to be home before the night. Filled with confidence that my anxieties were behind me, there was one last thing I needed to do. When we had left that house we did so in a hurry. As a child it was disorientating, even frightening, to leave everything I knew behind, but there was one thing left that I always wondered about.

At the bottom of the garden stood a sycamore tree that looked to be even older than the house. I was amazed at how unchanged it was. I had grown up, gone on to pastures new, but the old sycamore still stood, wise, warm, almost friendly in its appearance.

I think it's a rite of passage for any child to have a place to hide things. It's often his or her first experience with independence, something removed from any authority figure. For me, my "stash" was halfway up the old sycamore. I'm sure I must have looked like a fool, but I happily and gleefully climbed the tree with abandon. The configuration of the branches had changed in places, but overall the happy memories of playing among the limbs of the old sycamore, of having a little piece of the world to myself away from everyone else, seemed vivid as it was remarkable how much remained unchanged.

Halfway up I caught my breath and smiled to myself. In the central trunk of the tree lay a hollow. Whether it had been created by an animal or perhaps the tug of a gale on a weakened branch long ago, I do not know, but it was where I kept things. If I found something that I was sure would be taken from me for being "inappropriate," into the hollow it would go. The truth is, though, that the majority of the items inside were not very interesting, mostly just toys, and rarely exotic pieces of contraband like a slingshot or some smoke bombs. I had no reason to hide the toys, but when I was young it felt adventurous to have a secret.

The hollow was dark and filled halfway with rotting leaves, no doubt deposited there from countless autumns; nevertheless, I reached deep inside to see what remained. I couldn't believe it! I had found a toy that I had hidden there before we moved, all those years ago! I could feel the plastic in my hand, its sharp edges unmistakable, but the leaves and darkness of the hollow obscured its view from me as I struggled to remove it from the thick, wet mixture of rotting leaves and rainwater. It seemed to be caught among a collection of small twigs.

The reason I was so excited was that I knew when we moved that I had left one of my favorite toys behind, a small plastic First World War British soldier. It may not sound like much, but I had grown up on my family's stories of my grandfather's adventures during both wars, and though he had passed away before I was born, I would often act out exaggerated versions of the stories with this small soldier in the role of the hero: my intrepid grandfather. At the time I thought a hollow the perfect hiding place for a soldier.

My delight, however, quickly turned to horror. I felt sick to my stomach, for as I pulled the soldier out, I realized it was not my toy, but something else entirely. Stuffed into the back of the hollow among the sludge, and now in my hand, were the skeletal remains of a small animal. The bones crunched together in my grip as the few small flakes of hair and putrefied flesh left on it stuck to my fingers. I almost lost my balance as the rotten and potent smell of death escaped through my moist grasp, invading my senses.

I climbed back down carefully, dejected. There was nothing else in the hollow; my toy was gone, probably taken by another child during the subsequent years. What remained of the poor animal, I buried under some loose earth in the garden.

I left that place immediately.

Despite my unfortunate encounter in the hollow I still felt empowered. That I had actually plucked up the courage to revisit that place, to see how ordinary it really was, made me feel in control once more of my faculties. I did not at that time require anything other than a conventional explanation.

I said goodbye to the old neighborhood, to that bad memory once and for all, and began to make my way home. By the time I had driven onto the motorway, something had begun to filter through from the back of my subconscious. At first I disregarded it, dismissing it as my imagination, but as the sun shone its last and dipped below the horizon, I sensed the growing of a compulsion in me, an idea that seemed to have been born and nurtured for no good reason. No rationale, no sound causal footing, but one that had to be followed, at all cost . . .

I must get home!

I increased my speed, zipping sporadically between the slower cars on the motorway, looking in the rearview mirror, keeping an eye on what might be following.

I had to get home!

Again, I drove faster, constantly looking behind as if racing some unseen pursuer: 70, 80, 100 miles per hour! I tore along the road, I beeped, I yelled, the sweat lashed off of me. What was happening to me?

Please, just let me go home!

White-knuckled, I finally made it off of the motorway and onto the country roads that would lead directly to my town. The roads were narrow and wound around the now bleak and ominous countryside. Darkness seemed to blanket the road in front of me. I turned my high beams on and breathed a sigh of relief to see a bright light again, even if artificial. The manic anxiety that had seemed to grip me on the motorway appeared to have diminished; however, I still glared into the rearview mirror more often than I should have, just to make sure that there was nothing following me.

What a ridiculous thought! To think of something chasing my car! To put myself and others in danger by speeding down a busy motorway . . . Madness!

Still, madness or not, I had felt compelled to get away as quickly as possible, and even though I had managed to collect my nerves, the loneliness of the road I was on fueled my yearning for my own town, my own street, my own bed!

Nervously, I traversed the web-like winding roads that seared through the countryside, feeling relieved at the first sign of a lamppost, of civilization, and of the boundaries of my town. I pulled up outside my house, switched the engine off, and sat for a moment in silence. I had to stop all of this nonsense! Things coming out of walls, watchers smothering me at night, looking into someone's window like a prowler—all of this was lunacy!

Tomorrow, I would start afresh, no more writing about my childhood experiences, no more reliving of dread-filled nights. Just getting back to normal, carrying out my work, spending time with my girlfriend, and most of all reaffirming my belief, faith, and confidence in science and rationality.

Then the thing in the backseat leaned over, grabbed me by the shoulder, and breathed a foul, rancid breath from deep inside its lungs down the back of my neck.

I scrambled for the door, my arms flailing around looking for the lock. Fear possessed me, shook me—a fear I remembered all too well, a fear from all those years ago, lying awake at night in that sickening room. The inside of the car had grown much colder, but that was nothing compared to the icy fingers burrowing into my shoulder.

I honestly thought I was going to die, that this thing would finally get its way after all this time.

The door handle popped in my panicked grip and I fell out of the driver's seat onto the pavement. For the briefest of moments I thought I caught a glimpse of something in the backseat: vague, the form of an old man, yet twisted and distorted and grinning from ear to ear. Luckily there was no one around, as had there been I would have appeared a mad fool, for the car was empty. I grabbed the keys from the ignition and booted the door shut with my foot, locking it for the night.

I staggered down the path and into my house. I'm not going to lie to you: I drank myself to sleep that night. You may recall that I said I had evidence, actual physical evidence, of something unnatural. You might be wondering what that evidence is. Well, I could say that it was the marks on my shoulder that made me shudder with fear, or I could tell you that finding my bedroom window pried open this morning and claw marks on the sill has left me dreading tonight, or any other night. But no, none of that scared me as much as what I saw today upon waking.

Sometimes the most frightening of messages are the most simple, for lying on my chest as I awoke this morning was a toy soldier, the soldier I had hidden in that hollow all those years ago; returned to me as an adult, bitten in half.

Something Wicked This Way Comes

Last night was the most heart-wrenching and frightening of my life, so much so that I can barely bring myself to contemplate it.

By now I will have submitted what occurred during my visit to that cursed place I once called home; a visit that heralded the return of my childhood fears. No matter what foul thing befell me then, nothing could have prepared me for last night.

After waking up to the chilling sight of that toy soldier, bitten in half, I found that the window to my bedroom was slightly ajar. On closer inspection it looked as if the window had been pried open from outside. The latches were bent back, out of position as if subjected to an unrestricted, unbound brute force.

From the outside looking in, I could see three indentations where the unwelcome housebreaker had used some kind of tool to leverage the window unnaturally away from its latch. What was peculiar about those markings was that they seemed to cut across the outside of the window frame like an old uneven razor, unlike a crowbar or other implement that would have merely left a dent where it had been used as a wedge to force the window open.

Nothing had been stolen and I attempted to rationalize the markings on the window as human-made, and not "claw-like" as they appeared to be. The toy soldier, returned to me so violently, I could not explain. My heart sank at the very thought of it.

I knew it was a message, but it seemed to me to be more of a twisted joke, announcing the arrival of my childhood predator, rather than something to be puzzled over or interpreted.

I spent the morning checking each room of my house and its contents; nothing was missing. I could only hope that whatever that fiend had been in the backseat of my car the previous night, it had only wished to frighten me one last time and then be on its way.

Perhaps its reach would be weakened so far from my childhood bedroom.

It is all too easy for any sane person to persuade himself that a traumatic event is something more benign, but in this instance I could not; that broken toy was not a mere joke, but a promise. A promise that it would return; for what, I did not wish to know.

My thoughts naturally tumbled inward and back to those terrifying nights I had as a child. I was now re-introduced to the apprehension of bedtime, the longing for the day, and the anxiety of night. Like an old and relentless enemy, my fear grew throughout the day, festering inside of me, leading to strange and ominous thoughts about the consequences of unwittingly bringing that thing home.

Do not misunderstand me; my fear was not simply for my own safety. As a child I believed that my nightly visitor was transfixed and consumed by wanting me, but I did not feel that my loved ones were in any danger. This, however, had changed. I did worry. This time I did feel fear for my loved ones, because, you see, I do not live alone.

My girlfriend and I moved in together over two years ago. I have caused enough damage now that I do not wish to speak her name and will simply refer to her as "Mary." Mary and I had had a happy existence, and in fact, we were very much in love. This coming Christmas morning I was going to propose to her, but that beautiful moment has now been taken away from me by that rancid abomination.

I knew that Mary would be home that evening. She works in events and promotion and as a result is often away from home for days at a time, traveling around the country coordinating various conferences and exhibitions. I do not complain about this, as she and I both know that I am a solitary character, and that the odd few days of solitude normally do me good, allowing me to dive headlong into my writing, absorbing each and every word, undisturbed.

Despite this, I always miss her, and with the events of the past week, reliving those torturous nights and then allowing them to return, I had missed her far more acutely than I had ever done previously.

She arrived at around 6 P.M. and I greeted her with a smile, a warm embrace, and a passionate kiss. I tried to hide my perturbed state of mind from her, but Mary knows me better than anyone I have ever met and immediately inquired:

"What's wrong?"

I tripped and fumbled through my words as I explained to her that I had written a story about my childhood and that exploring those dark and twisted memories had left me distraught. Mary has an incredibly caring nature and she immediately laid her suitcase and bags on the floor, sat me down on our couch, and in her soft and gentle way, asked me to talk about the whole ordeal.

But I couldn't!

I couldn't mention this thing, this wretch that had now found its way to our home, an invisible and twisted invader that had been led there by my idiotic curiosity! At the time I felt that she would think me mad, but now how I wish I had told her the truth!

If there is one thing more damaging to a relationship than a lie, it is a half-truth. Not because it is deceitful, but because it is a corruption of the truth, perverted and abused to suit the teller's needs.

I told her my half-truth.

I told her about my story, of the thing in the narrow room and the watcher at the end of my bed, but that is where the truth ended and a lie began. I deliberately and deceitfully mentioned that it was of course just my imagination as a child, and neglected to talk of my experiences of returning to the scene of those depraved crimes. Knowing that she would see the damaged window latch and claw marks, I spun my web as I told a grand tale about waking up to a burglar attempting to break into our house, and having to chase him away.

I was quite the hero. I lied to her, and she showed me great sympathy and kindness for my deception.

I was embarrassed by the truth then, and I am ashamed of my lie now. If I had been truthful, then perhaps we could have faced this menace together, but instead that thing took advantage of my dishonesty and put a wedge between us.

> The events of last night desecrated the most important thing in the world to me.

Nighttime arrived in all of its bleakness, and was unwelcome. I lay in the darkness, waiting. Mary was sound asleep next to me, each breath a soothing reminder of companionship, but despite my growing aversion to loneliness, I would have no sleep that night. I knew from experience that when my uninvited guest showed itself, it would do so with subtlety, increasing its grip on me with each visitation as if requiring time to build up its strength—a leech feeding on my fear for succor.

My nerves kept me on edge, which fought back the oncoming onslaught of sleep admirably. In the end, though, biology won, and as my bedside clock lumbered toward 4 A.M., sleep took me; the relaxing blanket of nightly oblivion, anxiety washed away, my worries a distant memory, sinking deeper into the soft mattress below and finally into a long-sought-for rest.

Sleep, no matter how deep, is rarely all-encompassing. For as I hovered over the cusp of a dream, something began to bother me. Something invasive, yet distant. I slowly opened my eyes and allowed them to adjust to the darkness.

Mary lay soundly asleep and I calmed myself by listening to her breathing in the night. Inhale was followed by exhale, again and again, rhythmically, hypnotically. I began to drift toward sleep once more.

But, no. There it was, something else, distinct yet indefinable.

It was distant, out of the way, almost obscured or smothered as if coming from . . . behind something. I strained my ears in an attempt to define it, but it was all too quiet. I remained in the bed for several more minutes, but with each passing second that almost inaudible sound grated on me, like broken glass on a raw nerve.

Sleep was now abandoned, and with much frustration I decided to reluctantly investigate the source of the noise. I sat up in the bed and listened intently. It was unlike any other sound I had ever heard. Quiet, low, but as my mind adjusted to the noise I slowly began to piece its nature together. It was most certainly obscured by something, but the closest thing I could relate it to . . . was a repetitive murmur.

I had heard something similar when I was a child visiting my grandmother in a nursing home. The place had made an impression on me as I watched the wandering residents, confused and of fractured mind, meandering around the grounds like lost inmates, murmuring repetitively to themselves of days gone past, repeating nonsensical phrases and words.

This is what it reminded me of: a continuous stream of indecipherable words, uttered by someone in the throes of confusion.

I turned to check on Mary, watching her chest rise and fall with each breath. Assured that she was undisturbed, I left the bed. As I stood up I recognized immediately that the murmuring was louder. Although it was dark, I had left a light on in the hall as I always do, which crept under the door and allowed me to view the room, if in a dim way.

I looked around to see if anything was out of place, but the room appeared as expected. My mind ambled back to that night as a child in the second room, when noises could be heard from some unseen, yet ever-present menace.

I took a step forward and as I did so the noise once again grew in volume. While I was still at a loss to decipher the words, I could now hear the character of the voice. It was old, scratched by age, with a harsh, guttural undertone to it. The words were being repeated at a frantic pace and seemed anxious, yet muffled by some unknown barrier.

I was frightened, but I drew strength from Mary being in the room, and with a deep breath filled with trepidation, I took another slow and silent step forward, my bare feet cushioned by the cold floor below.

Again, the voice became louder. I wasn't sure if I was imagining it, but I could have sworn that it had become more agitated as I drew closer. The next step I took shook me to my very core, for as that murmuring, garbled voice grew louder still, among the rambling, graveled sound of it I heard a word. A word that shot an icy shudder through my bones. A word to be feared.

It spoke my name.

Dear God, it knew my name! To me it was as if knowing who I was somehow endowed that thing with an unlimited reach. That I may never be rid of it. That it could kill me at any moment.

Something suddenly caught my eye, a movement accompanied by a ruffle of cloth. I knew now where that rhythmic, agitated voice originated. I knew now why it was muffled and difficult to decipher. I could now see it, only a few feet in front of me.

Standing.

Standing behind the closed curtains.

The moon was in its ascendancy outside, and while its glimmer could not entirely penetrate the thick cloth, it could barely, and faintly, outline the thing watching between my window and the curtains. I cannot now convey the strangeness that then overcame me. My anxiety and terror had heightened, but an unusual compulsion, an untimely sense of purpose took me over.

I had to see what it was.

I took another tentative step toward the curtains. They swayed slightly as if caught by a breeze, but I could not tell whether the movement had been caused by myself or by the hand of that thing hiding behind a shroud of cloth. I was now close enough to hear its labored breathing, the displacement of fluid at the back of its throat palpable with each inhalation.

This was it.

I was going to confront this monstrosity from my past, this tormentor of children, this coward. Raising my right hand slowly, I accidentally touched the fabric of the curtains, causing a subtle ripple that parted them momentarily. I gasped, for through that temporary slit, only for a moment, I saw it.

My God, how can I describe what was standing there? Even now, I close my eyes and wish that I could erase it from my memory. It shivered and shook as it continued to murmur, repeating some indecipherable phrase, sounding like a bizarre mixture of numerous languages. Its emaciated skin stretched over an unnatural frame of brittle and prominent bones; vertebrae, ribs, and other inner workings nearly protruded through its paper-thin, pale, languidly pink, and almost bruised-looking husk.

As malnourished as it appeared, the stomach was distended in places and its bony appearance did nothing to diminish the feeling that it was capable of exerting itself with brute, perverted force on any of its victims.

Sickness swelled in my stomach, a tainted, offensive smell filled the air, and as it murmured and whispered in the darkness through what sounded like broken, fractured teeth, I could not help but feel pity for this wretch, quivering in the night as if victim of a long starvation.

I quickly came to my senses and realized that this thing was not to be pitied, but feared. Not to be understood, but exposed. It was not shivering because it was cold; it was shaking with excitement, like a drug addict anticipating his next dose.

Standing there contemplating what I had just seen between the curtains, I once again prepared myself to remove its shrouded, clothed protection and to reveal it for what it was: a cold-hearted vandal, a prowler of the worst kind, a deviant festering in its own delectation.

As I once again raised my hand to draw the curtain, something caught my attention. Its incessantly confused, gravelly, and inarticulate whispers squeezed through that broken mouth and uttered the three most terrifying words I have ever heard:

"Look behind you."

A cold breath slid down the back of my neck.

Momentarily I froze, but love is a powerful motivator. Had I been on my own, fear would have taken me, shaking any possibility of resistance from my mind—but with Mary sleeping soundly in the same room as that thing, shielding someone I loved from that wretch was my only thought.

I turned around slowly, and as I did so, I could hear it wheezing, gasping, groaning for air. At a quarter turn, I could smell its breath; the stench of death hung in the air, plague-like and foul. Then I heard another voice. It was not that horror in the darkness, but Mary. She let out a scream that startled and distressed me to my very core. A scream that will haunt me for the rest of my days.

I turned quickly and laid eyes on it, but it wasn't behind me, it was on the bed! It writhed and rasped, wheezing in delight, its bony spine curved with the anguish of countless years protruding through a ragged, torn piece of cloth that hung loosely over its torso, in a vain attempt to appear almost human.

But was it human? Had it once been human? Or was it something so vile, so despicable, so utterly and sorrowfully contemptible that no man or woman could ever attempt to quantify or understand it?

I sprung forward toward it, grabbing, hitting, pulling at that thing with every ounce of my strength. Its loose skin slipped through my hands. It squeezed and forced Mary's face into her pillow with glee, as its other limbs arched and contorted, tearing at her nightdress, running its long, starved fingers over her naked body with its sordid caress.

Mary's screams were muffled by the pillow and I began to fear that she was being suffocated.

I shouted, I yelled, I pleaded with that thing to leave her alone, to take me, to do anything it wanted, but that only served to animate the fiend to even greater depths of depravity. It was hurting her, cutting her . . . my beautiful Mary.

Suddenly it stopped attacking her, but it still kept one of its brittle, gangly, and gaunt yet weighted hands on the back of Mary's head, pushing her face further into her pillow. I had my hands around its putrid neck, trying as best I could to strangle the beast, but my efforts were in vain. Its scrawny frame belied its overpowering strength. I watched in sickly disbelief as it began to run its cadaverous fingers through Mary's hair, slowly, and almost with affection.

I could now hear the twisting and cracking of bone, the popping of cartilage, the snapping of tendons.

Thank God it was not coming from Mary! I was now on its back with my arm wrapped around its throat, and my chin rubbing against the abrasive skin of its shoulder. As its spine dug sharply into my stomach, it twisted its head in an entirely inhuman way. Its neck clicked and groaned under the strain with every arthritic movement, as if hindered by a thousand years of rigor mortis.

It was now looking at me.

I have heard it often said of some people that they cannot see the forest for the trees, but now I truly appreciate that sentiment. So close was I to its black, icy stare that I could not take in its surrounding features.

I increased my grip, I swore, I screamed, I would have torn its throat out if I could have, but my actions were all in vain as it continued to run its scrawny fingers through Mary's hair nonchalantly while looking at me.

I don't think I will ever truly recover from the sound that seeped out through what I assumed to be its approximation of a grin: a wheezing sigh; a grunt; something that sounded very close to a sinister, otherworldly laugh.

As its face touched mine, its eyes stared deep into me. Not even my reflection was returned; two looking glasses into a sanctuary for the dark, devoid of light, happiness, and love. It was staring as if it wished to say something, as if it was trying to communicate a simple idea to me.

Malice.

With a wrenching, stuttered, and violent movement, it tore an entire fistful of hair from Mary's head, leaving behind it an open wound. Then it was gone. Mary did not scream; she merely whimpered. I turned the bedside lamp on, but no words of care or sympathy could console her.

She wept uncontrollably.

The bed was soaked in blood that had seeped out from the numerous scratches on her back and the large cut where an entire section of her hair had once been. I hugged her and told her that everything would be all right; then she looked at me.

Looking at her tear-filled eyes I knew what she thought immediately. She thought I had attacked her, that I had done those terrible things to her. Of all the experiences I have had, the look of betrayal, disgust, and contempt on Mary's face will remain the most painful.

She is gone.

After composing herself, she gathered up some things and left. I tried to explain, I tried to tell her everything that had been happening, but she would not listen. Who would believe such a preposterous story? She simply said that she would not call the police, but that if I ever attempted to contact her, she would do just that. To her, I was the aggressor, not that thing. As she left, she turned to look at me one last time and then burst in to tears.

I know now that I have lost her forever. The woman I love more than anything on this earth thinks I am a violently hideous human being. If only she could understand that whatever did this was not human, and if it ever was, it had long since abandoned that nature.

It was 5 A.M. when Mary left me; it's 9 A.M. now. I am sitting here in the cold light of day at my kitchen table, writing this so that there is some record of what has transpired, so that people know, so that Mary knows, that whatever happens, that whatever occurs from here on in, that it was that despicable creature from my childhood, from that cursed narrow room all those years ago, that rained this misery down upon me, upon us.

I must now dispense with the sentiment. I could easily sit here mourning the loss of my relationship with Mary, or I could allow myself to be overcome with fear, to do nothing. But that simply will not do.

I can hear the laughter of my neighbor's children outside. At different stages in my life, I remember that same feeling of joy and happiness from something as simple as playing with friends, or climbing a tree, or kissing the woman you love, or even drifting off to sleep at bedtime to dream of what could be, in the safety of a happy family home. Memories, only memories . . . I fear I will never experience that happiness again. This thing has broken me. But I am resolute. Whatever that hideous wretch has in store, whatever it desires to do with me, I will not allow that thing to harm another person, or to invade another child's life as it did mine all those years ago.

I must leave you all now as there is much to be done before it gets dark, before it returns. My plans are made and with any luck they will succeed. I wish I could say we will speak again, but I think that is unlikely. I hope you understand what must be done.

Because tonight, I'm going to kill it.

Sleep Tight

I am shaking as I write this. I was released by the police less than two hours ago and I am compelled to record the events of the past day and night as quickly and as accurately as possible. In some ways I want to forget, but I know that I cannot, I know that I should not.

For my own sanity I must divulge what has happened; it is far too important. Should I ever allow myself to be swayed by the mechanical, rational nature of the world once again, these words should serve to remind me that what is unseen is both mysterious and frightening.

After Mary left, I knew that I had lost her forever, but rather than be consumed by depression and inaction, I was invigorated by one purpose, by one thought, by one idea that I knew I had to carry out. I had to destroy that thing, for I could not allow the chance that it may one day hurt my loved ones, or desecrate the innocence of another child.

I also knew that I faced death, but feeling that I had already lost everything, that was a small price to pay. It is said that revenge is a dish best served cold, but having waited my entire adult life to be rid of this thing, its memory, and the shadow that it had cast upon me, I met the proposition of killing this fiend, this corrupt and perverted force, with a smile on my face.

That night it would be dead even if I had to drag it to hell with me.

Busying myself for the next few hours, I packed a bag and wrote a letter to Mary and my family explaining what had happened and that they weren't to blame. I phoned my mother and father, then my brother, just to hear their voices one last time, but I did not let on that I thought I might never speak to them again. My mother's intuition led her to ask if everything was all right; I smiled and told her I loved her before reluctantly saying goodbye.

At about 7 o'clock I made my way out to the car. The sun had already set and the street seemed eerily quiet, as if the scene of an unattended funeral. I sat in the driver's seat and left the door on the other side open, awaiting my most unwelcome passenger.

By 9 o'clock nothing out of the ordinary had occurred, the place remained deserted, and the cold night air flowing through the open door was beginning to bite. As I sat there, contemplation echoed through my mind. I ruminated on the nature of this cadaverous parasite. One question rose out of a sea of thoughts, towering above all else, unmoving, and continuous:

"Can you kill something that is already dead?"

I did not know if this was a thing of the grave, or some unworldly specter that could be considered "alive" in some way, but just as I was re-evaluating my plan, there it was. It was subtle at first, but there was a small, almost indistinguishable shift in the suspension of the car. Had it been any other circumstance, I would have put this down to a gust of wind pushing and pulling at the chassis, but I was all too familiar with that feeling from all those years ago, as the bunk bed would shift slightly with that thing climbing into the bottom bed. I knew its foul calling card. The air grew denser as if contaminated by some nearby corpse.

It was in the car with me—unseen, yes, but there nonetheless. As I heard the slightest of whispered breaths from the backseat, I leaned over and calmly closed the passenger door. I turned the key in the ignition and as I pulled out of the street, I could have sworn I heard a quiet yet distinctly malicious snigger, as of something mocking me.

Did it know what I had planned for it?

Our destination was not far, but the roaming hills through which our taken country road penetrated rose up and diminished with regularity, a stark reminder of the ominous isolation of night. Occasionally on the way I could hear something from behind, but I refused to look for that thing in the dark. Patience; it would not be long before I would confront it.

The irony hit me: I was worried about scaring off the same thing that had terrified and tortured me as a child. I had to be resilient, so I drove carefully and calmly through the countryside, swamped by darkness, hoping that my unearthly passenger would not suspect me.

I arrived.

The wheels of the car struggled and slid on the undergrowth as I headed off of the narrow country road. The landscape had opened up, and as I looked at the broken and rotting trees around me, I felt that it was fitting to come to this bleak place in the cold night, to destroy that bleakest of things.

The land suddenly came to an abrupt end; a cliff etched out from an old quarry, looking deep into the black waters of the lake below. The cliff edge was relatively flat and had in fact at one time housed a road that had subsided into the lake decades earlier. The local kids would tell stories about the vengeful ghosts of those killed during the subsidence, but they were just stories. Or perhaps they weren't. In the past I would have disregarded such tales, but who would believe mine if I told it to them now?

I switched the engine off and parked several meters away from the cliff edge, switching off any lights and composing myself for what would come. I sat in that car for what seemed a lifetime, the only company given to me being the occasional splash of water against the cliff below.

I waited.

This thing was smart, of that there was no doubt. It had toyed with me, relishing the pain and torment it had caused as only something of a coldly frozen intellect could. For this reason I knew it would suspect me, and perhaps even flee if I brought the car too close to the cliff's edge. I had to wait for it to attack, let it feed, let it revel and gorge itself on me; perhaps then it would not notice as I slowly plunged the car into that dark, icy water below.

I was going to drown the bastard.

I had appraised the potential consequences in my head and reasoned that there would be a moment, a singular moment where I would have a slim opportunity to escape from the car just before it reached the edge. Mary and I used to go there occasionally, a place to be together away from everything else, and it did not look nearly as stark during a summer's day. I therefore had the place in mind and knew it well. The drop was at least thirty feet to the depths below and I did not want to be in that car as it hit the water, nor trapped inside with that abomination.

I waited.

Then I heard it. Slowly at first, and then increasing in rate and volume, a rasping, wheezing breath from behind. Strangely, it sounded more labored than before. Each breath a struggle, filled with fluid, rotten, and decayed. A shiver ran up my spine. A rank, foul smell began to fill the air.

The breath drew closer from behind.

My heart began to race, beating hard and fast as I looked up and saw the windshield begin to ice up from inside. I could see my breath, a natural thing indeed, but what was unnatural was the breath visibly moving across my face from the side. I turned slowly, I wanted to cry, I wanted to leave, run into the night, but I had to stay, I could not allow it to escape.

It was sitting in the passenger seat.

I was staring at it, and it at me. Hunched over, covered by darkness, contorted, gaunt, hands seized as if fighting rigor mortis, it slowly moved toward me. One bony leg cracked and groaned as it slid over my lap and onto the other side.

Oh God, it was sitting on me!

It pulled itself in close to me and, through a shard of light provided by the moon, I saw its face. Skin hung from its jagged features. Glassy eyes stared deep into me as its grin spread up through its face, unnaturally wide as the result of its half-rotten flesh, exposing the rotten muscles, broken teeth, and sinews of its rancid smile beneath.

Pulling closer, it opened its mouth, revealing a wet and putrid tongue that could be seen through part of its missing jaw. Wheezing, breathing heavily, it emitted a foul stench that stung my eyes and filled my mouth and made me retch as my body attempted to expel the poisonous fumes. As I did so it stopped for a moment, then cackled to itself, happy, content. Yet staring into its icy cold eyes, I got the impression of an afflicted and increasingly weak old man. It was still incredibly strong, but it seemed as though it had lost some of its potency.

Perhaps leaving that elongated room had somehow affected it?

Its long protruding fingers caressed my face and then, as a show of intent, it stuck one of them deep into my shoulder. I screamed as it bent and twisted inside of me, the rotting fiend moving its finger to cause the maximum amount of damage and pain that it could. As it did so, its other hand slid down against my body.

It touched me.

It was time. With my free arm I turned on the ignition, and though my shoulder was still pinned to the seat I managed to fight through the pain, put the car into gear, and take off as fast as I could.

The creature flailed and screamed. It attempted to climb over me into the backseat, but I held on with all of my strength, the thoughts of what it did to Mary enough to fuel my rage. We raced toward the edge of the cliff and I eyed the driver's door frantically. As we neared our icy plunge, I screamed in anger at its festering, rancid face and pushed it off of me.

It scrambled into the backseat for dear life as I scrambled for mine by unlocking the car door.

It was too late. The car careered over the cliff face, and before I knew it, we hit the dark water, splitting the black glass-like surface with tremendous force. I should have died then, but an airbag took the brunt of my impact, although I still managed to scrape my head across the door frame.

Dazed, I looked around. The sound that I heard coming from that thing was malformed yet familiar. The squeal of some demonic child soon gave way to the anguish and rage of an ancient intelligence that knew it faced almost certain death.

The water was freezing cold and poured in through the now twisted open car door with such force that it winded me. I gasped for air, as my unwilling prey now did. It writhed and twisted as it looked for an exit. Spying the open door, it pulled itself through the water toward me.

I curled up my fist and smashed it into that thing's face. Pieces of rotten flesh flaked off under the impact as a dark black liquid oozed from the resulting wound.

Again it attempted to get past me and I knew that to keep it in the car long enough to drown, I would have to die with it. I felt numb as the frozen water slipped over my chin; my heart struggled against the cold, and with a sudden surge I was submerged and had breathed my last.

I held my breath, but only to compose and ready myself for an icy, suffocating death. I hoped that it would not be painful. My thoughts returned to Mary and my family; an all-consuming sense of sadness and despair overwhelmed me, but as I struggled with that thing trying to get past me and through the door, grabbing and flailing with its arms, I looked down and saw it.

Its leg was trapped between the dashboard and floor of the car by the impact of the fall, and although it could move, it could not leave.

I turned immediately for the door. I could barely see but a foot in front of me in that black water, but there was enough moonlight to light my way. Just as I got to the door, the wretch grabbed hold of me and pulled me back to it. It had given up all hope of escaping, but it wanted to drown me with it.

We fought for what felt like an age in that cold bitter grave as the car slowly sank deeper and deeper into the darkness. I could now feel my body pleading with me to take a breath, to exhale my last gasp of air and then inhale the frozen water.

I am happy to say that I used my wits to get out of such a horrible fate. Orientating my body, I pushed my feet against the dashboard with enough force to at last escape the thing's slippery grasp. I do not remember much else, bar the anguished and hate-filled scream that my tormentor let out as I left it to die at the bottom of that icy lake.

I found myself walking through the wilderness, cold, wet, but alive. The wound in my shoulder slowed me down, but I kept the bleeding at bay by applying pressure to it with my other hand. It took me two hours to walk home, and I am amazed that I did not collapse from exhaustion or hypothermia. When I saw the familiar sight of the street that I live on, I was filled with a sense of accomplishment. A sense of pride and triumph.

I had beaten that thing once and for all!

That is, until I went inside my house and found a trail of large, wet footprints leading from the front door to my bed.

Disbelief took me. Despair so sharp and so overwhelming that I am unable to convey it with mere words. It was lying in my bed, waiting, a white sheet covering its emaciated body from sight.

The human mind is a wonderful thing. Just as you believe your body has reached a level of exhaustion that it cannot recover from, that your emotions are so frayed that you feel you cannot continue, a thought springs as if miraculous from a weary mind.

Let it rest, for now.

I quietly crept through the dark and picked up my wallet, which I had left on a small coffee table in the center of my living room. Leaving the door unlocked, I exited to attend to a new plan; I returned an hour later. With a moment's preparation I slipped into the spare room.

There I lay in that unsullied bed, waiting. I was sure that this was the end game, that instead of toying with me, it would come for the kill. How it had escaped that watery grave I did not know, but I would be damned if it would escape again. I could only hope that it would sense me from the other room.

I closed my eyes, pretending to be sound asleep. Time lumbered onward and although I fought it, exhaustion finally took me, sending me into a deep slumber.

I woke with its hands around my neck. It coughed and spluttered on top of me, a rancid black liquid dripping on my face as it oozed from the thing's facial wounds. I struggled, gasping for air and hoping that I had the strength in me to escape its grasp, but it was too strong and my hands could not grip it with any sense of conviction, as it seemed to be dripping wet from its plunge into the lake.

It may not have seemed rational at the time, but as my vision dimmed and the last light of consciousness extinguished within me, I did as so many animals do in their last moments; I played dead.

While I lay motionless, holding my breath, it shook me violently by the neck and then released me. I waited for my moment, my last chance to destroy this thing. Its labored breathing relaxed slightly and seemed to stare at me almost quizzically.

I waited still for a shift of weight that might have let me throw it to the ground.

Leaning down close to me, its wide, crumbling sneer puckered. Gathering its putrid saliva in its mouth and in what was left of its cheeks, it then showed utter contempt for the living, and the dead; it spat its festering fluid onto my face, the remnants dripping down onto me through a hole in its jaw.

I wanted to scream, to do anything to remove such a vile smear on my skin, but I dared not move; the time was not right. Leaning in closer, it prodded and scratched at the wound in my shoulder, the pain shearing through my body. With all of my resistance, I remained motionless.

Then, it slowly and patiently slid two of its long, distended fingers into my mouth. The taste was overwhelming, rancid, rotten, dead. The arthritic clicking of its knuckles shook my resolve. As it arched its back in glee, it suddenly pushed its fingers deep down into my throat.

I gagged, an instinctive reaction.

Instead of being shocked, a garbled laugh emanated through its broken teeth as it thrust its fingers deeper into my mouth. I felt its cold, hard flesh scraping against the inside of my throat pleading without words for it to stop.

In our darkest of moments, we sometimes find our true strength. I rolled to my side using its weight against it and finally managed to break free. I fell onto the floor. Its long reach grasping at my feet, I kicked and screamed and at last was free. It stared at me, only for a moment. Rising up on top of the bed, its brittle bones cracking under its own force, it now towered tall and gaunt ready to pounce.

Since I was a child I had been a victim. It had terrorized me, taken my innocence, attacked Mary, and broken my life.

I would not stand for it any more.

Sometimes the most dangerous prey is the one that can outthink you, the one that lulls you into a false sense of dominance or superiority, the one that has conquered any fear of you with a sense of anger and betrayal. It had fallen into my trap, one conceived by logic, reason, and an understanding of the world through the eyes of a scientific mind.

Fire cleanses all.

As it groaned, shrieked, cracked, and contorted, readying itself to pounce, in one swift motion I removed a blanket from the floor, revealing a bucket filled with gasoline that I had bought in that short time of preparation. I threw it as hard as I could, the liquid splashing all over that horror and the bed.

It grinned at me, mocking my very existence, making light of my pain and the agony it had caused.

From my pocket I pulled out a lighter, lit it, and threw it onto that wretched thing. It writhed and screamed in agony, parts of its flesh crumbling away, searing into nothing in front of my very eyes; I almost felt sorry for it.

Let it burn.

The fire got out of hand; thankfully a neighbor, hearing the screams and seeing the smoke, called the fire department. I remember nothing of how I escaped.

I spent several hours in hospital being treated for light smoke inhalation and painful burns to my hands. It still hurts as I type, but as with many superficial wounds, they will heal. Perhaps there will be a few scars, but I can live with that.

The police arrested me shortly afterward, believing me a murderer. They suspect that I killed someone in that fire and find it entirely suspicious that I have a deep wound in my shoulder and scratches over my body. I've been told not to stray far in case they wish to ask me further questions, but they can ask away, I doubt they'll believe my answers. They found no remains, nor any evidence that someone else was there, bar a strange outline of a figure etched deep into the bed and wall. It looked as though whatever had been there attempted an escape, but I do not think it accomplished this.

A weight has now been lifted from my shoulders, one that I now realize was always there—since I was a child, in fact. I believe that the thing had an effect on me even from a distance, and now that it is gone, I feel whole again.

I am devastated that I've lost Mary, and my house can be written off as I'll probably be charged with arson after they realize I started the fire, which means I can kiss goodbye to any insurance claim.

My hands ache, as does my shoulder, but my spirit does not. I am writing this from a hotel room; it's small and unassuming, but it will suit my purpose. Tonight I intend to sleep and dream, as I did as a child, before that wretch invaded my life.

I believe that it was my rationality that saved me, my logical thought that allowed me to destroy such an evil, but I will never escape the conclusion that there is much more to life beyond the veil, out there in the darkness. It is a world I have seen, and do not care to revisit, but tonight I will rest and tomorrow I will build my life again with the confidence that my unwelcome guest is gone forever. I can feel it, I know it!

It will take time for me to adjust, and perhaps my mind will play a trick or two along the way, as it is difficult to abandon the paranoia of a lifetime. I must learn to accept my safety once again. I refuse to be looking over my shoulder for the rest of my days, but I will always be cautious, as I was when I was in the hospital this morning. Lying on a bed in a quiet ward, I thought I felt the bed shake for the briefest of moments, but I know that it was just my imagination.

I am glad I have written down my experiences; it has illuminated much about myself to me. Most importantly, should anyone ever, God forbid, find himself in a similar situation, then maybe you will know what to do.

Now it is bedtime and I must rest, for I have never known weariness such as this.

Good night, and sleep tight . . .

JEFF THE KILLER: RIGHT ON TIME

Vincent V. Cava

He'd been watching her for a couple of weeks and in that time he had memorized her entire daily routine.

7:30 A.M.—Wake up and shower.
8:00 A.M.—Drive to Starbucks and order a tall latte, double shot.
8:30 A.M.—Arrive at the office. Make small talk in the break room for approximately ten minutes.
11:45 A.M.—Lunch—usually a salad at her desk, Cobb or Caesar.
And so on . . .

It hadn't been hard. He noticed almost immediately that she was a slave to her ways—the type of person who typically didn't deviate from her schedule—but that was fine by him. Her predictable habits had made planning her murder practically effortless. He checked the time on his watch as he pulled the stolen sedan up in front of her townhouse that night.

10:35 P.M.

That meant she had just finished watching television for the evening. *Probably one of those shitty reality shows she DVRs*, he thought to himself. If he had to venture a guess, she was most likely brushing her teeth at that very moment. Soon she'd be in the shower and after that it was bedtime. Except—he managed a smile—she wasn't going to make it to bed. Just a few more minutes and all of his careful planning would finally come to fruition.

He told himself that she deserved what she was about to get. All of his victims had. Sure, none of the women he stalked and murdered had ever done anything to cross him directly, but that didn't matter. Women like her sickened him—single working females in their late 20s and early 30s who claimed they were too wrapped up in their careers to be in a serious relationship, women more concerned with climbing the corporate ladder than moving into a house with a man who could provide and care for them. She didn't need a partner to feel complete and if she had a sexual itch she could easily scratch it with any number of the casual acquaintances in her Rolodex, yet men like him weren't even on her radar and that's what irked him most of all. In the three weeks that he'd been stalking her, she hadn't once looked his way. She would notice him soon enough, though. He was about to make certain of it.

His watch now said **10:47** P.M.

She would be in the shower by now.

10:45–11:02—Those were the golden minutes—his window of opportunity. He had decided that the best time to break into her place was while she was busy washing. He popped the car's driver-side door open, then headed around to the back of the house.

It had rained fairly hard earlier that day and now the air was unusually fresh. He swore he could smell the ocean even though it was five miles away. Part of him wished the weather hadn't cleared up. There was something peaceful about the sound of heavy rainfall to him—as if it drowned out the earsplitting roar of existence and brought a few brief hours of harmony to the world.

The lot in the back of the townhouse was so small he felt like he could stretch out his arms and touch the fences lining either side of it. There was a fake rock sitting underneath the yard's one rosebush. It stuck out like a sore thumb. Inside was a key to the back door. He knew it would be there because he had watched her use it before, but even if he hadn't, he surmised it wouldn't have taken him too long to locate the obtrusive thing.

"Idiot," he whispered to himself. "You think someone couldn't tell this rock was fake?"

He bent over and removed the key from the faux rock's tiny compartment, then slowly, quietly, he unlocked the back door and stepped inside. He was in the kitchen now. The shower was running. He could hear it as soon as he entered the townhouse. So far, everything had gone just as he expected, but this wasn't a surprise to him. After all, he'd been preparing weeks for this night.

He always planned his kills meticulously. The last place he wanted to go was prison. Most serial killers were in it for the fame. They left clues and calling cards so they could read about themselves in the paper. They wanted talking heads to argue about them on TV, and when they got caught they wanted to be celebrities. Not him, though. He was only concerned with maiming and torturing as many victims as possible. Getting arrested would ruin all the fun and he'd barely just begun to play. The woman in the shower would be the ninth casualty of his twisted game, but in his head he knew there were more that needed to die. So many more. Half the human race if need be.

He slinked through the kitchen and into the living room. Its shag carpet squished underneath the wet rubber soles of his shoes as he walked across it. He was moving through the shadowy house like a phantom. Darkness was his domain and he was the monster hiding in it. The sound of the shower was louder now. It was coming from the second level. He stopped at the base of the staircase and peered up. A yellow light was seeping out from beneath the door of the upstairs bathroom.

That famous scene from *Psycho* bled into his mind. He supposed jumping her in the shower was a little cliché, but at least he wasn't going to use a knife. *No, he preferred to choke the life out of women that ignored him.* It felt more personal that way. He crept up the stairs as silently as possible. Killing was the only time he ever truly felt good about himself. He was beginning to get excited, giddy even, but as soon as he reached the bathroom door, a sudden twinge of panic shot through his body.

The door! What if she had locked it?!

He had simply assumed the door would be unlocked due to the fact that she lived alone, but that didn't make it a sure thing. If she heard him trying to fiddle with the doorknob, she might scream. All of the townhouses in that neighborhood were packed close together. Hers even shared a wall with another one and the people living in the adjacent building would easily be able to hear her cries for help. A million frantic thoughts began to squawk inside his mind. Even if no one called the cops, people would be looking out their windows to see who came out of the house, maybe even snapping pictures on their camera phones. What if they got a clear shot of him? The police would catch him for sure once her body was discovered, and then his playtime would be over. How could he have been so careless?

He considered turning around and heading back down the stairs. There was always tomorrow. If he was quiet about it, he could rework his plan and come back the following evening. He started to leave, but only made it a few steps down the hall before a thought flashed through his head like a bolt of lightning. He stopped in his tracks and began to think about something that happened at the supermarket just two days prior.

There was a man. He was tall and muscular with a white smile and a perfectly manicured beard. The woman he'd been stalking—the one that was currently in the shower—was flirting with this handsome stranger. He had watched with disdain as the two traded phone numbers and went on their way. Their exchange had only taken a couple of minutes, but even in that short amount of time she had given the man at the market more attention than he'd received in weeks.

No, he decided to himself. She was probably in there thinking about him at that very moment. He spun back around and started back toward the bathroom. *She doesn't get to finish that fantasy.*

He wrapped his fingers around the doorknob. The metal felt like ice against his skin. The sensation of his heart beating wildly in his chest was tremendously apparent to him. He took a deep inhale. If the knob didn't turn he would break the door down. With a little bit of luck, he could crash into the bathroom and grab her around the throat before she could let out a shout.

He twisted his wrist a half-inch to the left and the knob spun with it. *Success.* A triumphant sigh emerged from his mouth. All of his worrying had been for nothing. The door was unlocked. He cursed himself for his stupid mistake, then turned the doorknob the rest of the way and slinked inside.

The shower sounded so loud, like snow on an old analog television when the speakers' volume is turned up all the way up. The air was so thick inside the steamy bathroom he could practically chew it. Cautiously he stepped, taking care not to slip on the floor's tiles that had become slick and wet with condensation. He moved slowly, but with a purpose, concentrating only on his target.

The shower's opaque, beige curtain had a pink, flowery design stitched into it. The sight of it offended him—he considered it tasteless garbage—but he didn't let it distract him from his purpose. His focus was keener than ever. Closer he stalked and now he was standing directly in front of it. He extended a hand out toward the shower curtain, but felt himself recoil before touching it.

Something was off.

The shower was running. Like the rainfall earlier that day, it dominated his ears, but this time he didn't find it comforting. He had come to a realization that made his stomach drop. Aside from the sound of the all-too steady stream spraying from the showerhead, there were no other noises coming from the other side of the curtain. No singing, no splashing, no sound of water occasionally sloshing around the bottom of the tub—*no nothing.* It was as if he was alone in the bathroom.

But then why was the shower running? He glanced at his watch; it read **10:58**. She had to be in there. In three weeks, she hadn't finished a shower before **11:02**. Had he missed her?

The shower's roar seemed almost maddening now. He stood in front of it listening, waiting to hear something, anything, emerge from the other side of the curtain, but nothing ever did. With a shaky hand he reached for the hanging fabric barrier, gripped it firmly, then in a quick, sudden motion, he jerked it back.

The woman was indeed in the shower, her eyes wide and gleaming. They sparkled with terror. Her panicked face looked as if she was readying a scream, except he knew it wouldn't come. How could it? She was already dead—a naked bloody heap at the bottom of the tub. Someone else had gotten to her before him and by the look of it, they didn't seem to mind movie clichés.

Her killer had mangled her with a knife. Each of her toes and fingers had been sliced clean off and her legs and stomach were riddled with deep cuts and gashes. For a moment he wondered if she was still alive while her assailant had been whittling her flesh. He looked away, trying to divert his eyes. That's when he saw the pink gelatinous lump laying next to the drain. He stared curiously at it. To him, it looked like a blood-soaked jellyfish. It wasn't until he glanced back at the woman that he realized her murderer had carved one of her breasts from her chest and left it in the tub for him like some sort of grotesque Easter egg. He could feel his breath becoming frenzied and shallow.

He hadn't planned for this. He had taken almost everything into account, but he hadn't planned for this.

Fright's razor-sharp talons sunk themselves into his chest. He turned to leave, but stopped abruptly in his tracks when he saw the mirror. There was a message written on it, a string of crimson letters smeared across the glass surface. He had been so focused on the shower earlier that he hadn't even noticed it. He read the words. It was short and brief, but it sent a horrible feeling of dread through his entire being because—and this was something he was sure of—the message was written for him.

RIGHT ON TIME

The humidity of the bathroom was making him woozy. It was an odd sensation. The steamy heat coming off the shower in combination with his dizzy head made everything feel unreal—almost as if he was experiencing a bizarre fever dream. He opened the door and wave of cool air crashed against his face. With it came a heavy dose of reality.

It hadn't been an accident that the woman he'd been following was murdered the very same night he decided to make his move.

No, the killer had even sent him a message. The entire time he had been stalking her, someone had been stalking him. While he had been planning her death, *someone had been planning his.*

He didn't run out the bathroom; he galloped. It seemed like the staircase had somehow moved a hundred feet down the hall. The shadows were no longer his to hide in. They had a new monster and he feared it was coming for him. His legs stopped working as soon as he reached the top of the stairs, causing him to collapse onto the bannister. With all of his strength he hoisted himself up to his feet.

What had happened?

A couple of seconds later and a searing pain in his back answered that question. He reached behind and felt something sticking out of it—a cold metallic cyst that had suddenly sprouted from his spine. There was pressure pushing down on the back of his head now, a hand forcing him into a helpless position, doubling him over the bannister. For a second it felt like he was levitating as he dangled precariously, looking down toward the living room floor fifteen feet below. Then came another searing pain, even worse than the first. Slowly, his assailant began to pull the knife from his body and it felt as though his wound was being defiled.

How big was the blade? How deep had it been buried? It seemed like it took forever to remove. Once it was finally out, he could feel the hallway's cool, drafty air add insult to his injury as it licked at the gaping gash in his back. He tried to get back to his feet, but before he could, someone snagged hold of his ankles and, in an instant, he was toppling over the handrail. The living room spun around him as he fell down to the floor. He landed on his shoulder with a *THUD* and let out a groan. There was no doubt in his mind that it was dislocated.

He gazed up and saw the figure of a man crawling down the stairs on all fours like an animal and he wondered for the second time if he was dreaming. The only thing he could make out was his pursuer's bushy hair, blacker than the midnight sky and as wild as a savage. Desperate questions streamed through his head, all of which he had no answer for.

He watched silently as the man or animal or thing that had attacked him reached the bottom step and stood up on two feet, uncurling its spine like a cobra dancing for a snake charmer. The shaggy head of dark, matted hair turned in his direction and now he could see a face—a human face—or at least one that used to belong to a human. His stalker wore a skeleton's smile—no lips and a set of flat, white teeth that contrasted bitterly against purple gums. Like a rotting corpse it had no nose, and its pallid complexion looked snow white in the moonlight seeping into the living room. In its hand it held an eight-inch bowie knife, coated in blood.

It began to slither toward him again, watching him through a pair of bulging, yellow eyes, and it almost looked as if it was wearing a person like a Halloween costume. A teenager or young man perhaps. It was dressed in black pants and a white hooded sweatshirt, tie-dyed in the blood of the woman in the bathroom.

He tried to get up, but it put a foot on his chest and pinned him to the ground, then crouched on top of him and placed the point of the knife up against his abdomen. He barely felt it penetrate his stomach. But as the blade turned inside him a blazing hot sensation swelled throughout his core. He stared back into the ugly thing's unblinking eyes as his vision started fading to black. The last thing he heard was its horrible, croaky voice, just as awful and repulsive as its face.

"Go to sleeeeep."

He would not fight it. The angel of death had arrived and it had come in the form of the terrible nightmare crouched on top of his soon-to-be corpse. He wondered if Hell was real, then supposed he'd find out soon enough. His eyelids were getting heavy so he let them fall shut and waited for the darkness to take him . . .

CONTRIBUTORS TO THIS COLLECTION

Vincent V. Cava

Famed author Vincent V. Cava is one of the major names of the Creepypasta community. Some have referred to him as a savior of the genre or a pioneer. When it comes to new ideas in theming or story, or even pushing the boundaries of the dark, gruesome, and terrible, Vincent V. Cava has definitely led the charge. In addition to his work on Reddit/NoSleep and the Creepypasta genre, he's also self-published much of his work on Amazon.

Michael Whitehouse

It's hard to browse Creepypasta.com or the Creepypasta wikia and not know the name Michael Whitehouse. Whitehouse's tale, "Bedtime," is a short fiction story that has always had a great hold on the Creepypasta community. It was one of the first of its kind to really blend the line between professional writing and online meta-horror. And it did it so well; it became a classic of the genre. Whitehouse's books, including *On a Hill*, are all self-published on Amazon.

Aaron Shotwell

Reaching back to the golden era, Shotwell is known for his stories such as "The Owl" and "Blackout at Third and Main." As his career has developed, Aaron Shotwell has come up with new ideas for the genre that mix with science fiction and even biblical themes. He has also announced his first self-published book available on Amazon.

Max Lobdell

UnsettlingStories.com is a Tumblr blog that's gained a large amount of fame for its telling of strange, gross, and disturbing tales. These stories all feature themes of the strange and really fit meta-horror to a fault; they fit so well, in fact, that it's up for debate whether Lobdell is writing from fiction or experience.

Isaac Boissonneau

Rapidly gaining attention on the YouTube and writing sides of the Creepypasta genre is Isaac Boissonneau. Boissonneau goes by the online handle of HopefullyGoodGrammar and has yet to disappoint with his creativity in story and detail. Many eyes are on his writing career, as it's sure to grow.

Rona Vaselaar

Sleepyhollow_101, or Rona Vaselaar, is a name that was featured on the *Sixpenceee* blog and since has been knocking every story out of the park. Vaselaar's stories have all featured wonderfully mysterious themes that are fitting of this genre. As well, her stories feature a widely unseen versatility of well-constructed female protagonists. *Colors of Death* is Vaselaar's first published title and can be found both on Amazon Kindle and in paperback.

Michael Marks

DeadnSpread, or Michael Marks, is a rising star in Reddit/NoSleep. His stories have all pushed the envelope on the dark and gruesome, but unlike most modern writers for the online genre, Marks still keeps an air of the unseen and the unknown. "Voices in the Spirit Box" is a beautiful blend of gore, shock, and horror.

T.W. Grim

T.W. Grim is a veteran of Reddit/NoSleep by the handle theworldisgrim. Grim has created multipart series that have received much note from the popular online forum and great attention from the YouTube community as well. Grim's work with these series shows wonderfully in his published works, such as *99 Brief Scenes from the End of the World.*

WellHey Productions

WellHey Productions, or OldManMurphy, is an author, husband, father of two, and YouTuber. Murphy's writings and channel have gathered much attention in the online community for being very brazen in language and content. The YouTube channel of the same name, in addition to horror, also features animations, film tests, and comedy produced by the writer himself.

Sarah Cairns

Sarah Cairns is a popular author and artist in the online world of Creepypasta. Much of her work is seen on YouTube channels such as MrCreepyPasta and CreepsMcPasta. Her handiwork has also gone into creating some of the masks worn on the respective shows. Her writing talents have created such Creepypasta creatures as the Yellow Raincoat and Sneckdraw, all have which have been embraced by the fandom.

Goldc01n

Goldc01n is a mysterious name from around the Creepypasta community. Little is known of the author, but many stories have been told as audio dramas on YouTube channels such as MrCreepyPasta.

Matt Dymerski

Matt Dymerski of MattDymerski.com is an old legend in the world of Creepypastas. In the online circles, Dymerski's story "Psychosis" caught on like wildfire, but was, for the longest time, thought to have an anonymous author. "Psychosis" was later found to be a work of Dymerski along with many great horror fictions. Over his writing career he's self-published many of these works on Amazon.

Barnabas Deimos

Barnabas Deimos is a writer whose preferred medium is that of the macabre, maddening, and morose. He is a writer capable of capturing the essence of a Lovecraftian style to more contemporary urban mythologies. He does not shy away from commingling the concepts of gay and lesbian themes with his tales in a way that does not cause the audience to feel lambasted but rather as natural a part of the story as the horror itself is.